Stephen f...
desire that could not be stilled.

And he made no effort to try. Reaching up his arms, he pulled Fellis from the horse. With torturous deliberation he allowed her to slide slowly down the length of him, his hands molding the gentle swell of her hips. Heat rose in his belly, and he closed his eyes, breathing in the sweet, warm woman scent of her.

She was a heady mixture of innocence and spirit, and he felt drawn to her as no maid before her.

When he opened his eyes again, Fellis was looking up at him, her own lids heavy, her breath coming quickly through parted lips.

Suddenly, he knew he was going to kiss her—had to kiss her....

Dear Reader,

Since the release of her first Medieval, *Rose Among Thorns,* Catherine Archer has been gaining fans, and her new book, *Velvet Touch,* is sure to win her more. This sequel to her previous title, *Velvet Bond,* is the bittersweet story of a young nobleman who is sent by his king to arrange a marriage and settle a feud, only to fall in love with the intended bride. Whether you're a Medieval fan or not, don't miss this touching read.

Three-time RITA Award winner Cheryl Reavis is back this month with her heart-wrenching tale, *The Bartered Bride.* Set in Civil War North Carolina, it's the story of a pregnant woman who reluctantly marries her sister's widower, yet soon discovers the healing powers of forgiveness and love.

Multigenre author Merline Lovelace makes history come alive in her new release, *Lady of the Upper Kingdom,* the dramatic story of forbidden love between two strong-willed people separated by the treachery and distrust that exists between their two cultures, the Egyptian and the Greek. And from popular new author Linda Castle we bring you *Abbie's Child,* about a young woman who comes face-to-face with the father of the boy she has raised as her own.

Whatever your taste in reading, we hope you will enjoy all four Harlequin Historicals, available wherever books are sold.

Sincerely,

Tracy Farrell,
Senior Editor

Please address questions and book requests to:
Harlequin Reader Service
U.S.: 3010 Walden Ave., P.O. Box 1325, Buffalo, NY 14269
Canadian: P.O. Box 609, Fort Erie, Ont. L2A 5X3

Catherine Archer
Velvet Touch

Harlequin Books

TORONTO • NEW YORK • LONDON
AMSTERDAM • PARIS • SYDNEY • HAMBURG
STOCKHOLM • ATHENS • TOKYO • MILAN
MADRID • WARSAW • BUDAPEST • AUCKLAND

ISBN 0-373-28922-7

VELVET TOUCH

Books by Catherine Archer

Harlequin Historicals

CATHERINE ARCHER

has been hooked on historical romance since reading *Jane Eyre* at the age of twelve. She has an avid interest in history, particularly the medieval period. A homemaker and mother, Catherine lives with her husband, three children and dog in Alberta, Canada, where the long winters give this American transplant plenty of time to write.

This book is dedicated to The Aunts, who each had a profound impact on my life, Aunt Judy, Aunt Martha, Aunt Pat and Aunt Susan. I hope you can all appreciate why it was necessary to put you in alphabetical order.

I must also give sincere and heartfelt thanks to our friends, the DeGuilios, Sam, Sandi, Ernie, Taylor and Zachary, for everything.

Chapter One

Stephen Clayburn shifted in the saddle to ease his stiff muscles. With his free hand he drew his cloak more closely about his wide shoulders, taking a deep breath of the cool morning air. Its early spring chill served to waken him more fully and he prodded his stallion to a slightly faster pace.

The knight had slept in the outdoors under the stars rather than spend time locating another abbey the previous night, for he was much tired of the gruel that passed for sustenance with the religious sector. He had even wondered to himself if the orders served guests such gruesome meals in an effort to discourage them from returning.

His chestnut stallion, Gabriel, seemed to sense his master's thoughts, for he snorted and tossed his head. "A little skimpy on the oats, were they, boy?" Stephen laughed and patted the sleek animal's muscular neck with a gauntleted hand. He'd left his other mount, Dancer, in the stables of his home in Windsor, preferring to ride the chestnut on longer trips such as this.

Stephen was concerned about getting to Malvern castle to complete his appointed task and be on his way again. When King Edward had first told him of the duty he wished done, Stephen had seen the journey as the answer to his immediate problems. His former mistress, Helen Denfield, was not accepting the end of their liaison with good grace, and plagued him at every turn. When they'd first begun the affair, she'd professed her agreement that they keep their relationship on a casual footing. But as time passed, Stephen learned that Helen, a once wealthy widow, was determined that Stephen should become husband number two.

It did not help that Stephen's sister Elizabeth had gotten herself married unexpectedly. With Elizabeth at his side it had been more difficult for Lady Helen to be too open in her prodding.

Beth married. He shook his head in amazement.

He hadn't thought her leaving their small house in Windsor would affect him so greatly, hadn't imagined he would miss her so much. He told himself he should be glad to be rid of her. She was always meddling in his business, cleaning his rooms, asking him what time he would be home.

A man didn't need all that mothering.

But the truth remained that he did miss Elizabeth, dreadfully. His sister had given him someone to come home to, someone to talk with in the evenings when he wasn't away on the king's business. As messenger to King Edward, Stephen never knew when he might be called on to do some service for his sovereign.

Elizabeth had been a friend and companion without the decidedly unpleasant complications of being a wife. And truth to tell, he was lonely without her. The whitewashed house was much too quiet and not nearly so comfortable with her gone.

That loneliness had definitely contributed to his present circumstances. It wasn't his usual custom to see to such complicated diplomatic negotiations as the ones he must now arrange. But King Edward had professed great confidence in Stephen's ability to get one Welsh lordling wed to the English bride Edward had chosen for him. King Edward had flattered him then, saying Stephen was a man of great charm and tact and more than equal to the task.

Stephen shook his dark auburn head. Aye, it might be true that he had the gift of using his tongue. But it was equally true that he had been chosen because most of Edward's more seasoned negotiators were busy with the Scots and the French.

Not that Stephen doubted his own ability. It was simply that he didn't relish the notion of arranging a wedding for anyone. He couldn't imagine getting married and tying himself to one woman for life.

And that was what marriage meant as far as Stephen was concerned. His parents had been very much in love and, as far as he knew, had remained faithful to each other until they died of plague some six years ago. At that time his life had changed completely. One day they'd been a happy family, their home full of laughter, life and, yes, tears. Then it was all gone, his parents dead, the home keep a hollow reminder of what had been.

To love meant to offer one's self up for hurt, for one never knew when everything might be taken away. The thought of risking his heart and happiness in that way was disturbing at best. Mayhap that was why he was so set against the idea of marriage. He could not imagine allowing himself to care for any woman that much. His liaisons had been more out of convenience, to satisfy physical need both for himself and the lady involved.

He rode on, shrugging off such thoughts with determination. There was nothing to be gained by them. He knew what was best for himself.

Stephen's pensive mood retreated when he took note of the surrounding countryside. The fields were showing a new growth of grain. It was still early for there was little sign of activity in the farmyards he passed. Neat cottages sat back from the road, and chickens and pigs roamed freely in the yards.

But there was no sign of Malvern castle, even in the distance. A hungry growl erupted from his stomach, and Stephen began to wonder how far he had to go.

As he turned a bend, he unexpectedly met a farmer carrying a hoe coming from the opposite direction. Stephen stopped his stallion and hailed the fellow. "You there."

The farmer looked up, obviously surprised to see a mounted nobleman at this hour of the morning. "My lord," he replied respectfully.

"Do you know the way to Malvern castle?"

"Aye." The fellow pointed off down the road behind him. "It be some ten leagues hence. But if you've a mind to go through the wood it be only four leagues. Just head due north and you'll see Malvern when you come out of the forest. The road, you see, follows around the fields," he explained with a deferential nod.

Stephen looked down the road, then toward the forest as another grumble erupted from his flat belly. "You have my thanks," he said.

Stephen left the road and went off toward the wood to his left. The branches of tall pine and oak formed a lacy green canopy overhead, but the trunks were spaced widely, allowing for fairly easy movement, even mounted as he was. The sun had risen high enough to begin peeking through the branches of the trees, creating a pattern of golden light and dusky shadow. It illuminated the ground before him, which was covered with a thick carpet of fallen needles that crunched under his horse's hooves.

At the edge of the wood, Fellis Grayson checked over her shoulder one last time. There was no sign of movement on the path behind her. The only hint of human occupation was the tendrils of smoke that rose over the castle as the morning cooking was begun. From this distance she could not see the sentry upon the high stone wall, but she knew he was there.

Though the castle was a secure one, with its strong inner and outer bailey defenses, her father always insisted that a guard be stationed and alert at the portcullis. The outer wall was flanked by twin towers and circled by a moat. Inside were the granaries, gardens, animal pens, wells and armory required to withstand a siege. And surrounding the keep itself was another fortified stone wall.

Richard Grayson did not trust the wily Welshmen who raided his lands at every opportunity. Since the last episode only two moons past, when a band had burned the granary inside the outer wall, her father had been doubly careful.

Fellis knew that her father had again written King Edward asking for assistance in subduing his enemy. The harm that was wrought upon her father's vassals and lands by the hostilities was great, and she prayed that the king would soon come to their aid.

She wished for this to happen for one other more selfish reason. It was getting harder and harder to find an opportunity to be out from under her mother's watchful eyes. Mary Grayson was ever fearful that something untoward would befall her daughter before she was able to carry out her plans for her future.

This thought was followed immediately by a sense of guilt that she had again crept from the keep without her mother's permission. Fellis said a hasty Hail Mary and crossed herself over the breast of her drab gray cote. She could not deny that escaping was exactly what she was doing.

Hurriedly she stepped onto the forest path and made her way through the thick growth. There was no hesitation in her step, for Fellis knew exactly where she was bound. As the soft silky sounds of running water came to her, she quickened her pace in anticipation.

A wall of tall trees rose up to block her path, but Fellis knew of a narrow path through them. It wasn't a minute later that she stepped into the glade, her one private place, and felt her heart sing as it always did at the beauty of her surroundings.

The ground was covered with a thick bed of moss, and all around the quiet pool the trees grew tall and heavy with needles and leaves, creating a privacy screen of greenery. From the branches trailed tender vines of ivy and moss. Delicate white water lilies dotted the pool that was fed by a narrow, slow-moving stream which wended its way to this magical place.

This was Fellis's favorite location on all of God's earth. Never had she even heard anyone else speak of it. So inside her had grown the notion that she alone had the ability to find the magical spot.

It was as if God were giving her this one rare gift in order to make up for the twisted ankle that had ordained her destiny from the day she was born.

Only here could she forget for a time that she was not as other young women. In the water she need not walk with slow deliberation to keep from appearing awkward.

With her careful, halting gait, Fellis moved toward the wide shelf of moss-covered rock that jutted out over the pond. With a rising sense of anticipation tingling along her backbone, Fellis went forward, pulling the heavy gray veil and wimple from her head....

Stephen was dismayed to find the forest becoming denser and more difficult to traverse. The underbrush grew thicker as the land beneath Gabriel's hooves became rough and uneven. Finally he had to dismount to pick his way through the growth.

Yet another grumble from his stomach made his lips twist in self-derision. If he'd had the sense to stay on the main road, surely he would have been at Malvern by now, eating a hearty breakfast.

At the gentle sound of water flowing close by, Stephen turned to follow the burbling noise. It was always a good idea to locate a body of water if lost. It must invariably lead to somewhere.

When he had pushed his way through to the stream, he frowned as he saw how small it was. Mayhap he had made a second misjudgment on this ill-fated morn. Such a narrow trickle might indeed lead nowhere.

But as he had no notion of how to go back, it seemed that following this course was preferable to heading off with no particular direction to follow. He continued on for a time, then once again cursed himself as he came up against a thick stand of trees, grown so closely together that they created what amounted to a solid wall.

Stephen studied the situation with ever-increasing ire. Thinking there must be some way through the tangle, no matter how thick it appeared, he decided that he would tie Gabriel to one of the branches. After doing so, he was free to press past and attempt to find a better position to lead the horse from the other side.

Choosing a spot that looked only slightly less dense than any other, Stephen closed his eyes and pressed his way through.

When he opened his eyes, what met his gaze was a true wonder. A lily-dotted pool rested in the center of a verdant and otherworldly glade. It was a secluded spot, completely cut off from even the rest of the forest around it. He felt rather like a knight braving an enchanted hedge in a tale of chivalry.

Stephen wasn't quite sure why, but something inside told him to remain quiet. Mayhap it was the cathedral-like stillness he felt as he stood there and looked up at the arched canopy of treetops over his head.

He moved forward slowly, almost reverently, through the dense growth of brush at the edge of the glade. It was then he looked up toward the far end of the pool and halted. He stopped thinking of anything, save the nude feminine form poised there on a rock that jutted out over the water.

It was a woman, a nymph, a silver spirit of the forest. Jesu, what a woman.

She stood tall, bathed in a shaft of pure golden light, her hair hanging down her back in a silvery curtain that reached to her knees. She reached high, hands over her head as if basking in the sweet warmth of that single bright beam of sunlight as it pierced the treetops. It shimmered on the perfection of her high, full breasts, narrow waist and gently curved hips. Her legs were long, slender and shapely, the muscles flexed as she paused there on one slender foot. Her very skin seemed to glisten with incandescent fire.

Stephen was struck dumb by the sight of her. Never in all his twenty-seven years had he dreamed such a woman existed.

Something, some inner sense of caution, told him to keep his presence secret. Surely he had stumbled upon this bright silver fairy maid by accident and she would disappear, did she become aware of his presence in her lair.

Without pausing to reason out the wisdom or sensibility of his actions, Stephen hunkered down out of sight. But a need to see again that lovely creature, to reassure himself that she was indeed real, prodded him to move forward until he was able to part the dense brush at the water's edge.

When he did so, he saw but a flash of pale skin as she disappeared into the cool depths of the water scarcely a few feet from where he crouched. The only things to mark her entry therein were a faint splash upon his face, and the heady sweet scent of the water lilies that were disturbed by her passage. Stephen wiped at the water, feeling its wetness upon his palm, and knew that he could not have been imagining the beautiful woman.

This was no dream, he told himself, and thus she was no wood sprite that would disappear if frightened.

She was a woman, flesh and blood, and so beautiful his body ached at the thought of how she had looked only moments ago, poised upon that moss-covered rock. And that meant she would have a real woman's reaction to being spied upon by a strange man.

Stephen felt himself flush as he realized how it would appear to her if she discovered him here like this. Why, he must look like some lecherous knave lurking in the bushes.

He ran an unsteady hand over his face as the unchivalrous nature of his behavior became clear to him. What in the world had come over him? Not in his life had Stephen acted so despicably.

He realized he had to leave, and quickly, before the woman noted his presence. 'Twas surely the only way for her to keep her dignity.

She was swimming now just a few feet away, her arms cleaving the water with firm, clean strokes, the sound of her passage drawing his rapt attention. And unconsciously he found himself watching for a glimpse of creamy flesh.

Dragging his captive gaze away from her, Stephen chided himself once again. He had to leave now, though it was not easy. The thought of never seeing her again was more disturbing than he would have imagined, and his chest ached at the very notion.

Then he reminded himself that such thinking was skewed. He knew nothing of this female, had no knowledge of who she was or anything about her.

Besides, if she knew what he was doing right now, she would not welcome him. Of that Stephen was sure. It was obvious that she had come to the place in the utter certainty that she would not be seen. The very lack of self-consciousness in her gestures and actions gave proof of this.

Could he simply walk away, never to know her name?

And then he knew. He would have to find her again, no matter how difficult it might prove. He must discover what lay beneath that exquisite covering of delicate white flesh, must learn of the woman inside.

But that could not be done now, not here in this secluded place.

With cautious deliberation, Stephen edged away until he felt the wall of trees at his back. Only then did he turn and force his way through the tangle of branches to his waiting stallion. And away from the sensuous pull of that silver-haired beauty in the forest pool.

Fellis felt the cool water glide over her bare skin with a shiver of pleasure. She moved her arms in long, sensuous strokes that pulled her forward smoothly.

'Twas her greatest sin, this desire to swim without clothing to hinder her enjoyment of the water and air. It made her feel so alive and so much a part of the gentle throbbing hum of the forest around her to go naked and unrestrained in the glade.

The whole of her life was so ordered, so determined by her mother and others. This was the one place that she felt herself. And though she knew it was wrong to come here, there were times when she could not keep herself away. This morning had been one of those times. The day ahead of her stretched lengthy and filled with the many responsibilities that were her lot. Prayer, passing out alms and helping the poor, caring for her aged grandmother, these duties occupied her life.

It had seemed almost a sign that Fellis had wakened long before her mother would be up and about. Mary Grayson was ever ready to chastise her daughter for any thought of deviation from her appointed tasks. Never would her mother understand the sensual pleasures that beckoned Fellis to this glade, this pool.

With a sigh Fellis slipped through the gentle caress of the water, her eyes closed as she drifted. In the buoyant liquid she was neither cautious nor awkward, but supple and fleet, diving here and surfacing there. And each time she did, the water lapped at her skin, bathed her in silken kisses. Unbidden came the thought that a lover's hands might feel much the same way, slipping over her legs, her hips, her breasts.

Her eyes flew open and she gasped, shocked at the path her own imagination had taken. 'Twas wrong of her to give form to such thoughts. Never before had they come to her with such intensity and she knew not whence they had sprung.

The course of her life had already been determined and, no matter that her future was not of her own choosing, she had resigned herself long ago to the knowledge that she would do as her mother insisted. Fellis was never to know the touch of any man's hands, never to hear the cry of her own child.

Her mother had determined for her long ago that she must one day take the veil.

She turned toward the shoreline, knowing it had been a mistake to come here. Each time she felt the call of the forest, she told herself that she had gained the power to hold all lustfull thoughts at bay, and each time they crept back into her mind. Once again the sensuous pleasures of being in her glade had conjured up thoughts she must not succumb to.

And today they had more vividness than ever before.

Stephen entered the high-ceilinged circular stone hall directly on the heels of the guard who announced him. A row of arched windows ran the whole circumference of the chamber, allowing ample light even without tapers. Only the far end of the room lay in shadow, where a wide-arched opening led to a dimly lit stairway. He was tired, hungry and more than a little angry with himself for his actions of the morning.

What had he been thinking to allow himself to become so enraptured by a strange woman he had no knowledge of whatsoever? Surely she could not have been as he remembered. Though he'd madly roused up fanciful thoughts of woodland sprites, Stephen realized the woman must reside somewhere locally.

Stephen told himself he must stop thinking of her. His foolishness had already delayed his arrival at Malvern by no small length of time. After leaving her, the knight had been forced to backtrack and come by the main road in the end anyway.

But the instant tightening of his body as that silvery image flooded his mind for the thousandth time since leaving her told Stephen he was only fooling himself. With a silent growl of self-disgust he forced himself to attend to what was happening as he followed the guard across the rush-strewn floor of the hall.

The trestle tables had been set up for the meal as he had hoped, but by this late hour the serving women were even now removing trays which had earlier been loaded with yesterday's bread, cold roast meat and cheese. There was only a smattering of crumbs and bones to greet his hunger. He forced back a grimace of disappointment.

The few remaining occupants of the room looked up as he came forward to the high table where a well-favored man of some forty years sat. As Stephen moved closer, he saw the man's tanned face was marked by few lines though his hair was an all-over shade of iron. Far from adding age to the features, the gray hair only served to highlight two deep blue eyes that lit up as the knight approached.

Lord Richard Grayson welcomed Stephen to the morning meal with an open smile. "Ah, Sir Stephen," he greeted, "the guard tells me you are just come from the king's court. I feel fortune to have lingered in breaking my fast else I might have missed you. You are most welcome to our hall. News from court is always received with gladness." He went on with a frown, "We get few visitors so close to the Welsh border."

Seeing the other man's adverse reaction to even mentioning his enemies, Stephen wondered how the king's solution to his problems would be met.

Richard Grayson's features cleared. "Please take a seat and join us. Surely you have not broken your own fast."

Stephen nodded with a smile. "Nay, my Lord Grayson, I have not and I thank you for your hospitality." He was pleased that he would not have need to discuss the most delicate matter of a marriage between this man's daughter and his enemy without sustenance.

He took the place indicated to him at the high table to Lord Grayson's left, as the older man raised his hand and called for more food to be brought. The other seats at the table were vacant and Stephen could only assume that the other members of the baron's family had taken their meal and gone.

When the golden-haired and curvaceous serving woman arrived bearing a laden tray, her eyes held a flirtatious smile as she set it before him. Taking only cursory notice of her, Stephen took liberal helpings of meat, cheese and bread. He was too occupied with behaving casually with the other man's close attention on him. He was careful to keep a relaxed demeanor, for he knew not how Lord Grayson would take the news of his daughter's proposed marriage. From what he had been told by the king, Lord Grayson had been feuding with his closest neighbors, the Welsh, since he had taken over the running of the castle.

Judging from the tone of Lord Grayson's voice when mentioning the Welsh, it seemed he was no nearer to developing a tolerance for them. This did not bode well for Stephen's mission and he knew he must tread carefully here. Mayhap it would take more time and care to see the matter done than he had envisioned, but he was determined to accomplish what he had been asked to do.

With obviously waning patience, Lord Grayson watched Stephen as he began to eat.

Realizing that he had best get the initial disclosure out of the way without further ado, Stephen took a long drink of the watered wine that had been set before him. He smiled then and sat back in his seat. "I must thank you, Lord Grayson, for greeting me with such warmth."

Lord Grayson nodded pleasantly enough. "As I said, we are always pleased to greet a messenger from court. I am most eager to hear the news." As if he could not withhold the query any longer, he asked, "Has King Edward decided what will be done about our feud with the Welsh? I have waited long for his reply."

Stephen returned the nod, pleased that Lord Grayson had introduced the subject on his own. Obviously the problem was an important one in his eyes. Mayhap he would be eager to see any solution to the situation and would welcome King Edward's decision, though from what Stephen had observed thus far, this would come as a surprise to him.

"I have come with news," Stephen replied. "The king is indeed ready to see your troubles settled."

Lord Grayson smiled, looking pleased as he folded his hands together and leaned closer. "I am most eager to learn of his plans. Will he be sending troops to add to our garrison here? Or mayhap he intends to attack and put down our enemies without preamble."

The bent of Lord Grayson's thinking further confirmed that his mind and the king's were not following similar paths. Stephen answered with careful deliberation. "Nay, neither of those things will occur."

Lord Grayson frowned then and leaned back. "What then? Pray tell me. How will he make this aright?"

Stephen laid his hands flat on the tabletop and met Lord Grayson's troubled gaze without wavering. "His Highness has proposed a union between your house and that of Wynn ap Dafydd."

"A union?" Lord Grayson's expression could only be described as baffled.

Stephen went on evenly. "Aye, a marriage between your daughter and Wynn himself." Reaching into his sleeve, Stephen removed a roll of parchment.

When he saw the royal seal that held the document closed, Lord Grayson's mouth opened but no sound emerged for a moment.

The serving woman, who had, at that very moment, been pouring more wine into his cup, let out a gasp of shock.

It was as if the sound of her gasping helped Richard Grayson find his tongue, for he cried, "Nay." He rose, pushing back his chair and nearly knocking the luckily quick footed serving woman out of his way. "I will not have it.

Not my Fellis. Not while there is breath in my body.'' He hit
his chest with an outraged fist.

The reaction was even worse than Stephen had feared,
and seeing it, he was convinced that he was not going to
have an easy time of it. But he also knew that no matter how
Lord Grayson reacted at the moment, he had to come to see
that he had little or no choice in this. King Edward would
brook no defiance to his decree.

What Stephen had to do now was handle the situation
with as much delicacy as possible. He could understand that
Lord Grayson might be disturbed at this news and had no
small amount of sympathy for him. Carefully he returned
the king's order to his sleeve. Lord Grayson clearly was in
no state to read it. The knight knew that what he said now
could make the difference between an ultimately peaceful
outcome and a disastrous one. He chose his words carefully. ''I can see, my lord, that this news has come as an
unhappy surprise to you. I must tell you though that I cannot allow you to defy King Edward's instructions. As his
messenger it is my duty to see his orders carried through. I
can only hope that you will have some understanding of
where my duty and loyalty must lie and not force me into a
position that would be impossible for me by defying the
king.''

Lord Grayson looked at Stephen with rising anger. ''You
inform me that I am to marry my only daughter to that
barbarian, and then you have the temerity to tell me not to
put you in an impossible position.''

With deliberate concentration Stephen forced himself to
remain seated as Lord Grayson went on.

''How dare you come here and ask this of me! How dare
the king send you! He has no understanding of the problems we have faced trying to live here next to these people.

They raid my lands, burn my crops and my buildings. 'Tis untenable.''

Calmly Stephen answered his tirade. "I can see that you feel strongly on this matter. But I can only add that there must be some way to go forward with His Majesty's proposal. What has been going on for all these years must be brought to a halt."

"Even if I was willing to cry pax with the Welsh—" Lord Grayson glared at him "—they would not. And offering them my daughter will not gain that peace. They resent English rule to the point of hatred. Truth to tell, they would never even agree to hear such a proposal. They are too occupied with planning raids on my land and people."

Stephen steepled his fingers under his chin for a thoughtful moment. Perhaps what the other man said was true, but he also wondered if anyone had ever tried to speak to them about a truce. Then he looked up at Richard Grayson with arched brows. "If I were to bring about a cessation of these hostile activities, you could then feel more inclined to talk with Wynn ap Dafydd on the matter of his marriage to your daughter?"

Richard scoffed. "'Twould not happen."

Stephen shrugged. He knew much could be accomplished if one set his mind to it, even that which seemed impossible. It was something his father had always told him, and Stephen attempted to live by that creed. "I think you may leave that to me. I must also tell you that such an agreement on the part of your enemy wouldst of necessity have to be abided by on both sides."

"What do you mean, sir?"

"I mean, my lord, that you would also need stop any such activities as you have complained of."

Richard Grayson had the grace to look uncomfortable for a moment, then he smiled unpleasantly, his gray brows drawn together. "I will agree to abide by such a plan. But I must tell you, sir, that you are a foolhardy knight. The Welsh will in fact kill you before you can even present such a plan. Neither Wynn nor any of his folk have any respect for English law. King Edward's part in this plan will be as nothing to them. They understand nothing of honor and would not abide by any agreement entered into with those they consider their enemy."

Stephen shrugged. "As I said, you must leave that to me."

Richard looked at the younger man long and hard, then said, "Aye, I will leave it to you then. Know you that I will not assist you in this farce. If you must treat with the Welsh, it will be by your own wits. I will not help you to perpetrate this action against myself and my family."

Stephen frowned. "As you will, my lord." It was not what he wanted to hear, but Stephen refused to allow himself to become worried. A glimmer of a plan was forming in his mind, and he had no need of Lord Grayson's assistance to set it in motion. Later, once the baron had become accustomed to the notion of his daughter marrying Wynn ap Dafydd he would surely relax this hardened stance.

In truth Richard Grayson had no choice. He held these lands and keep by virtue of the king. In the end he must do as ordered, or risk losing all.

But Stephen did not mind giving him some time to adjust to the truth of the situation.

Slowly Richard reseated himself, putting his face in his hands as he did so. Then he looked at Stephen with an expression that could only be interpreted as sympathetic. "You have no idea what a task you have set for yourself, young man."

"What mean you?" Stephen asked him, surprised at this new turn of attitude. Surely he did not think Stephen needed to be further warned in the difficulty of convincing the Welsh to comply?

"I mean, sir, that even if you were to convince Wynn to go along with this scheme, which is nigh impossible enough, then you must face another even more insurmountable obstacle."

This time it was Stephen who frowned. "You talk in riddles, my lord."

"I speak of my dear wife." There was a hint of bitterness in the older man's tone. "The Lady Mary has her own plans for Fellis's future and she will not be easily deterred. And you will gain no ally in my daughter, either, for she has agreed to go along with her mother's wishes."

Stephen relaxed back in his seat. The man might be overconcerned with his wife's wishes; Stephen was not. Not that he planned to leave this situation with enemies at his back. He simply knew there was a way to work around this new impediment. The girl's mother must simply be brought to see the wisdom of complying with the king's decision.

Surely they would all come to understand that King Edward has proposed a very sound solution to the problems Lord Grayson had been complaining of for years. He was clearly ready to have the feuding at an end.

If they but considered, a marriage between the two houses might not be so very disagreeable. Once a babe was born to the young couple, attitudes would be greatly changed on both sides, Welsh and English.

Thus it was with slight amusement in his tone that Stephen asked. "What then is your wife's plan for the girl's future?" Then suddenly a rough edge crept into his voice as an unpleasant thought occurred to him. "You have not contracted for another marriage without notifying King Edward of the fact?"

Richard raised his hand in denial. "Nay, I wouldst not."

Again Stephen settled back. "Then, beyond your troubles with the Welsh what could possibly hinder the proposed marriage?"

The older man's expression remained closed. "That, Sir Knight, I will allow you to see for yourself."

Without another word, Lord Richard beckoned the serving woman to him. When she arrived, he said, "Go and ask my lady wife to attend me here in the hall. And tell her I wish for her to bring our daughter with her." He stopped her then as she prepared to leave, his eyes stern. "And make no mention of what you heard here."

The woman nodded briefly, then hurried off. She was making an obvious effort not to look in Stephen's direction, but her expression was resentful.

Stephen could see that this news had come as an unpleasant surprise for those at Malvern. In time they must all come to accept it.

As she left, Stephen realized that sending for the girl was a good idea. He would have need to gauge her reaction to the king's wishes. Mayhap the girl would not be as set against the plan as her parents. That would be of great help to his cause, for in the end she was the one who must agree to the marriage.

While they waited, Stephen did try but was unable to gain any further information from the Lord of Malvern. The baron seemed to take an almost perverse pleasure from withholding his secret knowledge concerning his wife's intentions for the girl. The knight decided to allow the matter to rest.

He would discover the facts soon enough.

But he was determined not to let whatever it was stand in his way. He had been given many tasks to perform in his duties to the crown. He knew that though this one be clearly difficult, he was not about to admit defeat at the onset.

Stephen felt certain he could see this through.

And once it was settled, there was the matter of the woman from the wood. Though he knew it was pure foolhardiness on his part, Stephen could not dismiss the notion of trying to locate her.

His body tightened at the very idea. Be she some nobleman's bastard, he would surely be able to come up with the coin to loosen any possible resistance.

But once more he dragged his thoughts back to the present. Not until Stephen had seen to his official duties would he be free to pursue his own interests.

With impatience, he turned to the doorway through which he expected Lord Grayson's wife and daughter to come.

Chapter Two

Just a short time later, Stephen watched as two female figures came to the arched doorway of the hall. The light from the narrow windows was not bright on that end of the hall at this hour and, as they paused at the other end of the wide stone chamber, the two were cloaked in shadow.

The first, a slender woman of perhaps forty entered after only a moment's hesitation. She was dressed in simple but well-made garments of dark blue samite, and her head was covered by a dark veil and wimple. A ring of keys rode the belt at her waist and she approached Richard Grayson with stiff formality. "You sent for me, my lord husband." She nodded, her brown eyes fixed on the one she addressed without affection.

Stephen could see that she had surely once been a pretty maid. But now her expression was tightly fixed and unyielding, leaving her features pinched.

Grayson turned to Stephen, no hint of his feelings on his face. "Allow me to present my wife, the Lady Mary."

She made no attempt at speech, simply stared at him coolly.

Her husband gestured toward Stephen. "My lady, this is Sir Stephen Clayburn, he is come here from King Edward."

Stephen nodded and uttered a polite greeting. "Lady Grayson." There seemed little about this woman to lend such awe in her husband, though she did appear somewhat ill-tempered.

Lady Grayson's expression was rife with displeasure, her lips set in a firm line. Considering the fact that her husband had expressly forbidden the serving woman to tell his wife of Stephen's purpose in being there, her attitude was surprising.

He wondered if her reaction was directed toward himself, her husband, or just a sign of a sour nature. He hoped she had not passed it on to her daughter if the latter was the case.

With curiosity, Stephen's gaze strayed to the other female who still lingered in the shadows beside the doorway.

Stephen became aware of Lord Grayson's attention and turned to the other man to find a smile on his handsome face. Not that there was any real humor in it. That grin bespoke more a sense of resignation and pity for Stephen.

Unsure as to the cause of either emotion, Stephen turned his attention back to the girl.

"My daughter, Fellis," the older man confirmed. His tone became one of impatience. "Come here, girl, into the light where we can see you. You have no need to fear."

She hesitated still, only her shoulders shifted as if with indecision.

Lady Grayson spoke and her tone was filled with suspicion. "Why are we here, Richard?" she asked. "Why have you sent for Fellis to come to the hall and meet this man."

When Stephen looked at her, she was staring at Lord Grayson with open hostility. "I hope you have not finally given in to your selfish desire to try to wed our daughter to some hopeful suitor. He will only end in leaving here disappointed."

Richard laughed, still without humor. "Not I, my dear. And this man is no suitor, so you may cast your righteous indignation toward him away. He has not come here to marry our precious daughter. Though you will be equally displeased when you find out why he has come."

Stephen frowned. The relationship between husband and wife was more openly antagonistic than any he'd seen. His own parents had indeed argued in their marriage before they had succumbed to the plague, yet there had been no hint of the bitterness that clearly existed between these two.

Yet that was not his concern. Getting their daughter married was, and he wondered at the strange remarks Lady Mary had made concerning her fears that Lord Richard had brought the knight to Malvern as a suitor. The subject was clearly a heated one.

But he stopped himself there. What had gone before mattered not in the least. The future was paramount and Stephen was not going to allow them to digress into an argument about the situation before he'd even had a chance to reason with the girl.

He was certain that, given an opportunity to see what her duty was, the maid would do as she must.

Thinking to expedite the process of explaining the situation, Stephen called out softly, speaking directly to the girl. "Do not shy from me, Maid Grayson, I am not here to do you harm. As your father has told you there is nothing to fear from me."

She stepped farther into the room and stood in the soft golden glow of one window's light. Still she did not raise her head.

Stephen was surprised to see the young girl dressed in a gray rough-spun garment much like that of a nun. A veil and wimple of the same dull hue covered her head and obscured any glimpse of her face from his view.

He wondered at such lowly dressing for the lord's own daughter and swung around to face her parents with a frown. Though the mother's cote was admittedly plain, he had taken note of the fineness of the blue cloth. "What means this garb? Did I not know better I would think your daughter had taken holy orders. Or that she must live by some vow of poverty unobserved by the rest of her kin."

Richard Grayson faced him with a frown of his own, though he made no reply. It appeared that the situation pleased him no more than it did the younger man.

His wife interjected with a self-satisfied smile. "Unwittingly you have hit upon the truth. Although my daughter has not taken vows as of yet, 'tis but a matter of time until that eventuality takes place. We wait only for her father to pay her dowry and the abbey at Hardwicke will receive her into their order."

Stephen gave a visible start at hearing this. Even though he'd said the words, he'd not thought of them as anything beyond reprimand for the girl's poor state of dress. Then he forced his shoulders to relax. He was not going to let this woman get the better of him. "I think not, Lady Grayson. Your daughter is to be wed, most certainly, but not to our Lord and Savior."

Mary Grayson looked to her husband as her daughter echoed her gasp of shock. "What says he, my lord husband? This is surely some jest on your part. Why you just said this man was not here to wed our Fellis."

"He is not," Lord Grayson intoned. "He is come to arrange a marriage betwixt Fellis and Wynn ap Dafydd."

Mary Grayson cried, "Not on my life. You will not marry my daughter to that Welsh barbarian."

Richard Grayson flushed, casting an angry frown Stephen's way. "Lady wife, you know my feelings concerning our enemy match your own. I have not given my permission for this event to take place. Only agreed to go forward with talks on the matter should the Welsh agree to comply with a truce. I have been left with little choice in the matter. King Edward himself has sent this man here to see to the deed.''

Stephen did not look at him but kept his gaze on the Lady Mary. ''What he says is true, Lady Mary. The matter rests little in your husband's hands, but in King Edward's. He has declared the marriage will take place if it can be arranged and there is naught that can be done to change it.''

He reached inside his tunic to pull out the document that sealed Fellis's fate. He passed the missive to the older woman, who took it somewhat gingerly. Slowly she opened the document to scan it, her expression showing her displeasure and horror, which grew steadily with every word she read.

Thinking to give the lady an opportunity to absorb the truth with some modicum of privacy, Stephen averted his gaze to the young girl. She had stepped back into the shadows by the door, her slender body poised as if ready for flight.

Stephen had had enough of this. She had no need to fear him. He spoke to her. ''Damsel, please come forward so that we might discuss this rationally. Naught can be gained by hiding.''

He moved across the room in long, purposeful strides and held out his hand.

But she refused to put hers in it. After only one more brief moment of hesitation she finally did come into the room, stepping around him carefully, her shoulders squared as if fighting for courage.

When she moved, it was with a strange halting grace that drew Stephen to watch her with interest. Slowly she came forward, pausing as she stepped beneath the direct light of the window along the outer wall. For a moment her face was profiled in a fine, clear shaft of brightness.

It was then Stephen caught his breath.

It was her! The sprite from the forest. There was no mistaking the fragile beauty of her profile haloed in the white-gold light. Though none of that glorious silver blond hair escaped her nunlike wimple and veil, he knew there was no mistake.

Nothing could make him forget those moments in the forest glade and what he had seen. Each minute detail of her face and exquisite form was etched forever in his mind.

With chagrin he recalled his resolve to find her, his plans to have her, no matter what the cost. For one long moment he knew a gripping tightness in chest, the intensity of which surprised and displeased him.

God, to find her here. And worse yet, to know he must arrange her wedding to another man.

But Stephen quickly quelled his reaction. He would do what he must. Even though this was the first woman he had ever felt such an intense and overwhelming desire to know, she was not for him. It was, in point of fact, ridiculous of him to even ponder such thoughts.

He had only just set eyes on the maid this very morning. Surely he was quite mad to even concern himself with her.

But no matter what he told himself, Stephen could not force his gaze from her.

Fellis halted and glanced at the tall, imposing knight with a frown of displeasure as she passed him. What did her father mean by saying he had come here to arrange a marriage between herself and Wynn ap Dafydd? Then, as she actually looked at the knight for the first time, Fellis unexpectedly found herself giving pause, for he was devastatingly handsome with his dark auburn hair that gleamed with fiery highlights and eyes so dark a green they made her think of her secret place in the forest. Her gaze swept upward over a hard, chiseled jaw, an aquiline nose, then was caught and held by his.

For the eternal length of that one long pulse-pounding moment, she was unable to turn away.

There was something different about him, about the way she felt as he looked down at her. It was as if he were gazing not just at her but into her—into that place she had long buried where she was a woman with needs and desires like any other.

Without her consent, her willful gaze slipped down from that lean-jawed face, over a corded neck and across wide shoulders encased in dark green velvet. Not even the heaviness of his tunic sleeve could disguise the power of his arms, nor of his sun-bronzed hands, with their surprisingly supple fingers. Those fingers looked as if they would be equally at home on the strings of a lute as they would be on the hilt of the sword that hung from his narrow hips by a gold-buckled belt.

This was a man who had turned the heads of many a maid. Even to her untutored eyes there was no doubt.

But what completely unnerved her and made it doubly difficult to catch her breath was the hunger in his eyes as he looked down at her. It was as if he were drinking in the sight of her as she was him.

Fellis could not credit that this man with his strong, hard body and handsome face could be interested in her. The idea was unthinkable. It was simply her own reaction to his incredible masculinity that made her feel so breathless.

She was not a woman to draw such notice. Her crippled foot set her apart from others. No man would desire a woman who was so marked, 'twas a clear sign of God's displeasure.

Why then *was* he watching her with such open intensity? Then the answer flashed into her mind like a painful poke at a sore tooth. Her deformity! The man knew of her twisted ankle and simply sought to carefully study one so afflicted.

She flushed a deep scarlet and dropped her gaze. Always it was so. They could not see that inside her she was a young woman like any other and that defect had not twisted the rest of her body and mind as it had her ankle. They did not care that inside her beat a heart like any other. And that heart was vulnerable to their stares and revulsion.

Quickly she swung away from him, unable to face his scrutiny now that she knew the reason behind it.

To her great distress, her limp seemed even more pronounced than usual as she made haste to seat herself at the trestle table. But she held her head high, refusing to allow the man to see how hurt she was by his appraisal.

Her surreptitious glance darted to her parents and away. Hopefully they had not taken note of what had just occurred. She knew how sensitive they both were to people's negative reactions to her.

Her mother was still much occupied with reading the roll of parchment and Richard Grayson was watching his wife with undisguised longing.

Fellis forced away her own feelings of hurt, aware of a familiar ache of sadness for her father, but knew she could do nothing to help. Her mother had long ago made her feelings on the marriage known to them all.

Fellis was aware that the Baron of Malvern was a lonely man, yet to his daughter's knowledge he had not taken a mistress. He still hoped for his wife to someday turn to him.

But then, as she sighed with regret, Fellis looked to her mother again. Her gaze came to rest on the missive in the Lady Mary's hands and her eyes opened wide as the old problems flew from her mind in the face of the new.

It had certainly hurt for the man to stare at her so. But that was naught in comparison to what his gaze had made her forget.

Sir Stephen Clayburn had said she was to be married.

She longed to look at the man who had announced such incredible news. But Fellis could not bring herself to do so in the event that she might once again fall victim to that probing green gaze. Her attention focused on the white-knuckled hands she twisted so tightly in her lap.

Married. And to Wynn ap Dafydd, her father's sworn enemy. She had never so much as seen him, though the deeds of his followers were well-known to her. They were wont to rob, burn and terrorize the English residing at Malvern castle at every opportunity.

Her father had been granted custodianship of the castle twenty years ago, two years before she was even born, and Fellis knew no other existence beyond this uncertain one along the Welsh border.

Fellis looked to her mother, who had now dropped her hand so that the parchment dangled from her fingers as she visibly fought for control. And find it she would, of that Fellis had no doubt. Mother was not one to be overset by any circumstance, no matter how disturbing. She had a way of forcing things to come out as she wished them to.

Then Fellis realized that she need not concern herself with this marriage. Never would Mary Grayson agree to the match. She was determined for Fellis to enter the convent. In the past years her mother had managed to keep her father from so much as suggesting any suitor, though he still refused to pay the dowry that would grant her admittance to the abbey.

In Fellis's eyes Mary Grayson was a more intimidating force than any distant king could ever be.

It did not occur to Fellis that she was more than an observer in these proceedings. She had been told, since she was old enough to remember, that she must enter the church.

Like Malvern castle, it was all she knew.

But her mother was not saying anything. Her pale cheeks were flushed with unhappiness as she looked from Stephen to her husband.

At last Mary Grayson spoke, and Fellis had the answer to the question of her mother's reticence. "King Edward has deigned to command this. Why would he be so interested in the affairs of one insignificant girl?" She asked the question out of obvious anger but her tone was one of awe and respect.

So even Mary Grayson was moved by the wishes of a king, Fellis thought, realizing that her world was indeed on the verge of forever changing.

Stephen moved forward and gestured to the seats around the table. "Perhaps we should sit and discuss this more comfortably." They followed his suggestion without demur, as if forgetting in their shock and confusion that they, and not he, were the hosts here.

Fellis's surprised gaze went to his face. He appeared totally in control of himself and sure of the outcome of this situation. Fellis could not halt a glimmer of grudging admiration.

She had thought her parents the two most commanding people in all the world, and they were obeying this handsome young knight as if they had no wills of their own.

He sat down across from her and she could feel him willing her to look at him. But Fellis did not meet his probing gaze, finding an unaccustomed sense of rebellion swelling her chest. She knew a desire to show him that she, for one, did not feel the need to obey him. Yet the effort to withstand that magnetic attraction was great, and she was grateful when she felt him turn his attention to her mother.

She looked to Sir Stephen only when he began to speak. "First I must address your question as to why King Edward would be interested in the affairs of your daughter. I assure you, Lady Grayson, that King Edward is always concerned with the well-being of the least of his subjects. He has thought long and hard upon this matter and believes that a marriage between your daughter and Wynn ap Dafydd will bring about a peace in this region."

"But why has he interested himself in this matter in particular?" she asked again. "How did it come to his attention?" The puzzlement on her once-fair countenance was obvious.

Richard Grayson cleared his throat. "You know, my lady wife, that I have asked King Edward to intercede in our troubles with the Welsh, though I had not asked for such a drastic solution. I had thought more of troops to help quell the knaves. This reply from His Majesty is most unexpected, to say the least."

"This is your doing then," she accused, eyeing her husband with a look of betrayal.

Lord Richard's gaze hardened. "How can you say so, wife? I wouldst not have had our Fellis put to this sacrifice. Rather would I have seen her enter the convent as you have pleaded with me to do."

Stephen halted further argument with a raised hand. "It is what the king wishes that matters. He is the one to have chosen this method of peacemaking. You know, do you not, that the Scots plague him without cease? And it is known to all that the war in France shows no sign of ending soon. The manpower could not be spared to send you military aid and he wishes to see this feuding done. For now and for all time.

A marriage is a sensible solution. Wynn will not be near as likely to raid and make trouble for his own in-laws.''

Although it was Fellis who might be forced to marry the Welshman, and she was not particularly pleased about the idea, she listened to the knight thoughtfully. She could see the logic in this reasoning.

She wondered why she felt so little reaction at discovering that she was to marry. But she could find no real satisfactory answer. Mayhap it was just the shock of it that left her feeling numb. Surely it had nothing to do with the fact that even the probability of her own changed future seemed to pall in the presence of this all too fascinating man.

Her gaze went to Stephen. Seeing that he had his attention fixed firmly upon her mother for the moment, Fellis took the opportunity to examine him more carefully.

Mayhap if she really looked at him, the knight would not seem as devastatingly attractive as she had first thought him. No man could be so compelling, she told herself.

But as she studied him, she knew her own eyes gave lie to the thought.

He had a face and form that would make any damsel sigh with longing. His hair was a strange shade she had never seen on a man, dark, deep auburn, but on him, with his straight nose, hard jaw and wide shoulders, it was completely masculine and gave him an aura of being filled with fire and energy. Thick dark lashes framed the eyes she knew were an intense shade of green.

Meeting this knight did indeed make even the threat of marriage to a stranger fade into insignificance. After all, she did not know Wynn and so had a difficult time seeing him as a real threat to her ordered existence.

Sir Stephen Clayburn was another matter entirely. He was here and, in the oh-so-tangible flesh, far more compelling than any alleged husband-to-be.

* * *

Stephen could see that accomplishing his purpose was not going to be easy. His first impression that Lord and Lady Grayson seemed to have little liking for each other was apparently quite accurate. Stephen couldn't help wondering at the cause of it.

It was obvious, despite their hostility for each other, that both parents loved their daughter, though in his mind they had an odd way of showing it. Did neither of them see that it was their child for whom they should show concern? She was the one who had just been told she was to marry.

Stephen did know that females were wed for political purposes on a regular basis. But he would have thought that, this coming as such a surprise to all of them, Lord and Lady Grayson might have felt some compulsion to assist their daughter in adjusting to the idea. After all, they must both see that ultimately, if Wynn agreed to the match, there was no way out of it. Once the king had set his hand to the idea it was done.

Stephen stole a glance at Fellis to see how she was taking the proceedings. The maiden flushed a deep scarlet and turned away.

Stephen spoke directly to her, ignoring the elder Graysons. She kept her face averted, and the edge of her veil effectively blocked her expression. "You do understand what I have said?"

She looked at him then, raising her brows as if in disdain. "Of course, my lord."

He studied her even more closely, drawn to that slight show of spirit, which made her blue eyes sparkle like sunlight on water. The image was a disturbing one, for it reminded him anew of the way he had seen her that morning. He forced himself to set the thought aside and say what he had been about to. "You seem little moved by the notion of your impending marriage."

She shrugged. "What choice have I? Though the outcome seems less assured than you would have us think, have you then already attained Wynn's agreement to this proposal?"

Stephen grinned, despite his own preoccupation with controlling his reactions to the Lady Fellis. The maid had thought faster than her mother. He watched her approvingly, shrugging his shoulders with confidence. "I have not met with Wynn ap Dafydd. But I have no doubt that I will be able to convince him as to the merits of the plan."

Lady Grayson interrupted, appearing decidedly pleased at this news. "You have not spoken with him?" She shook her head with a pity borne of condescension. "I am afraid, Sir Clayburn, that the outcome of this plan may not be so assured as you believe. Wynn ap Dafydd is not one to bow to anyone's coercion, even that of a king. He, like the rest of his countrymen, resents English rule and does not recognize Edward as his true sovereign."

"Hence your difficulties with him," Stephen supplied. "But have no fear I shall gain his agreement. That is not your concern." He turned back to Fellis, finding himself lost in the depths of her wide blue gaze. He forced himself to say what he must, to remember what his purpose here was. "I simply require your assurance that you will consider the notion of marriage to him."

She stared at him, her surprise evident in her eyes. Fellis replied, "I must say that I am most astonished that you would even think to ask. I will have no say in what happens." She flushed deeply as she faced him, looked down, then back at him. "What...who is to say that Wynn will have me? Does he know of me...of my imperfection?"

So occupied was Stephen in trying to put name to the exact shade of blue, azure, he thought, that it was a moment before he could attend to what she said. Then he frowned. "Wynn ap Dafydd is not so great a man that he might repudiate you." It amazed him that she would think that Wynn might not want her. What man could refuse such grace and beauty for his very own? It was difficult for Stephen to even contemplate another man having the right to touch the perfection he had viewed that very day. He spoke slowly, thinking of his own loss in finding she was unavailable to fulfill his desire. "Not every man has the right to expect or even hope for true perfection in a bride. He must simply accept the more common lot he has been given."

Stephen was surprised to hear Fellis gasp, and forced his attention away from his interior thoughts.

But the sound of Fellis's indrawn breath was followed by her father's angry words. "How dare you, Sir Knight!" Lord Richard stood to glare across the table at him.

Chapter Three

Fellis Grayson rose, her face turned away from him, but Stephen could see her displeasure in the rigid line of her back. With careful dignity she stepped back from the trestle table. Her mother reached out a hand. But the maid waved it aside and turned from them without a word.

Stephen sat for what seemed an interminable moment, unsure as to what he might have said or done. Only then did he see that Fellis seemed to be limping as she left the room. He didn't spare more than a glance for her mother, who was muttering under her breath as she cast the knight a glare of disapproval from her place across from him.

He could not stop a rush of confusion as Lord Grayson rounded on him with outrage.

"What think you, Sir Knight, to insult my daughter so? Have you no sense of chivalry." The gray-haired man raked an iron-cold stare over Stephen.

Stephen stood, holding out his hands, his expression perplexed. "My lord, I know not what this is about. If you would but give me some clue as to what I have done to offend you, I would be grateful."

Grayson looked at him closely, then obviously seeing the genuine confusion on the other man's face, he calmed. His

shoulders slumped down as he regained his seat. "You behave as if you actually do not know."

"I do not!"

"Fellis is . . ." The older man halted, clearly finding what
he was about to say difficult. He straightened his velvet-clad
shoulders. "My daughter was born with a deformity of the
ankle. It is commonly known as a clubfoot. Could you not
see that she does not walk as others?"

Slowly Stephen sank into his seat, finally understanding
what had upset them all so much. It seemed that by making
that remark about Wynn not being able to reject a woman
of such perfection he had inadvertently touched a painful
wound.

For a moment Stephen felt angry with them all. What did
it matter that Fellis had a twisted ankle? He had viewed her
completely devoid of any covering and there was naught
about that small imperfection to mar his memory of what
he had seen. In point of fact, the blemish could not be so
very disfiguring, for he had not even taken note of the fact.

And as far as his noticing that Fellis did not walk as others, he had been far too occupied with his own confused
feelings at seeing her again. Even now he knew a tightening
in his lower belly at the recollection of Fellis's silvery beauty.

Stephen glanced over at the other man, a flush staining his
throat as he realized his thoughts had gone where they had
no right to. Now that he knew who Fellis was, he must remember that he was here for one reason only. And that was
to have her wed with all possible haste.

He glanced toward Mary Grayson and saw her watching
him with ill-concealed contempt. He would get no support
from that quarter. Of that he was more than convinced.

Stephen's speculative gaze went back to the father. Making Richard Grayson his ally was one thing that might certainly aid him in his task.

He was not sure how to go about telling Fellis's parents that he had meant no insult to their daughter by what he had said. Assuring them that he had seen her naked in the forest this very morning would serve no purpose other than to fully convince them that he was a knave. He would likely be thrown from the keep.

But Stephen did know that others might not feel the same way about the deformity as he. Those who had not seen how completely lovely Fellis Grayson truly was.

But how to convince her father the slight imperfection was naught to him? He decided that it might help to say as much. "Learning of your daughter's ankle makes no difference to me, my lord."

Lady Grayson drew their eyes by standing with a sound of disbelief and condemnation. "Pretty words, my lord, when 'tis not yourself who would take her to wife. Methinks the conversation might have taken a different turn had it been otherwise." She swept back the trailing hem of her blue cote and left them, her head held high.

Stephen found himself frowning with frustration. What more could he do? The woman was determined to think ill of him. He turned back to her husband.

Grayson watched him. "My wife means nothing against you as a man. She, as you know, has her own agenda in this. Nothing you could say would make her see you as anything but her enemy at this juncture." He remained silent for a long moment, then shrugged. "As far as what you have said about meaning no harm toward Fellis, I believe you." He eyed Stephen levelly. "There is a ring of sincerity in your voice when you say so. Although you are of a strange minority. Her affliction does matter to many. Even among those closest to her." His mouth thinned to a line of frustration and, Stephen thought, perhaps, pain. "There are those who view such a malformation as the mark of the devil himself.''

'Twas no secret that many believed this way. Though Stephen himself did not adhere to that ridiculous school of thought, he could not honestly say if he would have felt the same way toward the girl had he not seen her as she truly was.

But the fact remained that he had. And he could not forget that Fellis was lovely enough to heat any man's blood, twisted ankle or no.

Stephen knew he should not allow these thoughts to spill into his consciousness.

With determination, Stephen recalled the path of their conversation. It appeared there was more below the surface of what Lord Grayson was saying as he spoke. Stephen had a sense that his attention was turned inward on some hurt of his own.

Stephen shook his head. It seemed what he did was trade one unwise mode of thought for another. What he must concentrate on was making Fellis's father see where the real obstacles to her future lay.

"My Lord Grayson," he began. "I must tell you again that it makes no difference to me, and should not to any sane man. Lady Fellis is lovely and seems of bright mind and good health. If you worry over some aspect of her, please let it be her mode of dress. That nunlike garb is more liable to keep a man from her than her ankle. 'Twould give any warm-blooded male pause to wonder if she would be more inclined to pray all night than warm his bed. Would you welcome a woman who came to you in such?''

Now Stephen could clearly see that he had struck some sort of nerve as Grayson growled in reply. "Nay, I would not. 'Tis her mother's doing. And make no mistake, though I do not approve, I have not been able to convince her otherwise." He gave the younger man a long, measuring look. "There is more here than you know, sir. Are you able to change things, I will mark you a better man than myself."

A heavy silence reigned as Stephen took this in. He had no desire to get himself involved in affairs between a man and wife. But if it must be so to see his duty done, he would have little choice. With trepidation, Stephen took a long breath and expelled it, then asked, "What mean you?"

"I mean, sir, that my wife will never allow this marriage to take place, even can you arrange it. You see, it began when Mary was a child and made a foolish vow to someday take the cloth. Years later, when her father arranged our marriage, she had not forgotten and balked against the union." He spoke, his tone without feeling, as if once started he no longer cared about the telling of a tale that had long pained him. "But we were young and our bodies strong." Only now did he take on a wistful intonation. "That was the happiest year of my life. Though reluctant at first, Mary became eager in her passions. For those months she gave of herself as I had not thought possible, especially when she had not wished to come to me, and had only acquiesced when her father forced her. But it was as if her desire, once awakened, could not be cooled. Even when we discovered that she was with child, our passions did not abate. It was only when the babe was born, her ankle twisted, that my wife turned from me. She was convinced that Fellis's deformity was a sign that God was punishing her for not fulfilling her vow to become a nun. Nothing could sway her from that thinking. She turned from me and our marital bed."

Stephen could hardly credit this story. That a mother should think this of her own daughter, and that a wife should openly refuse her husband and her duty to produce children went against reason. It would be different if she had found her husband distasteful, but from the account, that was clearly not so. "How old is Fellis then? She is no longer a child."

Lord Grayson frowned, looking down at his hands. "She is some moons past eighteen."

Stephen shook his head. It amazed him that the situation could have gone on for so many years.

"My lady wife is determined that Fellis will fulfill her broken vow. And naught I have said has ever convinced her that it shall not be so." The baron heaved a sigh of sorrows unspoken.

Stephen felt himself unwillingly being pulled into the web of their lives. He could not prevent himself from asking, "Why then is Fellis not a nun, if your lady is so determined that she will be?"

"I have refused to pay the dowry. It is the one thing I have had the strength to defy her on."

With that, he rose and left a pensive Stephen seated alone in the hall. He felt sympathy for the other man but knew he could not allow himself to become too involved in what was going on between the residents of Malvern castle. His duty here was to see Fellis Grayson wed to Wynn ap Dafydd.

Mary Grayson must and would come to see the facts as they were. It was for the good of her family and the people of her lands that she do so. Her own desires surely came second to that.

And it was best for Fellis, Stephen told himself. What must it have been like for her to live with the knowledge that she was responsible for paying for her mother's imagined sins? Marriage, even to her enemy, must be preferable to that. Fellis must simply be brought to understand this.

Stephen felt a tug of something uncomfortable in his chest at the notion of Fellis's marriage. He sat up straighter, telling himself that having seen the woman without clothing did not give him any right to her.

And such thoughts were nothing short of foolish, as it was. He did not know her. Only that he had seen her and desired her in a way he had not known possible.

But somehow he must make himself forget that desire. It was all he could do.

Not knowing what to do with himself, Stephen remained seated. He had no idea where he might be accommodated. Such things were always an issue in the running of an overflowing keep. Clearly the family members were too upset to have given the matter any thought.

It was only a short time later that Stephen was surprised to see Lady Grayson return to the door of the hall. Although he knew she viewed him with ill favor, he could not deny a feeling of relief and went to her quickly.

She looked to him with a frown of displeasure, which Stephen did his best to ignore. "My Lady Grayson," he said, "I am most gladdened to see you."

Her pinched expression told him she was anything but delighted to see him. She made no pretense at polite response. "I came in search of my lord husband. I am sorry to have disturbed you, Sir Clayburn."

He held out a hand to stop her. "Nay, you do not disturb me. I was hoping someone would come to tell me where I am to be housed."

She gave him a long, disapproving look as if housing him was of great distaste to her. "I am seeing to that at this moment," she replied with transparent reluctance. "If you will but wait for me to see to things I will attend you. Excuse me if the wait is overtaxing, I must first find my husband before I can do so. I have need of his strong arms."

"Is there aught I can do to assist you?" he asked pleasantly, at his most agreeable even in the face of her dislike.

She frowned at him. "I think it best if I find my lord husband."

She turned to go, but Stephen followed her. "Dear lady, please allow me to be of assistance. I feel as if I have inconvenienced you and wish to make myself useful." He nodded, unruffled by her disapproval. Now that he knew whence it came, he felt no need to take any personal responsibility for her displeasure.

Lady Grayson was in a hell of her own making.

Obviously surprised at his continued good humor, she gave an offhanded shrug. "Mayhap you can help, if that be your desire."

With a smile that had melted many a hard heart, Stephen motioned forward.

She only made a rude sound in her throat and led the way.

They climbed a narrow stairway to the second floor of the keep. Lady Grayson opened the door of a well-lighted, comfortable-looking chamber with a large bed and a tall window swathed in crimson draperies that matched those on the bed. A fire burned in the hearth and the room was somewhat overwarm for Stephen's comfort.

But he made no comment as she led him directly to the bed and he looked down upon a diminutive elderly lady who was dwarfed by the enormous piece of furniture. As she saw Stephen, she smiled, peering up at Mary Grayson curiously. "Is this the young man then who will sleep in my chambers?"

Immediately Stephen shook his head as understanding dawned. "Nay, Lady Grayson. I cannot put this lady from her bed."

The elderly dame turned her still-alert blue eyes upon him. "Do not be foolish, young sir, I will be most insulted if you refuse."

"But, my lady..." He looked to Mary Grayson, realizing he did not know to whom he was speaking.

Lady Mary answered the unspoken question stiffly. "This is my husband's lady mother, Myrian Grayson." She motioned toward the knight. "As you have guessed, Mother, this gentleman is Sir Stephen Clayburn, the very one I spoke to you about. He is come to make Fellis marry the Welshman." She turned to Stephen with accusing eyes.

"'Tis time Fellis married," the tiny woman said. "Too much of her life has been wasted already. The girl needs to give me a great-grandchild while I am still upon this earth."

Lady Mary made a noise of denial. "You, as well as anyone, know that Fellis will be God's bride and no other's, Mother." She looked to Stephen, her mouth set in stubborn rebellion.

"Now," she said to him, clearly trying to forestall any rejoinder on his part, "shall we go about moving my lady mother, or will we stand about discussing matters which have already been set?" She gave an impatient sigh. "If you will not, I must fetch my husband. For Lady Myrian will not allow the servants to carry her."

Stephen felt his ire rising and fought hard to quell it. He was not accustomed to being the brunt of such open antagonism and it irked him. But he was not going to allow this woman to see that. With carefully schooled features, he said, "I beg you, my lady, to allow this lady to remain in her own room. I will be most content with some other accommodation and have no objection to however humble it might prove to be."

She put her hands on her hips. "Sir Knight, do not press me further. This chamber is all I have to offer that would befit the messenger of a king. The keep is full to repletion and I must beg your cooperation. Lest, of course, you would choose to sleep in the stables and insult me and mine by doing so. And let me assure you, my husband's mother goes to a comfortable place. I would not have her tossed into the dungeons in order to make room for even you, Sir Clayburn.''

This time Stephen could not prevent the thinning of his lips. But he withheld the sharp retort that sprang to mind. It was clear that nothing he could do would melt the frozen exterior of this bitter woman. "What would you have me do?" he conceded.

Lady Grayson drew back the covers and stepped aside. "Please, will you bring her? I will show you the way."

Raking a hand through his dark auburn hair, Stephen bent and lifted the little woman gently into his arms.

As Lady Grayson led the way from the room without so much as another word, Stephen went after her. He was eager to get this task accomplished and find some respite from Lady Mary's sharp tongue.

They went to the end of the corridor to another oaken door, which lay open in welcome.

Thinking to settle the lady and be on his way, Stephen moved into the chamber eagerly.

Then he stopped as he saw who waited beside the bed.

It was Fellis. Seeing her so unexpectedly was more unnerving than he would have imagined. He turned away, aware of no more than the fact that she now wore black and that her hair hung down her back in a thick silver braid.

Trying to give himself time to recover his equilibrium, Stephen turned his attention to the chamber itself, finding he was indeed curious about where she spent her private time. The bed curtains were heavy and of good samite, but of a dark shade of gray, as were the window curtains. The floor was bare of any covering, but as clean as vigorous scrubbing could make worn stone. On a chest beside the window lay a plain comb, hair bobs or mirror conspicuously absent. On a table beside the bed was an unlit candle, a crucifix and a book of prayers. Everything was spotlessly clean and neat. Nowhere was there even one other item of a personal nature. Everything about it cried out with the same stark simplicity that her clothing did.

Stephen found himself wondering if there was one sign of the woman he had seen in the forest, that creature of light and magic who had bound him so effortlessly in her spell.

He looked to where Fellis stood beside the bed. And then he saw it, there, in her.

As he had glimpsed upon entering, she had removed her gray garb and was now wearing a long plain garment of black. Her silver blond hair was no longer covered by a veil and wimple, but hung down her back in a thick braid the size of his wrist. Soft wisps escaped to curl around her pale cheeks, which were just touched with a blush of pink.

He sucked in a breath, stunned by the sheer loveliness of her. Shocked at the intensity of his reaction to her, Stephen knew he must relieve himself of the slight burden of her grandmother and be gone.

What a fool he had been to think he could so easily dismiss the effect she had had on him in the forest. With determined strides, he moved to the bed and, although he was agitated, he took tender care to lay the elderly woman down upon the pillows.

As he straightened, he looked into Lady Myrian's blue eyes, which were so like Fellis's, and saw that she was watching him with great intensity and interest. Stephen knew she was seeing far more than he would have liked as she then cast a speculative glance toward her granddaughter, who was standing as if carved from stone.

He looked into Fellis's face to see if she had taken note of her grandmother's scrutiny.

When their eyes met for one brief moment, Stephen saw the pain there and knew how much he had hurt her with his remark downstairs. He had not meant to do so, but could not say that he found her more beautiful and desirable than any woman he had ever chanced to behold. It would serve no good purpose for Fellis to know how he felt about her.

But he could not help conveying his feelings with his eyes.

Fellis could hardly think past the racing of her heart. The way he was looking at her made it so very difficult to breathe, let alone reason.

Never would she have expected to see Stephen Clayburn here in her very chamber. No man save her father had ever even ventured inside when she was present. She reached up to place her hand over the naked vulnerability of her throat.

He was even more devastating to her senses than he had been when she had met him in the hall. There, the table had been in the way, putting a safe distance between them. Here he was standing so close to her she was able to see the faint stubble of dark hair upon his cheeks and the way the muscles flexed below the skin of his lean jaw. Though Fellis was not a diminutive woman, being a medium height, he seemed to tower over her, the wide breadth of his shoulders in dark green velvet drawing her eyes almost against her will.

Despite the fact that Stephen Clayburn had hurt her with his insensitive remarks in the hall, Fellis found herself mesmerized by the sheer size and force of him. Nothing in her life had prepared Fellis for the eventuality of coming into contact with this physically devastating man.

She knew she should be angry, but Fellis found it impossible to look away. She could not summon the spleen to protect her battered pride.

Only when her grandmother called her very softly was she able to regain her senses.

With a flush of shame she looked into the old lady's eyes. There she saw sympathy and that nearly did her in. What that sign of sympathy meant she dared not contemplate. Did her grandmother pity her because she could see how Stephen affected her and knew that such a man would not want her?

If Grandmother had taken note of her sinful preoccupation with Stephen Clayburn then mayhap he had, too. So ashamed was Fellis that she could not even bring herself to glance in his direction for fear he might be watching her. At best, pitying her, at worst, contemptuous of her.

Hurriedly she reached to pull the bed covers up over her grandmother's slight frame. Grandmother was often cold now and Fellis did not want her to catch a chill. She took her usual tender care in making the elderly lady settled.

Once Grandmother was settled on her pillows comfortably, Fellis reached forward to smooth her hand over the skin of her forehead, which was fine as onion skin. Myrian closed her eyes and gave a tired sigh. Gently Fellis asked, "Are you well, Grandmother?"

"Just a little tired, dear."

Fellis felt Stephen move from her side. Her emotions were a mix of relief and, unbelievably, regret, but she did not glance up.

Only when Grandmother opened her eyes and observed Stephen, where he now stood beside Mary Grayson near the doorway, did she allow herself to look at him. "You have my thanks, sir," the old woman said.

Fellis was surprised to see him give what appeared to be a start.

But if the reaction had been what she thought, he recovered quickly and nodded his head politely. "And you are most welcome, dear lady. I can only say that you have my thanks for allowing me to occupy your own chamber. 'Tis a most gracious sacrifice. I beg you excuse me now until I see you again.''

With that, he turned and left the chamber before more could be said. Lady Mary hurried after him and Fellis could only assume that her mother meant to see the knight settled in his room. Though she did not want him here, Mother would not offer insult in the hospitality she extended to the messenger of King Edward.

Busily, Fellis moved to the end of the bed so as not to think any further on Stephen Clayburn and how he had affected her. She reached for the extra cover that lay there. ''Are you warm enough, Grandmother?''

''Oh, yes, indeed. You have shown great care for my comfort, dearling, as you always do. I think I will just have a bit of rest now.''

Fellis could hear the weariness in her tone. Her grandmother had suffered with a bout of lung fever during the winter and was still weak and frail from the illness. She tired easily and needed a great deal of rest. They were all grateful to the good Lord for her recovery, though Fellis knew they must still have fear for her.

Saying no more, she took up her book of prayer to read while her grandmother drifted off to sleep.

But the familiar words on the page could not hold her this day. It was a pair of deep green eyes that lingered in her mind, making her very aware of the fact that for some time Stephen Clayburn would be a guest in this very keep.

How was she ever to bear it? Not only had he come here thinking he could arrange a marriage between her and her father's enemy, he had offered insult by saying Wynn had no right to repudiate such as she even if she was not a worthy bride.

There was no reason for anyone to remind her of her shortcomings. Fellis was not like to forget them even for a moment.

Her traitorous thoughts tangled on. Why then, if he felt that way about her had he looked at her that way when they first met—so... as if, oh heaven, as if he were hungry. Looked at her as he had only minutes ago in this very same room.

For those instants when his eyes had met hers something strange had seemed to pass between them, a feeling that made her belly tighten, a yearning to touch and be touched.

It made no sense. And even if the man had not made cruel reference to her defect, he would have no personal interest in her.

The knight had come here with the preposterous notion of seeing her wed to none other than Wynn ap Dafydd. Fellis had not so much as laid eyes upon the man. And he was their sworn enemy. She knew her father would not approve of such a match. Even if Richard Grayson could be convinced, there was no chance of such a thing taking place.

Her mother would not allow a marriage, was Wynn the most acceptable of suitors. Her plans for Fellis did not in any way include marriage and—it was hard for Fellis to even think the word without regret—children.

Resolutely she shook her head on her pain. Such was not for her. She knew her duty and would do it.

Stephen Clayburn and his schemes could mean nothing to her.

Stephen allowed Lady Mary to lead him to the chamber from whence he had just taken the grandmother, without really hearing most of what she said. So preoccupied was he with thoughts of her daughter and his own guilt at having hurt her, that he was not affected by her disregard of him or even aware if she continued to display it.

Inside the chamber, Lady Mary halted, turning to face him.

Focusing his attention on his hostess, the knight learned that he would be expected to attend meals in the hall with the other castle folk, unless he gave instructions to the contrary.

Muttering that he would be happy to share his meals with them and that he would require no special care, Stephen watched the door close behind her with relief.

He could not stop thinking that, though he had not meant to offend Fellis Grayson, it was his responsibility to set the matter aright.

The naked sadness in her eyes had near done him in. But there had been no opportunity to explain himself in her room. And if truth be told, he'd been too overcome by his own reactions to her beauty to think of trying.

He threw himself down upon the bed, his hand across his eyes as he remembered it was what had come afterward that really unnerved him.

As he had watched her tenderly caring for her elderly grandmother, Stephen had been assaulted by images of Fellis nude, the clear vision of her burned in his mind for all time. He'd thought of her soft slender hands smoothing over his flesh as he lay gasping beneath her.

The image had been so real and vivid that he was unable to stop the immediate rush of heat in his loins. Only the fact that his pourpoint covered his arousal kept him from completely embarrassing himself.

Dear Lord, he groaned. What was he to do with himself? He was a man full grown, well past the time when he had gained authority over his body. And never, he had to admit, however reluctantly, had he known such a reaction, even as an unschooled lad.

But somehow he must wrest control of this madness. He knew why he had come here, and it had naught to do with becoming obsessed with the baron's daughter.

For the good of himself and his mission, Stephen knew he would need attain enough mastery over this situation to carry on with his duties. It was imperative that he at least make contact with the girl and so obtain her acceptance of the way things must be. 'Twould help him immensely in gaining his ends.

Firstly he must certainly explain about what he had said in the hall. There was little hope of convincing her of anything if he did not try to ease that expression of pain in her eyes.

Stephen sat up, a scowl of determination on his face. How he would persuade her he had no notion, but do it he would.

He refused to acknowledge the voice inside him that told him he had more private reasons for wanting to see the hurt disappear.

It was that very afternoon that his opportunity arose. He had taken the noon meal without seeing even one member of the family. This was a sure indication of their continued discomfort with the idea he had presented them.

He was not concerned about this though. Given time, Lord Grayson would see what must happen. He simply needed an opportunity to adjust.

After the meal, Stephen decided to take a walk about the grounds as he was loath to spend one more moment in his chamber. Never one to enjoy too much leisure, Stephen had paced the chamber's every inch in the hours he'd spent there during the morning.

He did not wish to go to the Welshman until things were progressing more satisfactorily at Malvern. Hopefully Lord Grayson would be able to bring himself to at least attend Stephen with civility ere long.

He was directed to the castle gardens by a buxom serving girl with a cloud of dark hair and flirtatious eyes. For the first time in his life Stephen was not moved by such charms.

It was eyes of light blue and hair of silver that occupied his thoughts to the exclusion of any others.

He hurried in the direction the servant had indicated. Mayhap a walk in the fresh air would cure him of whatever ailed him. The knight had gone only a short ways into the well-tended gardens, with their neat rows of flowers that had not yet begun to bloom, when he saw her sitting on a bench just ahead.

Fellis.

Stephen drew up short, taking a deep breath.

Though it had been in his mind to speak with Fellis Grayson, he had not thought the occasion would come so soon. Uncomfortably aware of the way he had been thinking of her, he hesitated. Then he chided himself. He was not so faint of heart that he must cower from facing a woman— however lovely and compelling.

As he moved toward her again, he found he had mastered some control over his reactions to her, for he was able to smile with casual civility as she looked up from her book. Or mayhap, he told himself with complete honesty, his fortitude was greatly buoyed by the fact that she wore what he thought of as her nun's garb again.

Fellis looked up, her eyes widening, her mouth opening in an O of surprise as she bolted to her feet. Her readiness to make an exit was clear.

"Lady Fellis." Stephen held up a hand to halt her. "Please do not leave on my accord. I have a wish to speak with you, would you allow me."

She looked about as if seeking some excuse to deny him.

He rushed on. "I must explain what happened this morn in the hall. What I said."

A deep flush stained her cheeks. "I assure you, Sir Knight, there is no need for you to explain aught."

"Oh, but there is." His voice took on an almost commanding tone as he insisted she listen to him. "I must do this for my own peace of heart if not for yours."

Fellis stood looking at him for a long moment. Peace of heart was a concept she readily understood. It was the one thing that she hoped for in the future her mother had chosen for her. She nodded slowly. "I will hear you."

He smiled at her then, and her heart thrummed in her chest. Dear heaven, but he was handsome. The spring sun glinted in his hair, bringing out the fiery highlights and making her fingers ache to touch it. She tightened her grip on the book of prayers she was holding as if that could stop her from thinking such sinful things.

It did not.

He moved closer to her, indicating that she was to retake her seat on the bench.

When she did, Stephen settled himself beside her.

Fellis could not keep herself from noticing how very hard the muscles in his thighs appeared as he stretched out his long legs in dark hose. The sleeve of his green tunic was so near that it almost touched her own sleeve. When she allowed herself a fleeting glance upward she became certain that the shoulders of his white pourpoint bore no extra padding, for the throat that rose from the open neck was strong and tanned.

She was grateful for her heavy veil and wimple, for surely it helped hide the color that had risen up to heat her face and neck.

"Lady Fellis," he began, "I am afraid I made a most unconsidered comment this morn."

She looked down at his strong hands, which seemed to be gripping his knees. Fellis would have believed this indicated discomfiture, if the notion was not so far removed from her ideas of who and what this man was. There was no way this worldly and powerful knight could feel anxious at saying anything to her. He lived and socialized with the most powerful and sophisticated people in the land—the very king himself.

'Twas her own agitation that made her see such in him.

But Sir Stephen continued to speak, and what he said made all else fly from her thoughts.

"I must tell you," he said, "that I had no knowledge of your infirmity when I spoke. I meant then, and do now, that you are most agreeable to look upon and Wynn would be a fool to reject you. In spite of what I have learned of your physical condition since then, I cannot credit that any man, including the Welshman, would have the stupidity to repudiate you. The truth, sweet damsel, is that you are lovely beyond what my simple tongue has words to describe."

Fellis found her eyes caught and held by his dark ones as the words sank into her soul. The way he was watching her, his expression revealing the depth of his sincerity, left her with little doubt that Stephen Clayburn believed what he was telling her. Going over in her mind the words he had spoken, Fellis could see she might have misunderstood them. She was simply so accustomed to people's pitying reactions to her that she had placed the wrong connotation on what had been said.

She found herself unable to turn away from that searing intensity. His eyes were so green and deep and, for some reason she could not fathom, made her think again of her special place in the forest, the place she had resolved time and time again never to return to.

There she felt so different, freer than at any time in her life, but with it also came yearnings she had no right to feel. Mayhap that could explain why Stephen Clayburn called up those images in her mind. For he too made her feel things she had no right to.

Her heart was beating so loudly that she was sure he could hear it, and still she could not look away.

But a bird chirped nearby and Fellis came to herself with a jolt. With a hot flush she looked down at her hands, which were clasped around her book. They were white knuckled with the intensity of her grip.

Whatever had she been thinking to stare at him so? He was here to complete a task, and surely he would do what he must to see that carried through.

Not that Fellis doubted the truth of his not knowing about her clubfoot. That much seemed reasonable. But the rest, especially the part about her being lovely beyond words. That was too much to believe. She was more than relatively certain that Stephen Clayburn was no stranger to beautiful women and knew how to use his considerable charm to best effect.

She was disturbed to find her own voice sounding decidedly breathless as she answered him. "Please, sir, there is no need to go on so. I accept your apology and your word that you meant no offense."

Feeling that the meeting was now concluded, Fellis rose.

But Stephen reached out to detain her, putting his hand on her sleeve. To her utter confusion, Fellis felt a tingle of awareness even through the heavy wool of her long sleeve.

So surprised was she that she nearly gasped aloud as she jerked away from him, her gaze again going to his.

To her further amazement the knight seemed to be battling some emotion himself, for his eyes were troubled as he met hers.

But he appeared to recover quickly or perhaps she had been wrong in her first impression, for when he spoke, it was without any hint of emotion. "Lady Fellis, I need speak with you a moment more if you will allow."

She looked away, feeling awkward and wondering what more there could be. "If you will."

"Please sit." He indicated the place she had just vacated. "I would discuss the matter of your proposed marriage to Wynn ap Dafydd."

Unaccountably, Fellis felt a wave of disappointment, then told herself she was nothing more than a perfect fool. What had she thought he might wish to discuss with her? Such a man would not put himself forward for the likes of her without reason. Disappointment made her sigh as she answered, "So be it."

But she sat as far from him as the narrow bench would allow, her hands clasped primly around the book in her lap.

"You must see," he began without preamble, "that what the king has proposed wouldst be best for all, your family, your enemy the Welsh, and mayhap for yourself."

"For me?" She looked to him in surprise. "Tell me then, Sir Knight, how I would benefit from this match with a man I have never so much as set eyes upon?"

He took a long time in answering and, when he did, his tone was deliberately frank. "Lady Fellis, I know of Lady Mary's plans for your future. It has been made quite clear to me that taking holy orders was not of your choosing, but hers." His expression took on a reasoning cast. "This is your opportunity to do otherwise. To have a husband and family of your own. Can you tell me that you have not even thought of the possibilities?''

She remained mute, wondering how he had read her secret desires so easily.

He continued, ''You know, of course, that the union must be of your will, my lady. The church does not sanction the forcing of any bride. I know not what the king would say of your refusal, but that would be your father's concern, not yours. I only hope that you will make the right decision based on the responsibility of your position and the good you can do by it.''

She looked back at him, her smooth brow creasing as she understood the importance of her part in this for the first time. ''I had not thought.''

''Tell me then,'' he said, ''if you truly feel you are called to become a nun, and I will not continue this effort.''

She could feel him willing her to look at him and could not prevent herself from doing so. No one had ever asked her before what she desired for herself and Fellis found that her dreams were so long buried that the words to tell of them were hard come by. Finally she shook her head, whispering, ''Nay, 'tis not so set in my heart. But,'' she said, and was gladdened to hear the rising strength in her tone, '''Tis not such a bad life that I dread it. To serve the Lord is a right and noble decision.''

''I cannot argue that,'' he replied softly. ''But there are various ways to serve the Lord. And, you, by agreeing to marry the Welshman could help to bring peace for many folk who have lived in strife.''

What answer could she give to this? He was right in that the Lord could be served in many ways. But was this way the right one for her?

It was too difficult to think clearly. All her life she'd known what was expected of her. The possibility of her future taking a completely unexpected turn was daunting. She could not so easily forgo her mother's teachings.

Heaven help her, what could she do? And would agreeing to at least consider Sir Stephen's suggestion be a betrayal in itself?

Something of her confusion must have communicated itself to Stephen, for he leaned closer and said gently, "Lady Fellis, do not think that you need feel bound to anything by simply agreeing to think on the matter. There is no need for me to even discuss our conversation with anyone else. You have harmed no one, broken no trust by deciding to reflect on the possibility of a marriage to Wynn ap Dafydd. Again I say that ultimately this choice will be yours."

She raised her head, gazing out over the just awakening garden with its newly sprouted tender shoots and greening branches, but seeing none of it. Despite what he said to the contrary, talking like this with Stephen Clayburn felt like a betrayal of her mother's trust.

But Sir Stephen was most convincing in his assurance that it was not.

Mayhap for the first time in her life, Fellis would have to decide what to do for herself. Though often desired, the prospect was now somewhat unnerving.

Slowly she nodded. "I will think on it." And as the words were said, she felt a surge of self-assurance that she had never known before. "But hear me, I will not allow myself to be coerced into this marriage by you. It is clear to me that you have a stake in the outcome of this situation. And I have no wish to be swayed by that. Only if I can believe it will be best for my family and our folk will I agree to negotiate a possible marriage with this stranger."

Stephen watched her for a long moment, his eyes taking on an openly admiring expression.

Fellis felt herself flush yet again, at his attention, though she knew it was truly madness to feel anything toward him. But that did nothing to quell the wild racing of her heart.

"Fair enough," he answered, clearly unaware of her agitation. "I can ask for no more at this time."

Chapter Four

Over the course of the next days, Fellis tried hard not to think too much on Stephen Clayburn and why he was there.

But 'twas nigh impossible.

Even Grandmother seemed to have nothing else to talk about.

This was evidenced by the fact that she had returned to the subject of the knight even now as Fellis helped her to eat her midday meal of bread softened in broth.

Her blue eyes studied her granddaughter over the bowl Fellis held in her hands. "You should not be here, child, but taking your meal in the hall with the others. I'm sure Sir Stephen would be glad of your company. I do not believe either of your parents have put forth much effort to make him feel welcome here. And you need not avoid him simply because they do. The notion of your getting married is not without merit. Why must you dismiss the idea out of hand? As you have dismissed Sir Stephen simply because he carried the news."

Fellis tried not to show how even the mere mention of his name made her heart flutter. She bent her attention to the broth, telling herself that it was not Stephen's presence that so disturbed her, but his errand. No matter what Grandmother said, she could hardly think of the knight without thinking of the marriage.

Being no closer to deciding what she might do about going forward with the negotiations for the wedding, Fellis wished to avoid him, if for that reason alone. What should be done was still unclear to her.

Realizing she was taking too long to form a reply, she answered her grandmother carefully. "What would you have me do, Grandmother? I am at odds. You know that I only follow my parents' wishes. I have been taught to accept the prospect of one future and know not how to even contemplate another."

The older woman gave her a shrewd glance. "You follow your mother's wishes, you mean." She shook her head as Fellis opened her mouth to reply. "Nay, do not defend her. We both know that she has decided you will be the one to cleanse her guilt from her. She feels that it is her own fault that you were born with a twisted ankle, that I know. And I do have compassion for her. That is what has kept me silent all these years as I watched her groom you for a life of her choosing, not yours. But the time has come to speak out. There is no reason for guilt. You are a beautiful girl, kind of heart, intelligent and gentle of spirit. God has given you many gifts to make up for the one small fault. It is time your parents and you see that. Here Fellis is your opportunity to have a life of your own. Mayhap you should take it. In truth I would not have picked the Welshman for you. They have plagued us too long. But you might at least meet him and take his measure."

Fellis could only stare as she realized that her grandmother was echoing some of the very things Sir Stephen had said to her. Something else Fellis realized she must consider was the possibility that the feuding might actually end if a marriage took place.

Her thoughts were interrupted by the elderly woman.
"Now go." Her grandmother waved a frail, blue-veined
hand. "I am much improved and can feed myself. You have
hardly left my side since I was moved to your chamber. I am
of a mind to have a bit of peace from all this fussing." The
last was said with a teasing smile and Fellis knew the older
lady was only jesting.

But she could see the concern for her on her grandmother's countenance and knew she had indeed been overzeal-
ous in her care. She also knew part of her preoccupation
with the older woman's comforts had been caused by an
unconscious desire to avoid the handsome knight from King
Edward's court.

"Go now," the older woman said. "Before the meal
grows cold."

Fellis stood. "I will leave you alone for a time. But you
are to send for me, have you any need."

"I will do so." Myrian nodded her wimple-covered head.

With that, Fellis went to the door, though she knew as she
did so that she would not be going to the hall. She had no
desire to find herself in Sir Stephen Clayburn's company. As
of yet she had not been able to control her reactions to him
and had no wish to see the knight until she felt able to do
just that. Though at the back of her mind she wondered if
that day might ever come.

Trying to relegate Stephen and all things connected with
him to the back of her mind, Fellis went down the stairs and
out a small side door of the keep. Making her way to the
storage shed at the side wall, she took a rough-woven bag
from a hook on the wall, filled it with several shriveled apples from a barrel and headed for the stable. Although she
could not ride, Fellis did enjoy petting and spoiling the
horses with a little treat.

Since Stephen Clayburn's arrival she had forgone the pleasure for fear of meeting him. His stallion was stabled with her father's horses.

Certain now that he would be at his meal, Fellis felt relatively safe in doing as she would.

The stable was a long, low building with several stalls on each side of a center aisle. The inside was dimly lit and smelled of fresh hay and horses. She made her way to the first stall without hesitation, calling softly to its occupant. The gray stallion came to the sound of her voice eagerly, nostrils open as he sniffed for the apple she held out toward him.

After a moment Fellis went on down the row of stalls. She offered a soft word, a treat and a caress to each of the equines in turn as she came to them.

It was as she came to the last enclosure in the first row that she realized she was not alone. For inside the door was none other than Stephen Clayburn. He was standing beside his chestnut stallion. He had obviously been grooming the animal, for he held a stiff-bristled brush in his hand.

The knight had removed his tunic and wore only an open-necked white shirt over his dark hose. Her gaze moved over the thickly muscled arms exposed by the rolled-up sleeves of the shirt, then fixed on the deeply bronzed patch of smooth chest. She wondered if that skin would still hold the warmth of the sun that had kissed it with its heat.

Fellis flushed, realizing her thoughts had gone too far. She stammered, "I . . . pardon me, sir, I had no wish to disturb you. I did not know of your presence." She made to back away.

He halted her with a raised hand, seeming to cover the distance to the short doorway in an instant. "Nay, lady, do not leave. You are not disturbing me."

"Nonetheless…" she began. Heaven help her, she seemed to lose all thought of propriety in his proximity.

He made a soft noise of irritation as he reached for her arm. "Please, I have said you have not disturbed me. Do you mean to run every time we chance to meet?" As if realizing he was still holding on to her arm, Stephen released her slowly with a self-deprecating laugh. "I fear I am most unpopular of late. No one at Malvern seems to have the slightest interest in even passing the time of day with me." He pointed to his own wide chest, then to his horse. "Hence I am spending my time in the company of the only being in this keep who seems to hold me in high esteem."

Her eyes again fixed on that smooth flesh and she barely heard the last of what he said. Fellis felt her body flush with a surprising warmth that seemed to spread from her chest outward, and found herself unable to look away from the rapid beat of his pulse there.

"Am I so very disagreeable that none of you can even speak with me?" His troubled gaze beckoned hers.

As her eyes dropped, she blushed a deeper crimson.

Why did he affect her so even now?

She tried to force her mind to focus on what he had said. It was not fair of her family to ostracize him so. Stephen could not help that he had come bearing unwelcome news. He was only acting out of his own duty to the king.

But that did not mean her father or mother would be able to accept that news more readily. Fellis knew that her mother had been at her father to send Sir Stephen back to the king with a politely worded refusal. She had overheard them arguing as she passed her father's chamber the previous evening.

As for herself—Fellis sent the knight a quick glance from beneath her dark lashes—she had her own reasons for avoiding the all too attractive knight.

But compassion would not let her walk away now, no matter how difficult it might be for her. She must learn self-discipline where he was concerned. It was the only way.

Stephen Clayburn was a guest in her home, far from his own world. She could not treat him ill.

With the decision made, Fellis found she had little notion of what to do next. Entertaining young noblemen was something not in her experience.

But try she would.

Raising herself up straighter, Fellis said, "I am most sorry that you have been treated rudely." She was heartened to find her tone sounded quite sincere and polite, so she went on. "It is not our usual custom to be so inhospitable. I can only beg your indulgence toward my parents in that your visit, and its purpose, has come as a considerable shock to them." She looked at him then, her expression unknowingly dismayed. "And to me."

He appeared disconcerted for a moment, his eyes growing dark with what she thought was sympathy and it seemed as if he were about to speak. But he closed his lips and looked down. When he did reply, Fellis had the distinct feeling that what he did say was not what he had been going to tell her.

His tone was polite. "I am the one who should be asking for forgiveness. Your family did tell me of their feelings, so I should not be surprised that their hospitality has been...shall we say, lukewarm." He smiled at her then, the sheer charm of it making her catch her breath as she saw how it lit his dark eyes and made his angular face even more handsome.

Fellis tore her gaze away.

Despite her resolve to control her reactions to this man, it was a moment before she could trust herself to speak evenly. "'Tis not your doing, Sir Knight. You but follow the orders of the king..." She halted painfully.

"Let us change the subject, shall we?" he said, as if sensing her discomfort.

She nodded slowly, without looking at him. "Yes, let us."

Stephen indicated the apples she held. "The animals must surely love your presence here if you are always so generous."

Fellis looked down at the bag of fruit, long since forgotten by her. She removed one of the apples from the bag and held it up to his inspection. "These are getting a bit old." She had to make a conscious effort not to take a step backward when he moved toward her, resting his arms on the top of the stall door. Even with the gate separating them, she was incredibly conscious of Stephen as he studied the shriveled red morsel.

"It looks as though your apples might have suffered a touch of frost." He chuckled, and she felt the sound ripple pleasantly along her skin. The horse nickered at the sound of his master's laughter and drew her grateful attention from the knight.

"What is he called?" she asked by way of searching for a safe topic of conversation.

"Gabriel."

"Might I?" She turned to the stallion, who had come forward and was eyeing her curiously and her apple covetously.

Stephen stepped aside. "Of course, only be careful for he is a wily beast."

Her eyes widened. She couldn't help wondering if the term could apply to the man, as well as his horse. Gingerly she put forth her hand. But the stallion hesitated, and she spoke in that same soft tone she had learned to use with the others. The horse stretched his neck forward and took the apple from her fingers with dainty care.

Stephen made a soft sound and she turned to him, finding he had moved closer, his gaze on her with quiet intensity. Fellis's face was mere inches from his, her breath mingling with his as their eyes met and time stood still.

Her heart thudded in an uneven beat and she could not think past the swirling awareness inside her. Perspiration beaded on her upper lip and when she licked at it with her tongue, his gaze focused there.

Gabriel nickered again, breaking the spell.

Clearing his throat, Stephen leaned back but continued to watch her, saying huskily, "He is not like to make friends so easily. Mayhap you have charmed him as surely as all other males in your vicinity."

She could make no reply to such foolishness, knowing that it was nothing more than courtly patter. Even so she noticed that her hand was shaking and drew it close to her side so as not to let him see.

He went on more normally and she wondered if she had imagined the previous intimacy of his tone.

"You obviously have a way with horses," he complimented.

Her eyes widened in surprise. "Nay, I only give them a treat. I know not even how to ride."

Stephen simply looked at her, for it took a moment before the words sank in. She did not ride. The very idea was completely foreign to him. He told Fellis that most gentlewomen learned to ride at an early age. Else how could they go out hawking or travel from one place to another with any degree of comfort.

Fellis replied that she had not done these things. Mary Grayson had kept her from all such pursuit in her desire to see her daughter learn the ways of duty and poverty that she must experience as a nun.

Stephen's lips tightened, for this thinking was foolish. As a baron's daughter, and with a proper dowry to recommend her, Fellis could easily have aspired to become nothing less than an abbess in choosing the spiritual path. Such a woman wielded as much power as a man in her own world. She would be expected to manage not only the spiritual well-being of those under her guidance but also oversee the financial, physical and clerical details of her lands. She would be counted upon to entertain and also to visit other powerful church figures.

Unconsciously Stephen shook his head. No matter how one looked upon it, Fellis had been ill prepared for her future, whether it be as wife or nun. And that he could do nothing about. But he could do something about what occurred now.

He looked into her blue eyes and saw Fellis watching him with obvious confusion and question. He realized he had been lost in thought for too long.

Quickly he answered her unspoken query. "I was but thinking on what you said. Wouldst you care to learn to ride?"

She replied hurriedly, her eyes wide with surprise at the suggestion. "Nay, there is no need."

"Aye, there is need," he replied, wishing he did not find it so difficult to take his gaze from hers. "Your husband may wish for you to travel with him at some time. On horseback is much less tedious and slow than by wagon."

"I . . ." she began. "Then perhaps I should ask my father to see to it." She looked up at him, clearly trying to appear unconcerned as she shrugged. "In the event that I am married."

"There is no need to trouble your father," Stephen said, his tone deliberately casual. He chuckled with irony. "I have little enough to occupy my time. I should be happy to teach you."

She looked at the ground again.

The light in the stable was dim, and Stephen could not read her expression when she turned away, but he sensed that she was not pleased.

Leaning closer to her, he said, "Lady Fellis, please, I offer only out of friendship. I have been riding since I could walk. It is the same with the rest of my family, including my sister, Elizabeth. Truth to tell, she is a better horseman than the rest of us."

She glanced up at him in surprise. "You have a sister?"

A fond smile lit his eyes. "I do and there's none dearer to my heart. I've missed her greatly since she married some weeks ago."

When she continued to study him with surprise, Stephen cocked his head in question. "Do you find that so very difficult to believe?"

She blinked. "Nay, sir." She laid her hand over her chest. "It seems you know so much of me, and yet, I know naught of you or your life."

Stephen shrugged. "There is no mystery to me and if 'twill make you easier, I am happy to share what there is.

"I am the middle one of three brothers. Henry is the eldest, then comes me, and lastly Peter. Elizabeth was born between myself and the youngest. My parents died of plague some years past." He could not keep the sadness from his voice as he spoke of them, but he went on. "Elizabeth, Peter, and I went off to live at court. Henry, who was with the Black Prince's army in France at the time, returned home, married and had a child. Through our family's connections, I became a messenger to the king. After a time Peter was fostered to our father's friend, the Earl of Norwich, and it was just my sister and I.'' He shrugged. ''We had grown accustomed to each other.

''Now with Elizabeth wed, I am alone.'' He paused then, disconcerted at the loneliness in his own tone.

He nearly started when she laid her hand on his sleeve in sympathy. She said softly, wistfully, ''I have no siblings and thus no real certainty of what 'twould be like to be without them, but I can well imagine.''

He looked into those fathomless azure wells of empathy and found himself lost. He was envisioning high proud breasts glimpsed through a curtain of silver hair, a sweetly curving waist and hips, creamy limbs.

The reverie was interrupted by Fellis's own voice. Blinking, Stephen focused once more on her and realized that Fellis was not speaking to him but had turned to address someone behind her.

''Yes, Thad, I do wish for your assistance.'' She swung around, indicating Stephen with a wave of her hand. ''Sir Clayburn has graciously offered to teach me to ride. Have we a mount suitable for that purpose?''

Stephen eyed the pubescent boy, who had obviously just returned from enjoying his meal, for he still held a piece of roast fowl in one hand as he wiped at his mouth with the sleeve of his roughly woven tunic. Meeting the lad's respectful brown gaze, Stephen wondered self-consciously how long he had been occupied with his completely unwarranted thoughts of Fellis. He hoped it had not been for long.

But when he looked to Fellis he saw that her hands were clenched tightly in front of her, belying her even tone and expression.

Could it be that she was not completely unaware of his interest? And just perhaps, the notion was not entirely distasteful to her.

But Stephen knew it was wrong of him to even think such a thing. What could either of them possibly gain by acknowledging the awareness that seemed to exist between them? 'Twould be nothing short of insanity.

Opening the door of the stall, Stephen stepped out into the aisle. Being careful to avoid coming into contact with the woman who drove him to such madness without even trying, Stephen went to the boy Fellis had called Thad.

The boy had not answered his mistress and Stephen's tone was purposely brusque to cover his own disquiet as he asked, "Do you have a mount?"

"Yea, my lord." Thad nodded hurriedly, as if becoming aware of his tardiness in making a reply. "If you will but allow me, I will fetch it for you with all possible haste."

"That will be fine. We will await you in the yard." The knight spoke to Fellis without meeting her gaze. "My lady."

She nodded, though she looked surprised at his suddenly brisk manner.

Stephen had no wish to explain. It would be best to keep his distance, to allow her to think he was cold and remote if need be. But he wondered as he followed behind her, his eyes lingering on Fellis's gently swaying hips if he had indeed made a mistake in saying he would teach her to ride.

Could he keep his objectivity and be near her?

The only thing that prevented him from withdrawing was the knowledge that they would not be truly alone. The courtyard was as public a place as one could wish for and surely there he could keep his wayward thoughts from straying where they dared not go.

The dappled mare was clearly ancient and the only thing Stephen could see to recommend her was her extreme docility which was obvious as the serf led her out into the open.

Glancing to Fellis to gauge her reaction to this poor mount, Stephen saw the ill-concealed apprehension on her features and realized this horse might do well enough. It was clear that Fellis would only have been frightened of a more spirited animal.

Fellis moved toward him, trying to appear confident even as her fingers twined in the rough fabric of her gown. She stopped beside him, eyeing the stirrup that he held for her.

He retained the reins, making a respectful bow to Fellis, his gaze encouraging. "Shall we begin, my lady?" His resolve to remain aloof wavered momentarily as he saw her nervousness.

With grave trepidation, Fellis first listened to Stephen's instructions on mounting, then allowed the knight to help her into the saddle, settling her knee around the pommel with his guidance. All this was accomplished with stern resolve as she told herself that it was too late to cry nay at this point.

But her will to follow through wavered even more as she looked down and took note of how very far she was from the ground. Closing her eyes to still the swimming in her head, Fellis took a deep breath.

Looking to Stephen, she tried to smile as he nodded and said. "You do well, my lady."

Feeling the quaking in her limbs, it was difficult for her to believe that Stephen knew of what he spoke. But she did not tell him so. "I . . . thank you."

"Are you ready to begin then?" he asked.

She nodded, though she held tightly to the pommel as Stephen went to the mare's head.

At first Fellis was conscious of nothing save staying aloft. Then, as the minutes passed, she became less frightened and realized that 'twas not nearly so bad as she had at first thought. The mare stepped slowly and carefully as Stephen led her about the courtyard, giving Fellis an opportunity to become familiar with the gently swaying motion.

To Fellis it seemed that Stephen must have the patience of Job as he continued to lead her about, giving her more than ample time to become accustomed to this new experience.

Finally it was Fellis who begged his attention. "Is there more, my lord?"

When he turned to look at her, she grinned sheepishly. "I am no longer afraid."

He nodded, and for the first time since they began, Fellis took note of his expression. It was carefully distant, though polite.

She frowned in consternation, biting her lip, and Stephen turned away.

He spoke without looking back over his shoulder at her as he led the horse toward the door of the stable. "I will get Gabriel."

Thad was waiting for them and Stephen sent him for his mount with a cryptic order.

He made no effort at speech while they waited and for that Fellis was glad. Whatever had happened to cause him to become so distant?

She had no notion of what might have given Stephen reason for displeasure.

A horrifying thought leapt into her mind. Could he have seen her reaction to him and been repulsed by it? She flushed, mortified at the very idea.

Her gaze went to his broad back as he waited some distance away for his horse. The rigid line of his spine seemed an affront to her, as if he were dismissing her.

Well, Fellis had no intention of spending time with Stephen Clayburn if he was disgusted by her. Raising her chin high, she glared at the back of his dark head. She would simply end this lesson here and now.

So thinking, she made to swing her knee over the pommel.

But at that moment Thad came from the stable, leading Gabriel, and handed the reins to Stephen.

The tall man took them, while still holding on to the tether of Fellis's mount. After a muttered thanks, the knight vaulted up into the saddle without so much as a by-your-leave, causing her to struggle to regain the security of her position once more.

Thus, before she knew it, Fellis had been led through the outer gate and down the hill side from the keep. Their pace was a bit quicker than it had been when Stephen drew them along on foot, and Fellis was more occupied in learning to keep her balance at what she had to truthfully admit to herself was only a slightly faster walk.

But she did learn and again began to enjoy the ride, except for the nagging shame at the back of her mind of the idea that Stephen Clayburn was repulsed by her. Could his previous assertion that the deformity was not distasteful to him be nothing more than mere words, said to gain favor with her—to make her agree to do what he wanted her to do?

Finally she could stand the silence and her own tormented thoughts no more. She called out to him. "My lord, please, may we return now?"

He stopped and turned to her, looking as though she had called him away from some far distant place. "I...yes. If that is your wish, my lady."

She held her head high. "It is. And I believe I am ready to hold my own reins now."

"Do you..."

"I do," she interrupted.

With nothing more than a skeptically raised brow, Stephen stared at her. Fellis squared her shoulders.

She motioned toward the horse in irritation. "Do you see, Sir Knight. She is most gentle and hardly likely to carry me off. In fact I believe she wants nothing more than her own stall and some oats after this day's work."

Looking at the mare, Fellis knew Stephen could not help seeing the fatigue in the baleful brown gaze the horse raised to him. How could he imagine any threat from her?

Slowly he nodded. "You speak true. But mind stay close in case aught goes awry," he said as he maneuvered his stallion close and handed her the reins. Using his gloved hands to manipulate her fingers, he showed her how the reins should be held before swinging away.

Fellis barely paid him heed, so grateful was she to be free of his control.

Having watched Stephen closely as he guided his own mount Fellis pulled the reins in the direction she wished to go. The mare turned toward the keep, where it stood on the rise to her left. Feeling somewhat more confident, Fellis clicked her tongue in what she hoped was a clear signal to the horse.

Without warning, the mare surged ahead, leaping to a gallop as one possessed.

Gasping with shock that the docile creature had suddenly turned wild, Fellis let go the reins and grabbed for the pommel with both hands.

She heard Stephen call out behind her but was powerless to stop the animal's headlong rush as she raced across the greensward, then up the hillside. The land beneath the horse's hooves disappeared in a sickening green rush that made Fellis long to close her eyes to stop the rolling of her stomach.

But she could not. Though she was helpless to halt the mare, she was too frightened to take her eyes from their course lest some horrible fate take them.

And then as the force of the wind whipped at her, tearing the wimple and veil from her head, then tugged her hair from its pins and tossed it about her head in mad abandon, she felt a strange thrill. A rush of exhilaration heretofore unknown to Fellis Grayson, dutiful daughter and future nun.

As the mare raced across the drawbridge, Fellis realized the cause of their headlong rush. The animal was simply crazed to return to her own comforts and cared not for the desires of the two-legged being upon her back.

This knowledge drove the last of the panic from Fellis's mind. She even found herself laughing in glee as she caught a momentary glimpse of the guard's incredulous face when they raced through the gates.

Behind her she heard Stephen's voice call out. "I am coming, Fellis."

She found a grin widening her lips. The foolish man believed she was screaming in fright. Did they all think she was such a spiritless idiot?

This nearly dimmed her amusement in the uproarious ride as they raced toward the stable and Thad, who waited in the open doorway. But the look on Thad's face, when he saw what was happening and rushed to come to her aid, brought her humor back. The silly boy nearly got himself trampled when he placed himself between the mare and the door to the stables, his eyes widening till Fellis could see the whites all round them.

At the last possible moment Thad seemed to recognize the danger he was in, for he veered out of her path. After that Fellis was only just able to remember to duck her head as the horse dashed inside the stable. There the mad gallop came to an abrupt end, and her arms were nearly pulled from their sockets as they took the jolt. And even though she was holding tightly, Fellis came dangerously close to being tossed straight over the mare's head.

There was a loud thundering of hooves behind her, and Fellis swung around in the saddle to see Stephen draw up short, leaping from the saddle in one graceful motion.

Standing in the doorway behind the knight, and snow-white with fright, Thad seemed to realize how close he had come to being trampled and bolted from the scene.

Stephen ran to take the reins, his worried gaze searching her face anxiously. "Dear God, Fellis, are you all right?"

Looking down at his handsome face, his lips lined with fear for her, Fellis couldn't help contrasting Stephen's obvious concern to the remote detachment he'd shown over the past couple of hours. She was glad that he could not know the way the sight of him tugged at her heart. She lifted her chin, refusing to let him see how much hurt he had caused her. "I am well, Sir Clayburn. There is no cause for alarm. Once I realized the mare was only trying to get back to her comfortable stall and a meal, I quite enjoyed myself. It was most exhilarating."

"Exhilarating," he gasped. "You enjoyed yourself? Have you no sense?"

She straightened her slender shoulders, unaware of the fetching image she presented to him with her cheeks flushed, her eyes sparkling and her hair flowing about her. Stephen was hard-pressed to keep from pulling her down into his arms. He wanted to hold her until he stilled the anxiety he felt for her.

She replied cooly. "Were you afraid you had lost your precious pawn?"

Without fighting it he allowed anger to rise up and mask his more ragged emotions. "Are you completely mad, woman? You could have been killed. Even though the horse was only returning home, she could have taken a misstep in a rabbit hole, or veered over the side of the drawbridge at that pace. You are not dealing with a fleet-footed mount at her peak, but with a clumsy old nag who could easily have killed you or herself."

For a moment he saw apprehension darken her eyes but she covered it quickly. And despite the circumstances, Stephen was aware of an intense feeling of admiration for her spirit.

Her pink lips pursed obstinately, drawing his gaze.

His eyes fixed on her mouth, and Stephen felt a sudden rush of desire that could not be stilled. And he made no effort to try.

Reaching up his arms, he pulled her down to him. With torturous deliberation he allowed her to slide slowly down the length of him, his hands molding the gentle swell of her hips. Heat rose in Stephen's belly and he closed his eyes, breathing in the sweet warm woman scent of her.

Fellis. She was a heady mixture of innocence and spirit, and he felt drawn to her as no maid before her.

When he opened his eyes again Fellis was looking up at him, her own lids heavy, her breath coming quickly through parted lips.

He knew he was going to kiss her—had to kiss her.

But just as he bent to close the distance between their two mouths, there was a loud blaring of the horn on the guard post outside.

Confusion clouded Stephen's mind as she started away from him—confusion and thwarted desire. He looked to Fellis in question.

She answered his unspoken query. "We must be under attack."

Though Fellis was trying to concentrate on what was happening outside the stable, it was difficult. The interruption had come so abruptly that the yearning awoken in the past moments was still very near the surface. She found it impossible to meet Stephen's eyes.

For she could not deny the knowledge that he had very nearly kissed her, and far from rebuffing him, she had surely led him to believe she was eager for that event. She who had never so much as been alone with a man before Stephen came to Malvern.

Fellis's face flamed.

When she did raise her head to cast the knight a quick glance, he seemed equally uncomfortable. She watched Stephen rub his palms over his cheeks, as if he were not sure what to do next.

Without another word, she turned to go out into the courtyard and he followed. Outside, chaos ruled. A crowd had gathered near the main gate. As Fellis and Stephen moved toward them, she saw that a short, wiry man seemed to be at the heart of it. Fellis thought she recognized him as one of her father's crofters. Surely she had seen him at one of the monthly manorial courts.

Several of her father's soldiers and one of his knights had joined the group that clustered about the crofter. Their faces were grim.

She could hear the knight, Arnold, speaking as she pushed her way to the front. "We have sent for Lord Grayson in the event that he did not hear the horn. He is out inspecting the fields behind the castle. I am certain he will return anon."

At that very moment, her father, mounted on his favorite silver stallion, came galloping through the main gates.

He rode toward the group, pulling his mount up short as he reached them. Then with the lithe grace of a younger man, he slipped to the group, removing his gauntlets as he did so.

He greeted the crofter with a terse question. "What has occurred, Dan?"

The fellow began his tale without hesitation. "My Lord Grayson, my farm has been raided by the Welsh this very day."

There was an outcry of anger from those assembled, but Fellis's father raised his hand for silence. He was obeyed.

Dan went on. "I was working in the fields when I heard my wife screaming. I ran to the cottage to find that one of the outbuildings was afire." He gulped, his eyes welling as he looked to his overlord. "My lord, my eight-year-old boy, my only living son, was inside." His tone grew angry then. "If I had not grabbed the ax and hacked through the wall, he would not have lived. As it is, the smoke nearly took him. The lad's abed as we speak."

Stephen spoke up, drawing all eyes. "How do you know it was the Welsh who perpetrated this evil?"

Looking up at the knight with a frown, Dan seemed to wonder who he was and by what authority he would ask the question. Dismissing Stephen, he turned to his overlord to answer. "My wife saw the devils as they ran for the forest. What will we do, my lord? I will join the attack against them. I wish to avenge the harm done to me this day."

Fellis heard this with growing horror as she looked to her father to see what he would decide. In the past such acts had brought swift retribution from Richard Grayson and his men. She feared the fighting would escalate until more senseless deaths occurred on each side. The circle of rage and revenge had been going on all her life.

Why could it not end? As the question formed in her mind, she realized that mayhap it could.

She was the one who might make peace come about. Drawing her courage up from inside her, Fellis turned to her father, who had not yet made a reply. She said, "Father, please may I speak?"

He looked at her then as if just becoming aware of her presence. "Aye, Fellis. What would you have of me?"

Though the decision was made in her mind, Fellis found the words stuck in her throat as she tried to form them. "I would that you do not strike back for this offense." At his expression of shock, she hurried on. "Please, do not let us continue this feud with the Welsh."

Her resigned gaze went to Stephen. "Sir Stephen has come to offer a different solution, one that has been decided on by King Edward himself. Mayhap it is time to try his way rather than ours."

Richard Grayson only stared at his daughter for a long moment and she saw the pain that her sacrifice would bring him. "Do you know what you are saying, my daughter?"

She took a deep breath and let it out slowly. "I do."

Richard Grayson swung around to look at the confused faces of his people. "'Tis time I told you all what has occurred. The king's messenger—" he indicated Stephen with a wave of his hand "—has arrived for the purpose of opening negotiations for a possible marriage between my Fellis and Wynn ap Dafydd."

There was a horrified gasp from those assembled.

The Lord of Malvern raised his hands to halt any words of disagreement. "'Tis not my wish but that of King Edward." He continued, appearing as if the next words cost him dear in pride. "We will not act against our enemies at this time, but allow Sir Stephen to try the king's solution. If that is what my daughter truly wishes."

"It is, Father." She looked into his unhappy gaze. "All my life we have lived beneath this threat. Until Sir Stephen came I had not even considered that it might really be changed. Mayhap now it can be."

There was a murmur of dissent from the crowd.

Richard Grayson turned from his daughter and halted them with one look. "The decision is made to go forward with the negotiations. I am master here. I will hear no more on it until we see what comes about."

Fellis's gaze followed her father's as he turned to Sir Stephen, who appeared surprisingly dismayed to Fellis. She would have thought he would welcome this news.

Richard Grayson said hollowly, "You have our leave to go forward. But remember this—should Wynn continue to attack my folk after you have made your proposal to him I shall be forced to protect what is mine. On that be assured." With that he turned, vaulted into the saddle and rode from the keep.

Fellis watched him go, feeling Stephen's gaze upon her. Squaring her shoulders, she swung around to face him.

He spoke to her alone, as if he had forgotten the others. "This is what you want?" His troubled expression confused her even as it drew her to him.

Resolutely she turned away, raising her chin. She needed none of Stephen Clayburn's sympathy, had no trust in it.

How dare he continue to pretend she had any real choice in this. The good of the people of Malvern must come first and if marrying Wynn would assure the peace, then she must do so.

Still without looking at him, she answered in carefully controlled tones. "I have said as much."

Chapter Five

Stephen rode along at a comfortable pace as he left one patch of woods and the land dipped down into a wide stretch of pasture. The rain that had begun that morning had lessened to a slight drizzle, but the sky was low and dark gray. When he inhaled he caught the scents of damp earth and sharp wet pine.

Stephen felt no physical discomfort, as his green sable-lined cloak was more than warm enough to keep off any chill that April might offer. What he did feel uncomfortable about was the way Fellis had agreed to go forward with the marriage negotiation.

He wondered yet again if he had done the right thing in calling to her attention her responsibility to her people. At the time it had seemed the only way to help her to see the situation as it was. She had admitted that her heart was not fixed on taking the veil, that she would do so only because she had been told it was her duty.

Stephen's conscience was not salved by telling himself that Fellis might even end in finding happiness by wedding the Welshman. He had sensed her unspoken desire to have a husband and a family.

And even as he went over these things in his mind, Stephen knew his unhappiness was caused by his own discomfort with the notion of Fellis marrying anyone. He shook his head, knowing this was madness. He was here to bring about that very outcome.

Unfortunately, the more he knew of Fellis the more he was attracted to the silver-haired maid.

He remembered how she had reacted as the crofter told them the story of his son's near death in the fire. She'd gone as pale as ivory. It was clear to Stephen that the tale had weighed heavily on her mind. He could not help admiring her concern for the child, the son of a lowly farmer on her father's lands. He'd watched as she made her decision, then faced him squarely. There had been no visible sign of fear and uncertainty about what she was doing, but he had known it was there.

The courage she had shown in hiding it had made him all the more drawn to her. That show of quiet strength gave just another glimpse into the passion of her character, making him see her as a woman set apart from others, not only by her incredible beauty, but depth of character. She was a woman who would be a true companion to a man.

But he reminded himself that she was not for him. Even if he were willing to admit that he really did want her for himself, Stephen had long since decided that he would not allow himself to be so caught up in another person, so dependent on them for his happiness. To do so was to risk losing them and thus his sense of equilibrium. It had happened when his parents died, and he was not willing to experience such deep pain and disorientation again.

He feared that to permit himself to care for Fellis would be to chance all. She was not a woman he could love in half measures.

He was here to do his duty to king and country, nothing more.

That duty did not include allowing himself to have tender feelings for Fellis. He was ready to acknowledge the incredible physical pull she had for him. But naught else. And by his own will that bodily temptation could and would be resisted.

She would go to the Welshman. That fact must not leave his consciousness.

Prodding with his heels, the knight hastened the pace as they started up the incline that led to the next growth of timber. He would do well to pay heed to where he was going.

This day's meeting with Wynn ap Dafydd could prove to be more important than anything that had occurred thus far. If he hoped to make the Welshman see the sense of what he was going to say, Stephen would have need to keep his wits about him.

It was only after Stephen had ridden some distance into the wood that he noticed a peculiar stillness in the air around him. Up until this point he'd been aware, if only subconsciously, of the sounds of birds calling back and forth, the rustle of small animals in the underbrush as they scrambled out of the horse's path.

Now there was nothing, only a strange, heavy waiting.

He slowed Gabriel, looking about him carefully. The forest was thick and heavy with undergrowth. The tight canopy of branches had kept out most of the rain and the ground beneath his stallion's hooves was relatively dry. But an occasional drop did make its way through the greenery to dot his cloak and glisten on his hair. The eerie silence continued and only the sound of crackling brush underfoot marked the passage of horse and man.

For some time now Stephen had been aware that he was riding on Wynn ap Dafydd's land. Lord Grayson had been quite clear in his instructions on locating them, even though it was obvious that he resented having to do so. Lord Grayson's decision to move forward with the negotiations, as his daughter requested, had not changed his own resentment of the idea. Yet despite his obvious displeasure with the scheme and his former declaration that he would not assist the king's man in his efforts to arrange the marriage, Lord Richard had gone so far as to offer an escort for the knight.

Stephen had declined with grave politeness, knowing what the offer cost the other man. He had simply stated that he wished to give no sign that he was there for any purpose other than reasons of friendship.

He felt that Wynn might be more inclined to believe him if he came alone. And that might make him more open to listening to the king's proposal.

Stephen had little doubt that the man would come to agree to the king's terms. He, like the Graysons, had very limited choice in the matter, as peace could be close at hand. But a bitter draught was much easier to swallow if 'twas not forced down one's throat.

And that was exactly the way the Welshman would view the intended marriage. Speaking as a man, Stephen knew it would not be easy to allow another to pick one's bride, even under the best of circumstances, and the reality of this situation was that the bride in question was also the daughter of the enemy. But Stephen had every hope of making Wynn see that the solution to the troubles between him and Richard Grayson was a wise one.

He refused to allow himself to dwell on the notion that 'twould not be so very hard for him were Fellis not the bride in question.

With these disturbing thoughts running through his mind, he grew less alert than he might otherwise have been. Thus it came as more of a surprise than it should have when a man armed with a knife dropped from a tree to land on top of him. Stephen felt the impact jar him, then he was falling sideways to hit the needle-covered ground with a jolt that knocked the air from his lungs.

Reacting out of instinct, Stephen sucked in a gasping breath even as he rolled to his back. His attacker had already gained his knees, giving a trilling whistle as he turned on the knight. Though the man was small in stature, he was solidly built, and Stephen's attention was drawn to the knife in his hand as it flashed silver in the light.

Realizing the whistle was most likely a signal to others, Stephen did not waste any time in pressing his own attack. Reaching up as the other man fell upon him, he grasped his arms, effectively stopping the knife in its downward arch. They grappled for several moments, then Stephen, with the grace born of much practice at hand to hand combat, rolled around, pinning the other man beneath him. In the space of a heartbeat he had the knife pressed to his attacker's throat.

His breath coming quickly from exertion, Stephen looked down into the other man's eyes. Those orbs were dark brown, holding a spark of intelligence, and, in spite of the fellow's precarious position, there was no fear in them.

Stephen experienced a wave of respect. Although the knight had no intention of killing, the other man could not know this.

Still holding the knife against the other's throat, Stephen said, "Will you give me your assurance that we need fight no more. I have no wish to kill you."

Before the man could form a reply, there was the sound of an outraged gasp. Stephen looked up to see several other fellows as they moved to circle the pair on the ground.

Deciding to ignore them for the moment, Stephen turned to the man beneath him. "What say you?"

The man stared at him in surprise and spoke in richly accented English. "My friends will kill you if you harm me, English."

Stephen shrugged. "That will be my concern. Right now I am talking to you."

The man said. "Why should you believe me? I could lie to save myself and then have you killed."

Again Stephen shrugged. "I will take my chances. Suffice it to say that I will believe you. I have the notion that your honor is important to you." Something told him this was indeed true, mayhap it was the caution the man used in agreeing. If he had a desire to simply fool Stephen into letting him go he would have done so immediately.

The other man gave him a long, measuring look. "You have my word."

With that the knight shifted off him, letting the hand that held the knife drop to his side. Two of the other men fell on him, pinning him to the ground, even as the one he had just released called out for them to halt.

"I have given my word," he said, as they hesitated, then released the knight, but not before they had relieved him of the weapon.

They moved to take his sword, but the first man halted them in this, too. "If he had meant to use it, I would be dead." With obvious reluctance they backed away.

With a sigh of forbearance, Stephen sat and looked up at them. They were all dark haired and eyed. Each one stood poised for action with the keen balance of a trained warrior. He had no doubt from the comfortable way the six held their weapons that they knew well how to use them. Their clothing was loose fitting and reflected the colors of the forest around them. Appropriate for hiding up amongst the tree limbs, he thought.

Gingerly Stephen came to his feet, rubbing the back of his neck with one hand.

One of the men said something to him in a lyrically throaty language that Stephen knew must be Welsh. He held up his hands in friendly appeal as he said, "Your pardon, good fellow. I do not speak Welsh."

The man gave what was clearly an angry retort, though he still spoke his own tongue. The only word of this that Stephen heard and understood was *Saesneg,* which he knew was Welsh for English. The fellow ended with a threatening motion toward the knight.

Stephen held his ground, though he raised his hands even higher. "Nay, do not act so hastily. I have come in peace to speak with Wynn ap Dafydd."

The man who had first knocked him from his horse gave a mocking smile, though there was a certain amount of admiration in his dark eyes. "You ask for much, Englishman."

The other Welshman growled out a reply in heavily accented English. "We should kill him now."

Stepping back, Stephen drew his sword with a heavy sigh. "I had thought to avoid such conflict. I wished to do no harm. But if I must kill a few of you to protect my own hide, so be it."

The six men who faced him looked to one another in surprise. Then his original attacker smiled, this time with some genuine amusement. "He is brave, that much I'll give him. And he certainly fights well. Not like the other English knights we've seen who only know how to fight from atop their horses. There's no denying that he bested me even when I came on him by surprise."

The others looked to Stephen, obviously impressed by this. It appeared they held the wiry man in high regard.

Stephen gave silent thanks to all the wrestling he had done with his older brother Henry as a boy.

"You are either a fool or very brave," the second man said gruffly.

Stephen shrugged but stayed at the ready. "I am no fool of that I can assure you. As to the other?" He shrugged again. "I merely know that I will not allow you to kill me. If it is a choice between your lives or mine, the choice is made without much consideration."

Now one of the men began to laugh, and as the others joined in, Stephen sheathed his sword.

As they saw this they laughed all the harder.

The man Stephen had fought spoke again. "English, whether you be fool or nay, is left to be known. But I think you have earned the right to speak with Wynn if nothing else. Rest assured that it may be the last thing you do, but as my name is Haydn, see him you will."

They had insisted that he must wear a blindfold, and Stephen agreed. If it made them feel more secure to hide the exact location of their master's stronghold, he would not attempt to gainsay them. Perhaps he had pushed his fortune as far as he should for the time being. His only query was to make certain they would bring Gabriel with them.

He was assured that the horse would be cared for and they started off. As they led him along, he concentrated on what he meant to say to Wynn himself.

The group came to a halt and Stephen blinked as the cloth was removed from his eyes and the light assailed them. It was a moment before his vision adjusted enough to take in the low-built, long stone house before them. The roof was thatched and a trail of gray smoke rose from some point near the center of the high pitch. There were several outbuildings surrounding it, but he saw very little sign of activity around these.

The man who had called himself Haydn said something to one of his fellows in his own tongue. The man nodded and went through the narrow doorway.

Obviously they wanted to inform Wynn before bringing Stephen before him.

In a relatively short time the man returned and, speaking again in Welsh, nodded toward the door. Hands reached from behind Stephen to take hold of both his arms as they entered the stone structure and moved across the rush-strewn floor.

There were several trestle tables set up along the length of the dwelling and these were crowded with onlookers who studied Stephen with ill-concealed distaste and even hostility. Many of them drank from flagons that sat before them.

Obviously the rain had forced people indoors. From the well-tended fields he had passed earlier while riding, Stephen could not credit that these men were wont to sit inside and drink ale all the day through.

He was led to the far end of the room, where a man sat in a carved chair on a slightly raised dais. He, like his fellows, was dressed in the loose garments that bespoke a need for comfort and a desire to travel the forests unobserved. A thatch of dark hair curled about his proudly held head.

Though he was of slender build and rested back in his chair easily, the keen intelligence in his eyes marked this man as a leader. Surely this must be Wynn ap Dafydd himself.

Stephen moved forward more quickly, eager to speak with the man.

The unexpectedness of his action caught the two men who held him off guard and he pulled away from them easily. "I have no further need of your assistance," he said politely but firmly. Before they could move to stop him he strode directly to the dais.

As he did so he became aware of a woman dressed in flowing garments, who rested on the arm of the chair. She leaned against the man familiarly. Tossing a lock of wild dark hair over her shoulder, she watched the knight with disdain.

Obviously this was the lord's leman. Stephen gave the fact little thought. Though she clearly felt some sense of possessiveness over her lover, she would be of no importance in these negotiations.

He turned to the man, who studied him with keen hazel eyes.

"My Lord Dafydd." He bowed gracefully.

The man in the chair stared at him for a long moment saying nothing.

Stephen's voice seemed to bring the two who had led him to their senses. They came forward with angry cries, reaching to take his arms once more.

"I beg you indulgence," Stephen said, neatly sidestepping their seeking hands. "I assure you I mean no threat to you or your master." He turned and smiled with friendly reassurance at those seated at the tables near him.

There was no welcome in any of the eyes that met his.

A husky chuckle came from behind him and Stephen turned back to the dais and Wynn, who spoke mockingly. "You are a madman, English, to come here alone."

Stephen looked at him. "As I have already discussed with your men, I am no madman."

"So I have been told. I have also been told you are surprisingly brave for an Englishman. Or at least it would appear so to my men." Wynn studied the knight with those steady hazel eyes.

Stephen shrugged. "I know naught of bravery. There was nothing to fear. Test me in a real situation of trouble and you will see that I am no less or more bravado filled than any other man."

Wynn laughed, throwing back his head, strong white teeth flashing as he ran a hand through thick dark curls. "Have you not the sense to fear for your safety now?" He waved a hand around the crowded chamber. There was a murmur of agreement from his men that contained an undertone of threat.

Stephen remained relaxed in his stance. "Had you any real desire to kill me you would have done so by now."

Wynn jerked upright, his movement forcing the girl to sit up straight, as well. "And why should I not kill you?"

His dark eyes held a glimmer of danger. For the first time Stephen felt he was actually in jeopardy of making a wrong move, and that wrong move might cost him his life. Though Wynn seemed friendly enough, on the surface he was obviously dangerous. Any man who called the Welshman his enemy would have need to guard himself well. And though he wished it were not so, Stephen, being English, could consider himself an enemy.

Inclining his head to the other man with a show of respect as one would an equal, Stephen said, "My lord, only you can answer that. Could it be that you believe me when I say I mean you no harm? And could it be further, as a man of intelligence, you want to know why I have come?"

Stephen meant no idle flattery in the question. He had met many people in his travels and had learned to take their measure quickly and efficiently. He had no doubt that his initial assessment of Wynn was accurate.

But he did need to go carefully for the good of his mission—that of getting Fellis Grayson wed to one Wynn ap

Dafydd. To see this happen the knight must gain not only Wynn's tolerance, but also his acceptance.

He could not jeopardize his task by appearing too sure of himself.

Wynn seemed to sense Stephen's inner struggle, for he leaned forward, his elbows on his knees. "Why are you here, Englishman?"

Stephen faced him squarely, somehow knowing his case would best be served by being straightforward. "On behalf of King Edward of England and all of Britain, I have come to negotiate a possible marriage between yourself and Lady Fellis Grayson of Malvern."

A cumbersome silence descended on the chamber.

Then a loud gasp of fury erupted from the woman seated at Wynn's side. "The cripple?"

A startled Stephen looked to the woman. He had completely forgotten her and was surprisingly defensive at her contemptuous and vehement reaction.

His lips tightened as she leaned toward him with open hostility in her dark brown eyes, her cheeks flushed with fury.

Stephen fought his own rising anger at her scathing tone and her reference to Fellis as a cripple. Squaring his shoulders, he faced Wynn rather than the woman. It was difficult to control the rolling distaste for her in his belly, but by his will he nearly mastered the sensation. Yet try as he might the knight could not keep the outrage from his tone as he spoke. "My lord, Lady Fellis is no cripple. She is lovely beyond your imagining. A woman made to cause any man's pulse to quicken."

Wynn was just recovering from hearing that he was expected to wed. Clearly he had not leapt to question or even care about the condition of the potential bride quite as quickly as his woman. "The English king has sent you here to tell me this?" His tone was rife with shock.

"Aye," Stephen answered. "There has been unrest in this region for too long. King Edward wishes to see a peace and he feels this would be the most expedient way to attain that end."

Wynn leaned back and was silent for so long Stephen could feel the tension in the rest of the folk assembled in the room. Many of them were probably surprised that their leader had not immediately dismissed the idea as preposterous.

But, as Stephen had found with many men who had the strength and burden of leading others, Wynn could not do so. He, out of his duty as their chieftain, had to consider this and every other issue that arose, not only from his own personal perspective but from the view of being the one who is responsible for the good of many.

Finally Wynn said so softly that only those close by could hear him. "Why should I agree to these negotiations?"

The woman jumped to her feet, her dark tangle of curls flying about her wildly. "Wynn, why do you pay heed to this nonsense." Her voice broke on a sob. "You will not do this." She turned and ran from the chamber.

Wynn looked after her, his gaze unmistakably yearning, but he said nothing.

A loud voice erupted from a table near them. "Nay."

Stephen swung around to see a large man, the tallest and brawniest he'd seen since entering the country, rise to his feet. He banged his mug of ale on the table so hard it sloshed over the sides. "You cannot be serious, Wynn. What would your father say to this." The big man went for the knife in his belt, his gaze trained on Stephen with open hatred. "Recall, Englishman, what came of Henry de Shaldeford?"

Stephen was already reaching for his sword. He knew what the other man referred to and took the threat to heart. Henry de Shaldeford had been murdered in 1345 as he was traveling to Caernarfon on the prince's business.

"Stay," Wynn yelled. "This man has my protection. Touch him at my displeasure."

With a shout of frustration and anger, the man turned and stalked after the young woman.

"Now, English," the Welshman said with narrow eyes, "you will tell me of your king's proposition."

Stephen sheathed his sword. "My lord, you know well that things have been anything but congenial between yourself and your neighbors. There is evidence of that here this very day." He looked to the door through which the big man had just disappeared.

Wynn was watching him as he turned back to face him. "Think you the wrongs are all done by my folk?"

Stephen shook his head. "Nay, I do not. And that is the point. Do you not wish for this to cease, for your children to know a more stable existence? How can this feuding be to your good?" He held up his hands. "What King Edward proposes would bring about a peace, a state of safety for you and the people of Malvern."

"And Grayson has agreed to this?"

Stephen met his gaze. "He has agreed to abide by this in the event that you will, as well."

Wynn sent him a mocking glance. "And I am to believe this?"

Nodding, Stephen said, "You are. Just yesterday a hostile act was committed against one of Lord Grayson's crofters." Quickly he related the events of the previous day. The knight ended by adding, "Methinks Lord Grayson would have moved against you then if he was of a mind to do so. You may believe that he is serious in this matter."

Wynn had sat up straighter as Stephen spoke, his face taking on a thoughtful expression. "You say he told his folk that they were not to take retaliation."

"He did."

One of the other men sitting at a table nearby spoke then as if he could not prevent himself. "What have we to gain, by this, Wynn? We are not afraid of Grayson and his knights."

Stephen turned to Wynn, deciding this was the moment to lay out his most persuasive point. "King Edward has given me leave to offer you, Wynn ap Dafydd, a very special boon." He could feel all eyes upon him. "In the event that an agreement of peace is reached and this marriage takes place, you will be granted a license to build a crenellated castle. You will also be allowed to hold a market."

Again silence descended.

Wynn finally spoke and the slight hint of incredulity he was not able to keep from his voice gave lie to the blunt statement. "I must think on this."

Stephen was not surprised. Only the crown could grant such privileges as a fortified keep, and when it did it meant prosperity and added security to all in the area. Wynn could not simply dismiss such a boon, even if 'twas granted by a king he felt no real allegiance toward.

Some hours later, Stephen rode into the keep at Malvern. He ran a hand through his hair which was wet and heavy as the rain had begun anew. It had been a long day and he was damp, cold and tired.

Wynn had made no decision, but Stephen was sure the Welshman would come to see the merits of entering into talks on the matter. Stephen had felt the antagonistic stares of many sets of eyes as he left after first obtaining Wynn's assurance that he would be notified when a determination had been reached.

So occupied was he with these thoughts that for a moment he did not take note of the way the guard at the portcullis was staring at him. All knew where he had been that day. And it was true Richard Grayson had warned him that he was walking into certain danger. But Stephen had felt no fear and thus could not credit that theirs was real. He had thought Richard's warnings more a way of trying to convince him he could not succeed.

Now, seeing the awe on the guard's face, Stephen began to understand that they might have been in earnest.

The man called out in surprise as if he could not stop himself, "You live."

Stephen made a great show of looking down at himself. "Aye. I live."

Once inside the inner bailey he was greeted with more amazed expressions. Surely these people did not fear their Welsh neighbors so very much? Had they really believed he would be killed without provocation? 'Twas all the more evidence that an end must be brought to this feud.

The only ill that could come of this proposed union was that Fellis would be lost to him for good.

Stephen drew himself up short, not knowing whence this unwarranted thought had come. It must simply be exhaustion and discomfort that made him think such an impossible thing. Even if she was free, Stephen knew he could not make a commitment to Fellis no matter that she drew him as no woman ever had.

He entered the bailey, trying to concentrate on the warm meal and fire he would soon enjoy, and came to a halt.

Mary Grayson and her daughter were just crossing the courtyard on their way to the castle kitchens. Both stopped as he drew his stallion to a halt before them and dismounted. With his recent thoughts of Fellis uppermost in his mind, Stephen kept his gaze carefully averted from hers.

"You live." Lady Mary echoed the guard's words.

"As you can see," he answered.

Then, as he watched, he was amazed to see a grudging respect come into her eyes as she looked up at him. "I would not have thought it possible," she replied. "You astonish me, young knight. Mayhap there is more to you than a strong back and a handsome face."

Stephen looked to Fellis to gauge her reaction to her mother's assessment and found her staring at the ground. The edge of her wimple and veil hid her face, but Stephen felt sure she was blushing. Did she agree with her mother's judgment that he was pleasing of countenance? The possibility brought a rush of pleasure that warmed his blood. But he quickly quelled it.

Again he reminded himself that Fellis Grayson was meant for Wynn.

Tearing his eyes away from Fellis, who was now watching him with a pacific look that gave away none of her feelings, Stephen forced himself to attend her mother.

"So," she inquired cooly, raising dark brows, "Wynn has agreed to the marriage?"

Stephen stiffened at her condescending tone, wondering why he was letting this woman rile him when he'd faced a whole clan of hostile Welshman with equanimity. He told himself vehemently that it had naught to do with the fact that Fellis continued to watch him, those blue eyes assessing, only the flush in her cheeks giving away any hint of anxiety.

"Not as of yet," he answered levelly. "But he will do so, and ere long if I make my guess."

Mary Grayson smiled without humor, the momentary glimmer of admiration buried as if it had never been. "Methinks you speak with a great deal of assurance on a matter as yet so left to chance.''

"What say you?" he asked Fellis, trying to gauge more of her feelings.

"I know not.'' She shook her head, her gaze uncertain. And though she kept her head high, he was aware of her fingers twisting the drab rough wool of her skirt. "These proceedings are beyond my experience. But I must admit I wonder why he would do so,'' she answered.

He frowned at being reminded of how ill they garbed her and that hesitant expression tugged at him as he spoke from the heart. "The man has only to look at you and the thing will become fact,'' he said, then stopped himself. He had no right to speak so. Stephen swung back to the mother, who looked on with narrowed, speculative eyes.

Searching for something, anything to divert that good dame from what she might have inferred from his words to Fellis, he knew he could not have Mary Grayson guess at his feelings for her daughter. Looking again at Fellis's fingers worrying the cloth of her cote, Stephen introduced a subject that had been on his mind since coming to Malvern.

"You, my lady, will please have some suitable garments made for your daughter to meet with the man who may become her husband. We will offer no insult to Wynn ap Dafydd with these nun's habits she is like to wear.''

The scowl that clouded the older woman's face told him he had accomplished his goal. She stiffened. "How dare you, sir?''

"New garments?" Fellis asked, clutching her hand to the throat of her gray robe.

"Aye,'' Stephen answered with agitation, still addressing Lady Mary as he turned and swung up into the saddle. "And recall that I said they were to befit her station and wealth. Make no mistake, the king would be displeased with anything less. His interest in seeing this matter settled is most sincere. Wynn ap Dafydd must have no reason to think he is being offered insult.''

Lady Mary took an angry step toward him.

Surprised by her action, the stallion pawed the ground and Stephen pulled him back. Having nothing more to say, the knight turned his horse to make his way to the stables.

Fellis had worn naught but black, brown or gray in her life. Not even as a child had she owned anything brighter. 'Twas not proper for a nun to wear worldly clothes, and her mother sought always to prepare her for that life.

She looked to the older woman, who was frowning in disapproval as Stephen disappeared around the side of the keep. But her mother remained silent.

Fellis ran her hand over the coarse cloth of her cote.

Would Mother really do as Sir Stephen said? It hardly seemed possible and she was afraid to put any faith in the notion. Surely Mary Grayson would simply go to her husband and tell him she would not comply with the knight's orders. In the past Richard had always done what his wife instructed as far as Fellis was concerned.

For some reason Fellis did not understand. Her parents, though married, behaved like strangers. It was almost as if each feared the other. Ofttimes she wondered what had brought about this state of affairs, but she dared not ask. She would see the pain in one parent's eyes when the other was not watching and know she could do nothing to help.

She remembered once attempting to talk to her father about the situation at about the age of twelve. He had grown distraught at her even mentioning the topic and asked her not to do so again. He had ended by telling Fellis she should not interfere in something she did not, could not, understand.

She had taken his admonition to heart, though it seemed to her that, of the castle folk who were wed, most had more intimate relations. Most couples laughed and loved and even fought.

Fellis had often wondered if this was because the nobility was different from others. Mayhap only the common folk were allowed to show such displays of emotion.

But since Stephen Clayburn had arrived at Malvern, she'd come to doubt this explanation more than ever. Fellis couldn't help believing that marriage to Stephen would be entirely different. He had a way of speaking his mind that made her think he would not hide his feelings from the one he loved, be they good or bad. And there was no mistaking that he came from a highly placed and noble lineage.

She frowned then. For some reason the notion of Stephen married was distressing to her, and Fellis had no wish to dwell on the reason for it.

She turned to her mother, concentrating on trying to anticipate what her mother would do in reaction to Sir Stephen's declaration. To her surprise, Fellis saw a gleam of grudging respect. It appeared that, in spite of herself, Mary Grayson was struck by the knight's confidence.

And heaven help her, Fellis was, too. Even though Stephen had come to Malvern with the idea of causing complete upheaval in her life, she could not still a rush of something warm inside her every time she saw him.

Just the thought of the way he'd held her in the stable, her body brushing the hard length of his, brought a heady lightness to her heart.

The idea that he might have kissed her, had the alarm not sounded, was surely a product of her willful imagination. And as she had told herself a thousand times since, she had best put such madness to the darkest part of her mind.

Fellis would do well to keep a steady head. Though she'd dreamed of having someone to love her, she'd known it was just that, a dream. All the while she'd known that no man would want her with her twisted ankle. But Stephen's arrival had changed even that.

For had he not said that Wynn ap Dafydd had agreed to consider marriage talks?

Her heart thudded at the very notion. Wynn was a stranger to her. Never had she believed that he might actually go forward with the idea.

Now that he had, she felt a painful tightness in her chest at the very notion of wedding him. And even as the ache seized her, she could not help wondering why it seemed to be more closely connected to her confused feelings about Stephen Clayburn than her intended bridegroom.

Chapter Six

The next morning Stephen woke with a groan of frustration when he saw the weak strands of morning's first light upon his chamber window. He reached up to rub eyes that seemed sprinkled with sand.

In spite of his fatigue the night before, he'd been restless. The bed seemed too big and empty with thoughts of Fellis swimming through his head. No matter how he tried he could not erase from his mind those images of her naked and beautiful in the forest glade. They burned behind his lids, leaving him aching and lonely.

And if that wasn't enough to disturb his rest, Stephen was plagued by wondering if he was doing the right thing. Was marrying Wynn the best thing for Fellis? Would she be miserable married to her father's enemy, wife to a man who took her only to fulfill an obligation?

Something inside Stephen rebelled at the notion. Did she not deserve better, after all the isolation and self-doubt she had known in her eighteen years?

Or, Stephen forced himself to face the question, did he only balk because he did not want to see her go to another man? He could not answer, for much as he tried to convince himself the question was ridiculous and he felt nothing toward her beyond a simple attraction, it did not ring true. Oh, he found her lovely. There was no denying that. Again he was taunted by images of her bare, supple and creamy skinned. For the thousandth time the knight wished he'd not seen Fellis that way.

But worse even than those memories were the other ones. If only he had never seen the tender gentleness with which she touched her elderly grandmother, had not been the beneficiary of that sweet smile, had never held her body next to his and felt the awakening passion inside her.

Stephen sat up and moved to the edge of the bed with a groan. Would that he had never known what beauty and brightness of character was hidden by her drab garments and meekly bowed head.

But he did know and could not forget.

Which left him uncertain of his own motives. He must do nothing to sabotage his mission. His every action must be carefully considered in order that it be right.

He looked to the window and saw that hours had passed since he had awoken. Naked and golden, he moved to where he had tossed his clothing on the chest at the end of the bed. As he drew them on, he began to formulate a plan.

Having met Wynn, Stephen knew he was not ill-favored, nor crude or ignorant. Fellis would not be stooping far beneath herself to have him to husband. If they had not been enemies, the match might have been a natural one with their families living in such close proximity.

As he pulled his tunic over his short quilted pourpoint, then bent to put on his shoes, the knight told himself the problem lay in the fact that they knew nothing of each other. Stephen realized it would do well to tell Fellis of Wynn. Surely the more she knew of the man, the less he would seem like a stranger and an adversary to her.

Stephen refused to allow himself to dwell on the feeling that he was turning her over to the other man. She had never been his.

Fellis was not in the hall when he arrived there for the meal. As he sat down at the trestle table and helped himself to the light bread, cheese and meat on platters there, Lady Mary came from the passage that led to the castle kitchens.

"Good morrow." He nodded with deliberate politeness.

After what he had said to her the previous night, Stephen was sure she was even more out of charity with him. Thus his current change in demeanor. From this moment on, Stephen meant to make a conscious effort to show Lady Mary every courtesy and to win her over to his cause. Surely she could be made to see that the wedding must come about.

When no reply was forthcoming to his greeting, Stephen tried again. "Good morrow."

"Good morrow," she answered stiffly, her eyes hard.

"I would like to talk with Lady Fellis this morning. Can you tell me where I might find her?"

A scowl furrowed her brow. "She is in the chapel saying her prayers, as is proper for her, considering her vocation."

He had taken only a few bites of his food, but Stephen dropped the bread to his plate in exasperation, his resolve forgotten. "Have done with such talk. Your daughter is not for the church. This much you need come to accept, no matter how difficult. Can it be arranged, she must, and will end in marrying Wynn ap Dafydd. And she will do so not for her own sake but for all of yours." His brows rose with his ire. "You have been very diligent in your teachings, Lady Mary, and your daughter has learned to attend her duty no matter what the cost to herself. You could at least try to remember that marrying a virtual stranger is going to be, at best, difficult for her, and lend some modicum of support to your daughter in this. No matter how disappointed you must be at this turn of events, my Lady Grayson, I am most sure it is more so for Fellis.''

She only stared at him, her expression unchanging, and Stephen wondered if she had even heard what he told her. She seemed too intent on her own wishes to pay any heed to those of others.

Stephen could not still the anger that rose up in his belly. Anger, not only with Lady Mary, but also with himself. How could he ever hope to make Fellis see Wynn in a favorable light in this setting?

There had to be some way to get Fellis away from Malvern, if only for a few hours. Aside from the complications with her parents, Fellis appeared to spend all her time in service to others. Stephen had seen her about the castle grounds, handing out bread and clothing to the beggars that came to the keep.

And just the previous morning he'd come upon her helping her mother to set the arm of a small boy. The parents were not from the village but had been journeying to live with relatives some distance away. The child had fallen from their donkey along the route and injured himself. They had been taken in without question. While her mother had set the break, Fellis had held the child tenderly, soothing him as best she could, though he was none too clean and screamed at her to be released. Stephen had been touched by her fortitude in retaining her grip on the squirming child even though her sympathy for his plight was apparent in her expression.

Aye, Fellis would indeed benefit from getting away. In a more customary frame of mind, Stephen might be better able to help Fellis see things more clearly.

But how to get her away?

He looked at Lady Mary, his gaze coming to rest on her fingers as they worked at the sleeve of her dark samite cote.

The cloth was fine, if plain, and offered direct contrast to every garment he had seen Fellis wear other than the black robe in which she'd looked so fragilely beautiful the day he carried her grandmother to her room.

An idea began to form in his head. How it would be received he had no notion, but he was determined to get Fellis from beneath this woman's thumb for at least a few hours.

"About our conversation last eve." When she gazed at him blankly, he clarified, "As to Lady Fellis's wardrobe. Have you some plan of action in this matter?"

She answered through stiff lips. "I have not."

"That is as I suspected. Therefore it is most fortuitous that I have conceived one of my own that I feel you will find most satisfactory."

She continued to watch him.

Pleasantly he asked, "What is the name of the nearest market town?"

"Glenmarket," she replied when such a direct question was posed, though obviously with reluctance.

"I shall be taking your daughter there to buy cloth."

Her expression, if he could credit such a possibility, became even more stubborn and resentful than before.

"I will not attend you."

It was more than he had hoped.

Hiding his elation, Stephen nodded. "That will not be necessary. Knowing how busy you are, seeing to the many details of running this keep, I would be most happy to attend the duty myself. It is the least I can do to assist, since the notion was mine."

He stood, determined to give her no time to argue the point. "I shall beg escort from your husband. He has agreed to allow me to see to this situation as I see fit."

That halted her even as she opened her mouth. Richard Grayson had made that much evident and she clearly had no will to defy him when he was obeying the wishes of his sovereign.

With a final nod, Stephen added, "No harm will come to Lady Fellis. Of that you can be assured."

The knight then strode from the room.

The chapel was not difficult to find, being down a long hall at the very far side of the keep. From outside the keep, one was easily able to locate its arched and steepled roof.

As he went, the knight wondered what ill Fellis had done that her mother had told her to remain so long this day.

Coming to a heavy carved oak door at the end of the passage, he pushed it open. He entered the church and looked about, expecting to see Fellis in one of the pews. But she did not appear to be there. Mayhap her mother had been mistaken, he thought as he took a few steps farther into the high-ceilinged stone chamber. But as he did so he realized he was wrong. There, kneeling on the floor in front of the altar, was Fellis. A rainbow of colored light filtered through the stained glass windows that ran along the outside wall and played over the silver blond hair from which she had removed the customary gray veil.

Stephen caught his breath at the sight of her. Her delicate profile bathed in that same gentle light was sweet as any he had seen on statues of the Madonna.

Something must have alerted her to his presence for she turned at that moment. Fellis's blue eyes went round with surprise even as she reached for the veil that she had set on the floor next to her.

With obvious agitation, she placed it on her head and moved to rise. But as she did so, Fellis stumbled, nearly pitching forward. Stephen frowned as the damsel righted herself. She had been kneeling there for hours if he didn't

miss his mark. And no wonder she was stiff, the stone floor
was surely cold as ice.

"What are you about?" he asked in disbelief, reaching
out to help her to her feet. Only the most zealous of religious devotees would suffer such discomfort in prayer,
without even a cushion to protect them from the hard stone
floor.

Her slender fingers were frigid in his and Stephen could
not keep from pressing them between his two warm hands.
The feel of her soft skin against his made him want to draw
her close, protect her from discomfort and harm.

Fellis looked up at him in confusion, feeling as if all her
hours of prayer that morning had been for naught. Now the
few moments of peace she'd achieved seemed as a dream.

Stephen Clayburn had only to touch her and she tingled
with awareness despite the cold in her torso and limbs. All
those hours praying for the strange feelings he awoke in her
to be taken away had accomplished nothing.

Had the Lord deserted her now when she needed Him
most?

Her mother had told her often enough that the sin of lust
was the worst of all. It could entice you away from the true
path by the very pleasure of it. That the feelings of sweetness it brought confused the heart and soul and made one
believe that wrong was right.

Fellis could only stare at Stephen with wide eyes and
wonder why she could not be delivered from her own sinful
thoughts. Just the feel of his strong hands on hers made her
wish for him to touch other more intimate parts of her.

Flushing brightly, Fellis jerked her hand from his grasp.
Whatever was the matter with her, she could not fathom,
but it could go no further. She did not even know this man.

For all she knew, he could be the very devil himself come to tempt her.

But as her eyes met the genuine concern in his dark ones, she knew inside herself that this was not true. There was no fault in Stephen.

What really had he done but be kind to her, taught her to ride, helped her from her horse as he would any woman. But even as the last thought came, Fellis bit her lip in shame. How she had reacted, her pulse pounding while at the same time a heated languor made her want to mold herself to the hard planes and curves of his body.

Stephen Clayburn could surely have his pick of court beauties. And though the knowledge was painful, she forced herself to remember that he could have no interest in her, a green maid with a twisted ankle.

Nay, Stephen was no devil.

He was exactly as he appeared, a gently reared knight bent on doing his duty. It was she who had misunderstood his actions. Her infirmity had further added to her isolation from members of the opposite sex until she knew not how to interpret a man's kindness toward her.

The difficulty between herself and Sir Stephen lay only in herself and her own reactions to him and his nearness.

But even as she told herself all these things, he stood looking down at her and the longer he did the more difficult it became to breathe, her breasts seemed to swell to aching awareness. A shaft of light pierced the stained glass windows and caught in his hair, caressing it to fiery brilliance. Her heart thudded in her chest as she fought an urge to reach out and touch it, to see if it would burn her. For surely it would, if the feelings inside her were any indication.

It was Stephen who broke the spell by shaking his head.

"Fellis, I don't know what to do about you."

"About me?" Could he know her feelings toward him? The thought was mortifying.

He smiled softly, the tiny lines at the corners of his eyes crinkling attractively, and her heart turned over in her breast. "Aye. If only there was some way for you to see that you need not do this." His gesture swept the chapel. "Never have I met a woman of more gentle and good heart. The Lord in His heaven can see the sweetness inside you. He could not expect you to kneel for hours on a cold stone floor. To shut yourself away from sunlight and laughter."

For a moment she could only stare at him, shocked that he would think such things of her. He had no idea what lustful thoughts burned inside her each night as she thought of him there in his bed just down the hall from her. Thoughts that plagued her even now in this holy place.

She turned away, looking at the floor. "Mayhap I am not as you see me, Sir Knight."

She felt his compelling gaze on her down-bent head and could not resist the pull of it. When she faced him, those green eyes were dark with some indefinable emotion.

He spoke then, softly. "Respectfully, I must disagree. The more I know of you, fair lady, the more I know that you are indeed a precious jewel among common stones."

Fellis could form no reply. For even though she found it difficult to give credit to the words, how could she say so in the face of the knight's obvious sincerity. Her heart swelled and grew warm within her.

He looked away, then swallowed before turning back to her, as if he too were fighting to control his emotions.

Again he made a sweeping gesture that took in the beautiful chapel with its carved ceiling, polished dark wood and carefully crafted stained glass. With stronger tone, he said, "You need not hide yourself here, Fellis. The world will not be any more cruel to you than to others. Do not be afraid to join us in our struggles.''

The words came as a jolt after his previous sensitivity. Hide herself away? As she looked about her, Fellis knew a sense of resentment. How could he say such a thing?

But then she began to ask herself why the words struck such a painful nerve. Was it because there was truth in them? Had she placed the church between herself and everything that might hurt her—between herself and men.

Surely it was not true. It had been her mother's wish that she join the church. Fellis had only gone along with her wishes because she had no choice.

Or had she? Had the fear that any man she might meet would reject her because of her twisted ankle caused her to acquiesce too readily?

Fellis did not know the answers to these painful questions. Her tormented gaze went to Stephen's.

Oblivious to her thoughts, he continued, ''You have done much to show your strength and courage. In agreeing to marry Wynn ap Dafydd you will make a supreme sacrifice for the good of your family and all the folk of Malvern. It is time you began thinking of yourself, your future as a wife—and mother.''

Fellis's stomach turned with disappointment. He'd had her marriage in mind all along. Everything he'd said just now had been directed toward that and nothing else.

He waved a hand to indicate her mode of dress. ''Do you not desire lovely things . . . to make yourself ready for your bridegroom, as any expectant wife might.'' The last words were said so slowly it was almost as if it pained him to say them.

But in her confused and disappointed state, she could fathom no reason for that, so she dismissed it as nothing more than wishful thinking. Instead Fellis concentrated on what he had said. Is that what he wanted for her, that she should care for nothing but her own appearance and pleasure?

"I..." she started, then hesitated at the fragility of her tone. Fellis had no wish to give away any more of her agitated state than she already had. When she began again, she was gladdened to hear her voice emerge more clearly. "The marriage is not a given, as yet." She held her hand to her heart. "I have given my whole life to prayer and devotion to duty. What would you have me do, throw away all of my own values? To take up the life of some idle maiden? I know not how."

He shook his head. "Nay, I would not wish such for you. I can see how intolerable it would be." He held his head at an angle as he looked down at her, his gaze willing her to heed him. "But you can begin to fill your life with things other than this." He motioned toward the floor where she had knelt so long. "I have something to tell you. You know I have asked your mother to have a new wardrobe prepared for you?"

She nodded, wondering what this could mean.

"Well, there is need to purchase fabric for the garments to be fashioned. And we will go to Glenmarket to see to that."

She gazed at him in surprise. A trip to market for the sole purpose of buying cloth? For her?

'Twas ridiculous. And she said so. "It is too much bother for such a petty thing."

He put his hand on her arm and she started at the unexpected spark the contact caused.

Stephen too seemed to be aware of something passing between them, for he looked away and quickly drew his hand back.

But he made no further sign other than to run a hand through his hair as he went on. "It is not a petty thing as you term it. When Wynn asks for a meeting with you, you will have need of something suitable. As I told your mother, he must have no reason to feel insulted. As a nobleman he has the right to expect his bride to show him honor."

She gave him a long stare. "What had my mother to say to this outing?"

He shrugged. "She said she would not be free to accompany us, but I assured her I could proceed without her assistance. And I am most certain your father will supply an escort of his own men so that the proprieties are met."

She was tempted to deny him. Stephen would not force her to go, and heaven knew he had enough confidence to purchase fabric without any assistance from her.

But something stopped her from saying the words.

This was an opportunity to go away from Malvern without her mother's constant watchful attention to guide her every action. The thought was an unexpectedly heady one. She loved her mother dearly but did regret that more of her decisions had not been her own. More so since Stephen Clayburn had come than ever before.

She looked back to Stephen. Even though she knew the outing was simply a way to further his own plans to see her married to Wynn, Fellis could not stop a thrill of excitement. For the first time in her life, Fellis would know what it was like to be escorted about by a man who was not her father.

"I will accompany you."

She did not look up as he spoke, but she could hear the approval in his voice. "If it can be arranged we will leave on the morrow."

Still she did not look up, only nodded.

He said, "Until then."

Fellis could not keep her eyes from the door through which he passed. Biting her lip, she suddenly wondered if she had made an error in saying she would go with him.

Chapter Seven

They left as he had planned at first light on the day of the market. Richard Grayson had made no demur about giving them an escort of four mounted men. He felt there was no way of knowing when they might be set upon by a band of Wynn's men.

Looking at the mounted guard who moved to surround Fellis as they readied themselves for leave-taking, Stephen was fully aware that her father's men would act not only as protectors but also chaperons on this journey. He was sure they had been given direct instructions not to leave the young lady alone with the knight.

A fact for which Stephen knew he should be grateful.

In spite of everything he told himself about his duty and what he must do, he could not control his attraction to her. It was as if Fellis were a flame and he a wick. Every time he brushed against her, he flickered to glowing life.

Why had he brought up the subject of her fears of coming out of the safety of her old life? It was none of his affair. Why must he always show the depth of his interest in her and her actions, when all he need do was get her away from the keep, find a way to bring up the subject of her future husband without distraction?

That was his true connection to Fellis.

But he hadn't been able to stop himself from saying the things he had. He found himself wanting her to understand that she was the one who must choose the way she should live. That when she showed the world what she was made of, it could not help being awed by the spirit and strength of Lady Fellis Grayson.

Her ankle would not matter to others when it no longer mattered to her.

But Stephen knew he had no right to speak on such a personal subject.

So thinking, he purposely kept his gaze from lingering on Fellis as he bade farewell to her father in the courtyard. Richard Grayson had one final instruction to add to those of making sure his daughter was well cared for and that they be back that very same night. He looked at Stephen, his blue eyes unwavering. "Mind you see that she has all she needs to go from my house as befits her station. The girl has not had much in the way of vanities. I wish her to purchase aught she desires."

He held out a fat purse, which Stephen took from him with a nod, saying, "I will see to it."

Richard Grayson backed away and Stephen went to Fellis's side, where she sat mounted on the gentle bay mare. The knight looked up into her anxious blue eyes, and when he did, he saw not only that anxiety but also a glow of excitement. At that moment he resolved to give her a day unlike any she'd had.

"Are you ready to depart, Lady Fellis?" he asked with all the courtly grace in him.

She rewarded him with a grin of anticipation. Stephen felt himself captivated by her despite the fact that she wore her usual drab costume, including the hated wimple and veil that hid her glorious hair and much of her lovely face from his view. She replied, "Aye, Sir Knight, I am ready. And have been this long time."

He could not help reacting to such enthusiasm with a smile of his own. "We will away then." He strode to his horse and leapt into the saddle, even as he motioned them onward.

Fellis could not help casting repeated glances in the knight's direction where he rode beside her.

Stephen was dressed in a fine cote of dark blue velvet and a black tunic with matching hose that hugged his long muscular legs most lovingly. She couldn't help but see the way he held the reins so confidently in his long supple fingers. And she could not be found completely at fault when she was transfixed by the way the sun shone in his dark auburn hair, streaking it with fire.

Nor could she answer for the way her heart fluttered at the sight of him.

Quickly she reminded herself that she could. Such a reaction was completely uncalled-for and Fellis forced herself to look away.

She made herself think about riding. Was she holding the reins properly as Stephen had shown her? Was she giving commands with the appropriate tone?

The mare was the same gentle bay she had first ridden, and practice had given Fellis a certain amount of confidence in handling her. Admittedly she was still not overly so, even though she now knew that the animal must surely be quite ancient. She must have once been her mother's mount, and Mary Grayson had not ridden in years.

For a moment Fellis knew a feeling of guilt at thinking about her mother, but she swiftly quelled it. Fellis was aware that Lady Mary had approached her husband about stopping the proposed outing. She had heard them arguing from her mother's chamber, but for the first time in her memory her father had not capitulated and done as his wife wished.

More and more Fellis was coming to understand that things would not be the same as they had been in the past.

At that moment she looked up and found Stephen watching her, his dark gaze thoughtful. His close scrutiny was strangely unsettling.

Surprising her with his directness, he said, "What, may I ask, has brought such a pensive frown?"

She bit her lip, then answered him honestly. "I was but thinking about my father." She paused then went on. "He will have to do as King Edward says, will he not? I mean, there is really no choice in the matter."

Stephen looked at her, realizing his opportunity to speak of Wynn had come. Slowly he nodded, knowing there was no point in being anything but straightforward. "I must speak true, my lady. Does Wynn agree, he will have no choice."

"But W...Wynn." She hesitated, as if finding it difficult to say his name. "Will he agree?"

Stephen's gaze was unwavering and honest. "I believe he will." He looked away then, frowning. "Do you wish to hear what happened the day I went to see him?"

She hesitated again before replying. "I do."

Stephen took a deep breath, unexpectedly discovering that he was having a difficult time finding the words he wished to say. Drawing himself up straighter, he began, "First allow me to say that I think you will find Wynn a pleasant surprise from what you are imagining. He is, I believe, not ill-favored and is unlikely to strike fear in your heart on your...your wedding night."

Stephen could barely make himself say the last part, but he compelled himself to go on. It was madness for him to feel resentment toward Wynn or any man who might take her to his bed. He forced himself to attend Fellis, who seemed to listen to this with close enough attention, but there was little expression on her face.

She shrugged, "I suppose I should be glad of that."

Stephen did not ponder her strange lack of concern as he related the events of that day. By the time Stephen had finished telling her what he had seen and learned of her future husband when he visited him, Fellis had still said very little.

He made certain she knew that Wynn was a man who cared for his people, as her father did, as she did. Mayhap on that subject, if no other, they could find some common ground. They would surely have need of something. For if Sir Stephen was correct in his assessment, Wynn would eventually agree to the marriage.

Fellis cast a thoughtful glance toward Stephen, but she said only, "I thank you for telling me of this. I must think on it."

Stephen wondered if he had been open enough, if he should make the rest clearer. Mayhap he should have done more than gloss over the obstacle of Wynn's having to convince his allies to support the plan? Stephen had done no more than offhandedly mention the subject as if it were of little importance. And he had mentioned no other complications. Certainly not the fact that Wynn had a lover.

Looking over at her, Stephen knew he could not do so. Once Wynn saw Fellis, he would forget any other had ever existed. What man would not?

Unexpectedly she turned to him with a shrug. "I know not what tomorrow will bring, but for this one day, I wish to put it aside. I wish that more than anything."

How could Stephen deny her? Such a chance at freedom would not likely come for her again. He nodded, his gaze unknowingly gentle. "Let us forget then," he replied.

Though even as he said so, Stephen knew that the last thing he could allow himself to do was forget Fellis's coming marriage. To do so was to court certain disaster.

But for her sake he would pretend.

Glenmarket was truly an amazement to Fellis and she could scarce focus her eyes upon one wonder before they were drawn to another.

Even as they had come closer to the busy market town, the roads had grown more crowded with carts, horses and travelers on foot. Country folk in their best homespun garments, farmers in field clothes, and merchants in the finest velvets, each vied for their own portion of the busy thoroughfare.

Not since early in the journey had there been any real conversation between Fellis and Stephen. It had taken her some time to think on all he had said of Wynn. If what the knight had told her of the other man was true, the notion of marriage to the Welshman was not so fearsome a prospect as she had previously thought.

Could most of the troubles that had gone between their two peoples really be settled by them joining together in wedlock? She certainly hoped they could be. Especially because of the price she would be forced to pay did it come about.

Deciding that she was not going to let thoughts of her future marriage or anything else ruin this day, Fellis pushed them to the back of her mind. She also tried not to think on how being with Stephen made everything seem more exciting, the sun brighter, the breeze more gentle. But these thoughts were much more difficult to control than the others.

She knew the glory of the countryside awakening afresh to spring's call should be more than sufficient to keep her occupied. New leaves waved delicately from the oak, birch and elm trees that grew along their route, as if competing with the evergreens for attention. Delicate flowers for which she had no name had begun to sprout in amongst the underbrush that was also greening.

As they moved closer to town and the press around them became more dense, Stephen drew his mount a bit closer to her own, motioning for one of her father's men to do the same on the other side. She felt precious and cared for as never in her life, though she knew there was no need for such cautiousness.

Stephen seemed to sense her feelings, for he nodded with courtly grace as she looked over at him.

Fellis could only smile her appreciation, for no words would serve to make him understand how much this day and his attentiveness meant to her. Would always mean, even when Stephen was far from here and she bound in a loveless marriage.

They entered the town slowly, for the press of travelers had become great. In her excitement she was not able to fully take in everything she saw. Fellis had an impression of wattle and daub houses built along meandering streets. The common was divided into neat rows that lay between the forest and the impressive cluster of houses and public buildings. Looking at the many faces in the crowd around them as they made their way to the market at the center of Glenmarket, Fellis could see many Welsh mingling with her own countrymen. They were marked by their dark coloring and more loosely fitted garments, and also by the deep richness of their native language as they spoke to one another. None seemed to even give more than cursory attention to the fact that they mingled freely with folk who would have been their enemy in another setting. Here, as nowhere else in her experience, nationality came far behind commerce.

Seeing this gave Fellis her first real glimmer of hope that a peace might be brought about by her marriage to Wynn. Surely if the two peoples could get along for the purpose of trading, they could do so in other circumstances.

She could only hope so.

Soon it became difficult for Stephen to keep his stallion even with her mare and he looked toward her with questioning eyes. "I think we are in no danger here. Would you care to dismount and look at the wares more closely."

His thoughts echoed her own, and, without hesitation, she nodded. "Oh yes, please."

He gained the ground in one fluid motion, then reached up to assist her. But remembering what had happened the last time he touched her, Fellis made a pretense of holding tightly to the saddle pommel as she slipped down to join him. She had given herself leave to enjoy this day, but she had no wish to further make a fool of herself where Stephen was concerned.

If he took note of her action he made no comment, and for that she was grateful.

Stephen handed the reins of their horses to two of her father's men. "You can see that all is well here. Please take the horses to the forest at the edge of town. There, I'm sure, you will be able to find a cool place to tie them until they are needed. The first man nodded and said, "Yes, my lord."

Fellis then watched as the two moved off through the crowd, leaving their two fellows to act as guardians over Fellis. They remained mounted, each looking for signs of danger to their mistress.

With a smile that was merely polite and that nonetheless did wild things to her heart, Stephen held out his arm. His dark eyebrows rose high when she hesitated beside him.

"Wouldst allow me to guide you, my lady. I will feel less fearful of losing you, should I have your hand on my arm."

With a delicate flush she nodded. "Oh course." She reached out and rested her fingers ever so lightly on the soft velvet of his sleeve. "You have my thanks, Sir Knight." After all, he was thinking only of her safety. 'Twould be churlish of her to refuse him.

With her hand on his arm they started off through the bustling crowds. Though Stephen seemed mindful of keeping the guards in sight, he was not overly so.

It was not long before she began to take note that the other occupants of the market made way for them as they passed. Fellis felt herself standing taller at the attention they drew. She felt like a great lady for the first time in her short life. Even her limp seemed less pronounced as Stephen matched his pace to her slow one.

Stephen knew Fellis was aware of the stir she caused, her head held high as any queen. Even with the gray veil and wimple covering her head, many a man's gaze was drawn to that delicate profile and the light of excitement in her azure eyes.

Fellis was filled with life and it shone from inside her, making him wonder that she could have been kept from experiencing her true self for all this time.

He had almost a sense that they were co-conspirators in a forbidden adventure. He did not even ask himself why this notion so pleased him. Following his inclination, Stephen drew her along until they came to the booths he sought.

Before them along the route were several stalls set up to display bolts of cloth to best advantage. From here all looked bright and inviting. But Stephen knew, through his sister's learned tutelage, to look more closely for the one that would suit.

And then he saw it, near the end of the row, a booth like the others with brightly colored wares draped attractively over the counters and hanging elegantly from the corner posts. But what set it apart was the scarcity of customers. This told him it was most likely the very one he should seek out.

Elizabeth had taught him that few could afford the very best of fabrics and thus he must be wary of buying from those sellers with many customers. He drew Fellis forward with him.

Paying obvious attention to the quality of Stephen's own garments, the merchant hurried forward with a ready smile. "How may I offer assistance, my lord?"

Stephen saw the man's gaze pass over Fellis's plain gray clothing with a critically knowing eye, but his expression did not change as he spoke to her. "And, my lady. I hope I have some goods that might not offer insult to such noble customers."

"As you have guessed, we wish to see your finest goods," Stephen replied evenly, though he was gladdened to see the man defer to Fellis so readily. Clearly the man was clever and Stephen knew he would do well to stay on his guard so as not to pay too much for what they purchased.

When he looked to Fellis, he was amazed to find her eyes wide with what he could only describe as horror. She squeezed his arm as if in warning and made to draw him away.

When he resisted, she leaned close, her eyes beseeching. Stephen bent down to her as she whispered in his ear, "Sir Stephen, we must not stay here. The goods in this booth are far too dear." Her unconsciously yearning gaze moved over a length of pale green samite, the color of new grass. "We must go elsewhere."

"Nay," he told her, trying to concentrate on her words, even as her warm breath on his earlobe sent a shiver of awareness down his spine. "We will buy our cloth here. This booth is clearly the best and that is what you shall have. The best and nothing less." He said this softly, for her ears alone, as he did not wish it to be made even more difficult for him to get a fair price.

As if sensing his need for a moment of privacy with his lady, the man busied himself at the other side of his stall.

Fellis looked up at Stephen, biting her lip in consternation as if what she were about to say was more than a little difficult. "My mother would never allow it. 'Tis a sin to deck oneself in such finery."

He frowned in irritation, though it was not directed toward Fellis. Would her mother ruin this time even from a distance? He spoke carefully. "'Tis no sin to dress as befits your station. Your mother wears fine garments, even if the cut is a bit severe."

She shook her head. "My mother is a great lady, the wife of the Baron of Malvern. She must garb herself as befits her station."

"And you are his daughter." His tone was harsher than he intended and he saw her raise her chin in reaction. He chided himself even as he admired the show of spirited resistance. Here again he saw that they had not cowed her completely.

He went on more gently in deference to her pride. "Fellis, your father gave me more than sufficient funds to see you well equipped for your coming marriage. Do not worry over this. I beg you choose what you will. It is only right that you do so."

She looked down, stung by this further reminder of her coming marriage. As ever, Stephen thought of that eventuality and no other.

Allowing Stephen to call the merchant back to them without further comment, Fellis cast her gaze over the lustrous fabrics the man began to lay out before her. A saint would be hard-pressed not to admire the fine samites, sendals and damask the man brought forward. And despite her disappointment in Stephen and his motives, she found herself reaching out to run her fingertips over a lush gold velvet.

Fellis thought long and hard on which pieces of cloth would serve the purpose of being beautiful, as well as practical. Tentatively she then chose the green samite, a length of palest blue damask and another of deep peach in samite. That done, she turned to Stephen with a smile of accomplishment even as the merchant moved to set them aside.

To her surprise the knight was scowling.

To her further amazement she found herself scowling back at him in consternation, her hands going to her slender hips as she peered up at him. "What is the matter now, my lord? What have I done to bring about your displeasure this time?"

He gestured to the piles of fabric lining the booth. "If it takes you as long to decide on the rest we shall be here for days."

She gave a delicate snort. "Decide on the rest. What mean you? I have made my decisions." Surely he would press her no further in this matter.

He simply looked at her with grim resolve on his handsome face as he folded his arms over his chest. "Nay, you have barely begun, my lady. We shall purchase enough cloth to garb you as the wife of a nobleman should be. Does it take you the rest of the day, I will not leave until we are done."

She folded her own arms, appalled at the very gall of him, to think she would be so wasteful.

With a sound of complete exasperation, Stephen turned to the patiently waiting merchant. Without deigning to consult her further, he began to point at whatever caught his gaze. "We will take that, and that, and a length of this, and most certainly that one..."

He went on until Fellis was fair dizzy with trying to recall all the fabrics and colors he had chosen. At some level of her mind she was aware that the knight seemed to have taken note of her preference for soft colors, for he selected many delicate and lovely pastels, shades that made her think of spring.

The most notable deviation from this theme was a bolt of bright red damask that fair cried out to be noticed.

In spite of her horror, there was nothing Fellis could do to stop it. In the end she could only watch with wide eyes as he removed a sizable handful of gold from her father's purse and handed it to the bowing merchant, who did not seem to be able to stop smiling.

Turning to the mounted guards, who had waited with patiently blank expressions through the whole exchange, Stephen told them to collect the goods and take them to where the others waited at the edge of town. And as they obeyed, the soldiers made not so much as a murmur to question him. In the face of Stephen's self-assurance they seemed to have forgotten that Fellis might have need of protection from this very man.

Looking up at Stephen as he led her away from the cloth seller's booth, Fellis wondered at his easy ability to govern others and his unshakable self-confidence.

She could only imagine what it would be like to feel so completely sure of yourself and those around you. 'Twas a thing she'd never experienced or even thought to.

Then knowing that she must be honest with herself at least, Fellis gave pause. She had to admit that since Stephen had arrived at Malvern she had found herself rebelling with near open hostility to his high-handed ways at times. She did not know why, but it seemed the knight brought out hidden depths of defiance inside her. And far from shame her, as the realization should, Fellis was pleased by it. She rather liked the notion of defying this arrogant man, who she was sure did not meet with such resistance from many.

But even as she was considering this amazing fact, Stephen turned to her with a self-satisfied grin. "Now, my Lady Fellis, what shall we do next?" His gaze swept the busy throng before them.

That streak of rebellion resurfaced. "And where would we go from here, sir? It would seem you have no need of my presence to see your way. You are clearly more than equal to the task of seeing to what must be done without my assistance." She averted her face from him as she spoke.

He stopped short with a frown of irritation, then nodded. "I am guilty as you have charged. Forgive me, I saw that you were having a difficult time of it and sought only to make things easier for you. 'Twill not make you feel near as guilty to wear your new garments once made if you have me to blame for having purchased the cloth that made them."

With an angry gasp, Fellis started away from him, even as the truth of what he had said struck home.

Before she had gone more than a few steps, Stephen was at her side, his hand closing around her arm. And as always when he touched her, she knew a tingling awareness. But she hurriedly pushed it away as she swung around to face him. "My lord, please take your hand from me?"

He did so, but with obvious reluctance. She refused to meet his probing gaze, looking out unseeing at the people around them, who seemed to pay no notice to the two of them, since they were no longer accompanied by a mounted guard. For all the attention they attracted from the busy strangers surrounding them, they might have been alone. That made her feel an odd sense of disquiet that she could not put name to. To cover her confusion, Fellis said, "My lord, I am no child to be treated thus. I have my own mind and would act on it. None of you seem to understand that."

He raised his hand in a gesture of acceptance. "I admit I am at fault. You speak true."

When she only studied him without answering, he added, "May we begin afresh. I had hoped to see you enjoy your time of freedom. I vow to treat you as the woman you are for the rest of our time together. You may do as you will."

He bowed with fluid grace, catching the eyes of several maidens nearby, causing Fellis to realize once again that many women would look upon one Stephen Clayburn with favor.

He appeared not to notice the covetous gazes cast his way as he looked into her eyes. "I await your pleasure."

She could not halt the heady rush of blood to her face and neck. Fellis was infinitely grateful that the knight had no idea of the provocative memory of her body gliding along his that the words brought to mind.

Stephen really was trying to be agreeable. In all honesty, Fellis had to admit that it was not his fault she could not control her own impure thoughts.

Surely she must take his offer of friendly companionship as just that. It would serve her best to form a reasonable reply to his suggestion. "I do not know where to go," she admitted, biting her lip in consternation.

"Then allow me to attend you." He held out his arm for her to take. "And if at any time, where I lead is not to your liking, you must only tell me and we shall venture forth to some other point of interest."

He appeared so earnest that she could not restrain a laugh, a soft melodious sound that drew Stephen's gaze to her lips. And for a moment neither of them moved or even breathed as a shaft of longing so sweet it stilled her pulse shot through her.

Stephen found himself drowning in those blue eyes, so innocent yet so intoxicating. Fellis had no idea how desirable she was and the soft sound of her laughter slid over his skin like warm honey, leaving him achingly aware of how much he wanted her, how much he needed to put his mouth to those soft pink lips.

Chapter Eight

Stephen looked away even as he swallowed hard past the lump of desire in his throat. When he spoke, his voice was unexpectedly husky. "This way then, my lady. Mayhap we might find some ribbons and baubles to go with your wedding garments."

For Fellis the words were like a dash of cold rainwater. For the second time since she had known him, Fellis had felt that Stephen Clayburn might kiss her. But of course that was foolish. Whatever was the matter with her?

By turning all her attentions to simply walking beside the knight without awkwardness, Fellis was finally able to bring herself under control.

It was simply a matter of calling on her own sense of pride, she told herself. She knew that she had to find some mastery over her reactions to Stephen if she was to know any peace.

This day she meant to enjoy, come what may. And after a time she began to do just that.

They saw a troop of acrobats, tumbling for what coin might come their way, and stopped to watch. When the performers were finished, Stephen took a copper from his own purse and tossed it to them.

Fellis could hardly catch her breath as they moved through the throng, her gaze lingering on the people and sights with avid interest. Never had she seen so many folk all together at one time.

Strolling along slowly upon Stephen's arm, her limp was so slight as to be imperceptible and Fellis drew not a second glance. For this day she was not Fellis Grayson, crippled daughter to the Baron of Malvern, but an anonymous young maid in the company of a handsome knight. A maid who drew the envious glances of other young women when they passed close by.

The feeling was a heady one.

After a time they grew hungry, and true to his word, Stephen allowed Fellis to pick from one of the many merchants selling food. She was drawn by the pungent scent of savory to choose a booth that sold freshly baked pastries still warm from the oven, as well as another where they purchased two apples roasted with cinnamon. Breathing in the spicy scent Fellis moved with Stephen to the edge of the crowded court to eat them.

Never had she enjoyed herself more.

As Fellis was finishing her last bite of apple, she took note of a young woman with a mane of tangled dark hair, who stood at the edge of a crowd gathered around one of the stalls selling food. The girl was lovely, to be sure, but what drew her attention was the way the woman was watching herself and Stephen.

Having now grown accustomed to the covetous glances brought by the man at her side, Fellis was unaccountably made uncomfortable by this particular stare. The expression on the woman's face was not so much admiring as others had been but seemed more of a look of anger or resentment.

Looking toward Stephen with a puzzled frown, she was relieved to find the woman gone when she turned back. Stephen seemed not to have noticed the exchange and Fellis did not wish to explain her own uncomfortable feelings about the situation.

Surely she had been mistaken in thinking the young woman was angry. She did not know the girl and did not believe that Stephen could, as he was so recently come to the area.

With little effort Fellis was able to forget the incident, for Stephen continued to present himself as a charming and attentive escort.

Next they wandered toward the edge of the town, where a group of men were gathered around several horses tied out in the open.

Pulling her gently along, Stephen made his way to a particularly lovely black filly. Stopping before the mare, Stephen held out his hand and softly urged Fellis to do the same.

"Slowly now," he instructed, holding Fellis's hand forward in his own. "Let her get your scent."

With a thrill of excitement that was a direct result of Stephen's strong fingers curved protectively beneath her own, Fellis found herself holding her breath as the mare leaned forward to sniff her hand.

Then Stephen's hand was gone from hers. Trying not to show her disappointment, Fellis reached up to trace her trembling fingers over the mare's delicate nose as the midnight head dipped toward her. Now a thrill of pleasure raced through her at touching the beautiful animal.

"She is quite an ebony beauty, is she not?" Stephen spoke quietly, his voice filled with admiration.

"Yes, she is," Fellis answered. "What a lovely girl you are," she said as she caressed the noble head.

Feeling Stephen move away from her, Fellis looked up to see him engage in conversation with a man who had stood close by. He seemed to be discussing the merits of the mare, for the two men glanced toward where Fellis stood beside her, nodding and chatting amiably.

It was only a few moments later, as Fellis saw Stephen remove his purse from his belt and count out what seemed an inordinate amount of gold, that she realized what was happening.

Why ever would Stephen buy the mare? Fellis knew it was against the codes of chivalry for any knight to ever be mounted on a filly. The horse could not be for him.

And then realization dawned.

"Nay." She shook her head, moving to stop him even as he came toward her. "'Twill not serve, Sir Knight. I cannot accept. Verily, even if I could, 'twould be a crime. Having so little experience in riding never would I be able to ride such an animal."

He halted before her, his jaw setting stubbornly even as he tried to reason with her. "'Twill be no great trouble. The breeder assures me she is most gentle and has been specially schooled for the needs of a lady. Besides, you are growing more accustomed to riding. You did journey here this day by that very method."

"On the old mare from my father's stable. A blind man could do so." She waved a hand toward the horse seller. "What if he lied about the mare's training?"

Stephen's gaze hardened even as she looked up at him, and Fellis knew a moment of compassion for any who dared to dupe Sir Stephen Clayburn. Then his face cleared and his expression became his usual pleasant one. "He did not. I have some knowledge of horseflesh and this mare is of the best."

"And there," she said, "we have another problem. I cannot accept such a gift. My father is not expecting any such purchase. He made absolutely no mention of such an extravagant thing."

Stephen looked down at her with unshakable obstinacy. "That is why I have paid for the mare of my own coin. I would not expect your father to do so without consulting him."

Her own will rose to her defense and she stood as tall as she could though her head still came only to his shoulder. She did her best to keep her tone polite but feared she was not quite succeeding. "That I cannot allow. You have no obligation to buy me such a dear gift. 'Tis not right and I would be wrong to accept."

"It is no great matter. I can well afford the horse."

She crossed her arms over her chest. "I will not accept."

A look of complete consternation crossed his face. And for a moment, Fellis felt a rush of almost childish pleasure. She was more certain than ever that Stephen Clayburn was quite unaccustomed to anyone defying his wishes.

He glared at her, but there seemed a contradictory glint of amusement in his eyes as he spoke. "It is becoming clearer to me by the very hour that you have played some unexplained hoax on all of us. You are not in the least the milk-cheeked maid you pretend. Beneath those overmodest garments lurks a will of iron."

She could find no reply to such an outrageous statement. He had no right to accuse her so. And even worse than his having accused her was the unmistakable impression that the knight seemed shockingly pleased by his observations.

Without another word, Fellis moved away from him, intending to seek out her father's men and make ready for the journey home. This latest conversation had left her feeling she'd had enough of Stephen's company to last her for some time.

Fellis refused to acknowledge his presence in any way as she made her way back through the press of the market. But even as she ignored him she was completely conscious of the knight keeping perfect pace with her as they made their way through the throng. If she slowed to let someone by, he slowed. If she hurried to get away from him, he sped up. Finally she gave up trying, though she was aware of a feeling of disappointment in the way the day was ending.

Now that she was tired and angry, the town seemed not to hold its former fascination for her. All she wished to do was return to Malvern and her ordered life there.

As her thoughts calmed, she reflected on what he had said. Inside her she knew Stephen had not understood the truth of things. She had not sought to mislead her family. She was agreeable and slow to react in anger. Fellis was the very damsel they thought her.

Only with the advent of Stephen Clayburn had she found this hidden well of stubbornness. In all the years of her life she'd never experienced as much animosity and aggression as she had since his coming.

It was also true that she'd never felt so alive.

Suddenly through the haze of her thoughts, Fellis heard someone call out behind her. Stopping, she turned, something in the tone alerting her to danger.

What she saw brought a frown of confusion to her delicate brow.

Stephen was standing on the path behind her. Another man, tall and burly, with a head of shaggy gray hair, had moved before him, blocking his path. As the man addressed Stephen, Fellis realized it was he who had spoken, but to the knight.

She watched the two of them and took note of a girl standing near the gray-haired man. It was the same young woman who had looked upon them so coldly in the market. There was no mistaking that mane of dark hair that framed her exotically pretty face in an attractive tangle.

Even as Fellis studied her, the girl turned to face her. Fellis nearly recoiled at the expression of rank hatred on the other's face, and she searched her mind to discover a reason for it.

She found none. Fellis knew this woman not and could fathom no cause for her ill will.

But she did not linger on the puzzle as the gray-haired man spoke to Stephen in a voice of rage. "Go home, *Sais*. You are not wanted here." His English was spoken slowly and with the deep lilt of the Welsh.

Stephen held up his hands in a gesture of peace. "I wish you no ill, sir. This is a public thoroughfare and I wouldst thank you to allow me to pass unmolested."

The man made a deep growling noise in his throat. "I said, *Sais,* that we do not want you here. You should take yourself back to your *Saesneg* king and stay there, if you know your own good."

Stephen's jaw hardened in repressed anger at the verbal attack. He knew this man.

'Twas the same one who had spoken against him at Wynn's holding the day he went there. Wynn had called him Owain, saying that he had been his father's closest friend. This was not a fellow who could easily be dismissed, but someone Wynn obviously trusted and had a close relationship with. It was not a part of Stephen's plan to become involved in a public brawl with one of the very folk he hoped to come to terms with. He must not allow himself to get into an altercation with one of Wynn's close allies.

But neither was Stephen about to let any hint of danger threaten Fellis. Even as he risked a fleeting glance toward her, from the corner of his eye, Stephen saw her start forward. Desperately he wanted to tell her to keep her distance, but he had no desire to call attention to her.

As Stephen watched, he saw a woman move to block her path. He was not reassured as to Fellis's safety when he noted that it was the same woman who had sat on the arm of Wynn's chair the day he went to see him.

"Do you hear me, *Sais?* Are you so much a coward that you have naught to even say to me?" the Welshman chided in a voice of scorn.

Stephen answered him with forced patience, trying to see what was going on with Fellis while keeping this bear of a man in control. "As I said, I wish you no ill. This conversation would be better left to a more private place. Do you wish me to attend you at some future date, I would be most happy to oblige."

The man let out a bitter, scoffing laugh. "Hear me well, *Sais,* I wish naught to do with you or your kind other than to be rid of you. I sought you out to tell you that if you continue on the course you have set, you would do well to watch your back. You just might find a Welsh arrow sticking from it."

Stephen heard an answering laugh from behind him and looked to see that quite a crowd had gathered.

They were in what seemed to be an area where a large number of Welsh countrymen had gathered to talk and trade. He'd been so occupied with following Fellis that he'd not seen this heretofore.

Besides, Stephen told himself, he would not have taken any particular notice of the fact. Hadn't he already seen that there was an unspoken truce amongst the people in the town?

But it had taken only this one furious man to change the attitudes of many. Their animosity was more than apparent now.

Witnessing the angry and resentful faces pressing close around them, Stephen knew that there was no real peace even here. Their hatred had only been thinly disguised in order to conduct what commerce must be done before the people went thankfully back to their own lands. There might even be added resentment that they were forced to come here to English lands to do business.

All knew that the right to hold a market town could be granted by the king or one of his powerful supporters. And it was a right that was guarded most closely.

Stephen knew King Edward sought to bring the Welsh into his law under the guise of granting the rights to build such towns to those loyal to him. When the Welsh moved closer to these towns in order to conduct business, they would be brought directly into the path of those loyal to him, their bailiffs, sheriffs—and the royal justice.

But even as this realization passed through his mind, Stephen had no notion that the crowd would erupt into violence. Then he felt something hit the back of his head—hard.

His head reeling from the force and the unexpectedness of the blow, Stephen staggered to one knee. Bile rose in his throat but he forced it down, willing himself to stay conscious.

He must protect Fellis.

But directly on that thought, he heard her voice beside him, even as her gentle fingers moved through his hair. Unerringly she located the growing lump on the back of his head.

"How do you dare!" she cried in outrage. "This man has done nothing to any of you. Besides 'tis a coward's way to strike a man from behind. I had thought better of the Welsh sense of honor."

There was an angry growl from the gray-haired giant who leaned over them. "Stay your tongue, girl. There is no honor in treating with the enemies of Wales. And this knight is our enemy, as are you. But he's come to meddle in affairs that are none of his concern."

Stephen looked up to see Fellis standing over him. Somehow in the heat of the moment she had lost her veil and wimple and her silver blond hair fluttered about her like a halo. She appeared as some pagan goddess of old, become flesh, but not of this world. He recalled again in a flash of vivid detail the way she had looked that first morning in the forest and he felt a desperate yearning to possess her, her body, her spirit—all of her.

He felt a swell of pride in his chest that this glorious woman would come so quickly to his defense. Though he also wished she had not placed herself in the midst of this.

He heard Fellis answering Owain, her tone confused. "I know not how you are aware of his purpose, sir. But let me say that he has come only to do his duty to the king. As a man he has no ill feelings against you or any of your folk. Can you blame him for the wishes of a king? He has no more say in that than you or I."

Angrily Owain replied, "I care nothing for the wishes of your English king. He has no say over me and mine."

She faced him without a hint of fear. "Be that as it may, you have broken the peace of this place to attack a man who meant you no harm."

Owain took a step closer to her, raising his fist in threat.

Stephen felt fury such as he had never known reach out and take him in its grip. Hard upon it came a flash flood of strength that flowed into his veins, washing away any hint of weakness.

Eyes dark with rage, Stephen rose and placed his hand on her shoulder. Fellis did not look around as she continued to face the large burly Welshman without flinching.

He rested his other hand on the hilt of his sword. Stephen spoke in a voice made more threatening by the very controlled rage behind it. "Touch her and you shall never raise that hand again."

Even as he watched Owain swing away after a moment with a growl of rage, Stephen knew he dared not allow himself to think on the depth of his fury. Or what it might mean.

With Owain's retreat from confrontation, the rest of the crowd seemed to have lost their thirst for a fight. They stood silent, none of them meeting his gaze as he cast a glare over them.

Then he turned back to Fellis, thinking only that he must get her away before there was more risk to her safety. Gently but possessively Stephen drew her back against him. "Come."

She faced him, her eyes searching his even as she tried to reach up to feel his head once again. "Are you well, my lord?"

"Aye," Stephen said, her concern causing a sweet tenderness to rise up inside him. Uncaring of what anyone else might think, he reached down and swung her up into his arms without effort. "I am fine."

Fellis gave a gasp of surprise even as he started down the path to the edge of town.

Stephen paid no heed, only knowing that he need see her away with all possible haste. He was hard-pressed not to cuddle her against his chest as his instincts bid him, to claim her as his woman before all and sundry. What a prize she was, this fiery little Fellis.

At this moment it was near impossible for Stephen to care for anything save having her close to him.

Stephen halted only when they came to a small orchard at the edge of the market town. He moved in amongst the trees and leaned against one of the trunks as he buried his face in the silken tumble of her hair.

Fellis made not a sound as he held her close. And after a time, Stephen was moved to speak, his voice husky with emotion. "Why did you not run?"

She continued to hold her head against his chest, not looking at him. "I could not leave you."

"I was in no danger," he told her gruffly, finally letting her slide down to stand on her feet. But he did not remove his arms from around her.

She looked up at him then, her blue eyes wide. "It did not appear so to me." Fellis shook her head, not breaking the contact of their gazes. "I do not know what came over me. I was so angry that I did not stop to ponder my actions. I only knew that I could not leave you to face them alone." She halted, her blue eyes misting as she looked up at him.

Her silver hair was spread around her like a cloak, hanging like spun silk to her knees. So often Stephen had longed to see it this way again.

He reached out a hand and ran it softly over the tresses that reminded him of moonbeams. To his surprise he saw his hand was trembling and he was powerless to stop it.

She sighed, closing her eyes as she leaned into his hand. "Oh, Stephen." Her mouth parted and her breast rose more quickly with each breath she took.

His eyes came to rest on those sweetly curved lips, lips he had been ofttimes tempted to kiss.

From the moment he had seen Fellis he had known that he wanted her, and now he had no will to resist his own desire. He lowered his mouth to hers, brushing that delicate flesh with his own. She was so soft, so warm. He kissed her more fully, fitting his mouth to hers, his lips opening when she returned the pressure.

Stephen felt the familiar tightening in his lower belly. A pleasant heaviness grew in his arms, which he drew more tightly around her as he urged her mouth to open with his tongue.

She made no protest, simply pressing herself more fully against him as she opened to him. Inside she was damp and luscious as warm custard. Her tongue slid along his, and he groaned deep in his throat. Stephen arched against her, unable to control his body's urgent response to her.

She only held onto him more tightly, her hands gripping the front of his tunic more urgently.

God in heaven, he wanted her. And knew she wanted him. There was no mistaking the way she reacted to their kisses. Her slender form was molded so closely to his that his head swam with the feel and delicate woman smell of her.

He knew he had to stop.

With a force of will he had not known he possessed, Stephen drew back, pulling her head down to his shoulder. "Fellis, Fellis, we must not."

She looked up at him in confusion, her eyes dark as cobalt. "Stephen, what mustn't we do? I feel so... I do not understand what is happening to me."

This finally brought him to his senses. She was completely innocent of what had just occurred. Only Stephen knew where these kisses could lead.

And down that path was utter ruin for her. He could not allow that to happen.

Stephen held her away from him. "Fellis, what just happened here was a terrible mistake. We must find your father's men and return to Malvern."

She frowned up at him, her eyes clearing slowly. "A mistake?"

He looked away from her, the muscle in his jaw flexing. "Aye, and we must take every care that it does not happen again."

Her voice was rife with confusion as she stiffened. "What are you saying?"

He looked down at her then, forcing himself to face her without showing any of the tumult of emotion inside him. "I am saying that we both overreacted to what happened in the town just now. I was frightened for you and you for me. It made us behave in a way that was completely inappropriate."

When she did not reply he went on. "For God's sake, Fellis, you are to be married soon. What I just did was inexcusable. Surely you can see that." His own disgust at himself for forgetting made him sound more angry than he intended.

She started as if he had slapped her and jerked away from him, turning her face. "I see, as ever we must remember my coming marriage."

"We must," Stephen replied. He knew that the determination in his voice was brought on by a drastic need to keep his distance. He had no right to touch Fellis, no matter how it pained him to admit it.

She took a deep breath. "So be it." Without another word, Fellis started back through the orchard. He watched her stride away from him, her back rigid with resentment and hurt.

Deep inside he desired to call her back, to tell her he was sorry. But he could not do that. It was better for her to be angry with him and remain at arm's length than have what just occurred happen again.

For Stephen was not sure he would have the strength to turn her away again. The line between his duty and his emotions was growing less clear as the days passed.

In all honesty Stephen had to face the truth that his noble action in halting their kisses had very little to do with the fact that Fellis should not be besmirched as the future wife of an important ally to the crown. It had more to do with his not wanting any hurt to come to her. And that realization brought him only turmoil.

Chapter Nine

Over the course of the next days Fellis found it far easier to avoid Stephen than she would have dared hope.

During the long ride from Glenmarket, she'd been able to think of little save getting home. And away from Stephen Clayburn.

When she finally located her father's men, she had known he was right behind her. Thankfully he'd said not one word to her. Stephen had simply gone about readying them for the return journey to Malvern. Even when he had sent one of the men back to fetch the horse he had bought for her, he'd not so much as looked at Fellis, a fact that had eventually begun to irritate her however irrational it might be.

She felt almost as if she were the one at fault. In her heart of hearts, possibly she knew that she was. Hadn't she secretly longed for what had just occurred.

Stephen might believe the kiss had been brought on by a reaction to the threat they had faced together. Fellis knew differently. Thus the shame must be her own. She had wanted him to kiss her, wanted it more than anything in her life.

When he'd taken her in his arms, she'd lost all thought of anything besides the pounding in her blood, the honeyed sweetness that rose up in her belly. Stephen's lips had been so sure, so supple. Her nights since had been filled with the memory of the touch and taste and feel of him.

This very afternoon, a full week later, Fellis could not stop thinking about what had happened that day. As she stood looking down at her mother's head, where she knelt measuring the hem of yet another new cote, she wondered what Mary Grayson would say about the thoughts that heated Fellis's pale cheeks even now.

In shame and frustration, she wiped a hand across her furrowed brow.

"Mary, you must see that the child is exhausted." Her grandmother's chiding voice came from the bed. Fellis looked over at the dainty little woman who was propped against the pillows. With the warm weather had come a decided improvement in the elderly lady's health. Fellis was warmed by the love that shone from the blue eyes that met her own, but she was surprised at what Myrian said next. "Let her go out and ride that new mare she's told me about. 'Tis not right to have it cooped up in the stables, nor Fellis here in the keep on such a lovely day." She indicated the cloudless blue sky that was visible through the open window.

Mary Grayson looked up from the hem of the samite cote that perfectly reflected the color of that summer sky. "Tired is she. Fellis has done little but stand while garments are fitted to her since she came back from Glenmarket a week gone. And please do not even mention that animal. Were Richard not a fool, he would have sent it back to the thief who sold it." She rolled her eyes heavenward to emphasize her point.

Fellis grimaced. When her father saw the horse Stephen had purchased for Fellis, he insisted on paying for it himself. On learning of the gift her mother had made her disapproval most clear.

Yet Fellis was grateful that her father had chosen to give her the horse. Only then had she felt free to accept the animal as her own. On realizing the animal was indeed hers to keep, Fellis had promptly given her the name Ebony, remembering the way Stephen had called her an ebony beauty.

If she was honest with herself, she knew in the days after Stephen had accomplished his purpose and gone back to his own life the mare would remain special to her. For in spite of all that had passed between them afterward, he had made her feel different that day he purchased the horse. He made her feel like a woman.

Fellis looked out the open window with longing. "May I go out, Mother. Ebony does need the exercise."

Mary looked more closely at her daughter's face in surprise. "It is the first time I've ever heard you question me, Fellis. Do not tell me you are grown too full of yourself to wait on your mother's pleasure."

Fellis flushed and did not meet her mother's eyes. "Nay, Mother, I meant no disrespect." Then with an unusual show of spirit she raised her head high. "I only sought to go out for a short time. And, truly, how am I ever to become more accustomed to riding, if I do not ride?" She held up her hands. "I've hardly seen the mare since Father bought her and 'twould be a great waste of her price to leave her unridden."

"Go then," Mary said in a tone of flat disapproval. "I am finished here for the moment." Without looking at her daughter, she began to gather up her sewing accessories.

Hurriedly Fellis removed the gown and drew on an old one. She bent and pressed a grateful kiss to her grandmother's soft cheek. She whispered, "You have my thanks."

As Fellis headed for the door, her mother stopped her, and for a moment Fellis feared she might have changed her mind. She was not sure she would be able to bring herself so far as to openly disobey, but she felt as if she would go mad if she was cooped up here for one more minute.

But all her mother said was, "Mind that you are back here ere long." She indicated the stack of brilliant and beautiful fabrics that littered every surface except the bed. "All this waste is for your benefit alone." Her lips thinned. "Your father has assured me that he feels you have need of such luxuries even if the marriage does not come about. Which it will not. And I can only meet such foolishness with bewilderment, knowing how you will have no use for such finery once you enter the abbey. But the task has been undertaken and you must be willing to at least allow yourself to be fitted for the garments." The last was said with raised eyebrows.

Fellis felt herself balk at the unfairness of her mother's disdain. And from somewhere inside herself she felt rebellion surface. She raised her head high. "Mother, however respectfully, I must disagree with you. Sir Stephen does believe the marriage will take place, and I can only think that he has some reason for such certainty. He is the one who met with Wynn. And let me also say that unless Wynn refuses, we will have no choice. Father holds these lands only by royal decree. He cannot, even to please you, refuse the wishes of King Edward."

Her mother only watched her in mute horror, then she said, "Fellis, never did I think to hear you speak so to me."

Fellis felt her defiance leave her, to be replaced by regret, regret that her mother could not unbend from her stance even now. She spoke gently. "Mother, please, I do love and respect you. I have no wish to hurt you. I want only for you to see that I am a woman now and must face my fate without childish fantasy."

Mary Grayson said nothing. She only stood staring as if Fellis were a stranger.

Unable to bear the aggrieved expression in her mother's eyes, Fellis turned and left. She pushed the problems with her mother to the back of her mind. They were not likely to be solved this day. She hurried to the stables and, as she did so wondered what Stephen Clayburn was about.

Since the day they had returned from Glenmarket she had seen him only at a distance. He seemed to have attached himself to her father and she had seen them ride from the keep together this very morning. What interest the knight could have in the daily running of her father's lands Fellis had no notion. But she was grateful for his absence.

Stephen had assured her that the mare would be gentle enough to act as mount to her. Fellis did not stop to even question why she had such faith in his judgment. She simply did.

And true to what he had said, Ebony was the epitome of obedient horseflesh as Fellis mounted and rode her slowly around the courtyard. The horse's complete compliance soon led Fellis to decide she was ready for more.

Like the first time she'd ridden a horse, Fellis was conscious of a complete sense of freedom upon Ebony's broad back. Here she was no longer forced to be cautious in her movements to keep from appearing awkward. She could trust in the mare's sure feet to take her where she would go.

There was no telling when her mother would agree to another riding session and Fellis meant to enjoy this one. So thinking, she told a wide-eyed Thad where she was going.

He nodded quite sagely for a twelve-year-old and said, "You are doing right well, my Lady Fellis. Who would have thought it?"

His comment only served to boost her confidence further and she held her head high as she made her way from the keep.

Fellis wondered what Stephen would think of her now, mounted on this fine mare. Surely no court lady would have a better mount than the black beauty beneath her.

That thought halted Fellis in her tracks.

Whatever was wrong with her. There was no way she could even hope to compete with such women. She was as nothing to those women of the world who knew all about luring and keeping a man. Did such a female want Stephen Clayburn, she would surely know how to show him without disgusting him with her uncontrolled passion as Fellis had.

For a moment the knowledge was grating.

Then she straightened her shoulders as pride came to her rescue. Though it was near impossible to set her feelings for Stephen aside, they were far too complicated for her to understand or define.

That day in the market town when she had gone to his defense it had been purely on instinct. She'd given no thought to the wisdom of her actions.

Stephen had come to her rescue, facing the Welshman down with great courage even though he'd have been severely outnumbered had the crowd chosen to attack him. She'd been filled with pride and awe in him.

Fellis had been even more swept away by her feelings when he'd taken her up in his arms as if she weighed nothing more than a child. He'd held her with a care and tenderness that had been clearly communicated to her.

She had felt the same toward him, not even questioning the feelings they shared. Simply knowing they were there had seemed enough at the time.

When he'd stopped to rest in the orchard she had not known what was to happen. Not until Stephen had looked into her eyes. And then ...

She blushed even now, prodding Ebony forward. Why must she keep thinking on this? 'Twas only madness to do so.

What had gone between herself and Stephen could make no difference to her. It mattered not in the least what Stephen thought of her. It was of Wynn she must think, him whom she must hope to please. He was the one who should look on her with favor.

If he ever contacted them.

Fellis refused to allow herself to even think about how she might actually feel if that eventuality finally came about.

But in truth, no matter what she tried to tell herself, everything palled in comparison to the way she felt about Stephen Clayburn.

Fellis rode on unmindful of her direction or the passage of time.

Stephen dismounted and handed the reins of his stallion to Thad. He had returned to the keep alone as Lord Richard had asked him. The request had been made very politely and the knight had not taken offense, as he could see that the village steward had some private business to discuss with his master.

Over the days since the trip to Glenmarket, Stephen had spent much time with Lord Grayson. Although the baron had not been completely welcoming at first, his attitude had thawed somewhat as the week progressed.

Stephen knew he had no need to put himself to such lengths with Lord Grayson, but anything was preferable to the possibility of running into Fellis. In the end, he had begun to almost enjoy his time with her father.

In his own element, that of running his lands and commanding his people, Lord Richard was more than competent. He was in fact a model overlord, strong but fair. The kind of man Stephen's brother Henry was.

It seemed that only with his wife was the baron unable to exert himself. Though from the evidence of late, he was making an effort to do so.

At least as far as his daughter was concerned. It seemed as if he wished to somehow repay her for her sacrifice in agreeing to marry Wynn. Even though Lord Richard had not openly admitted that the wedding would take place, neither did he behave as if it would not.

Stephen raked a hand through his hair and wished he was far from here and the problems he'd encountered at Malvern. Yet as he thought this he knew it wasn't true.

He could not imagine what his life would have been like not to know Fellis, to see her smile, to hold her pliant form in his arms.

His body tightened at the mere memory of the kiss they'd shared. He'd known from first seeing her in the glade that day that she was a woman of rare passion. It had been obvious in the lack of self-consciousness she displayed, her nakedness being a completely comfortable state to her.

The reality had been even more devastating than he'd imagined. Though he was certain that the kiss was her first, after only a brief hesitation she'd given of herself without restraint. She'd met his passion with her own, unashamedly.

God, but he wondered what it would be like to call such a woman his own. Would he be willing to give up his freedom and face his old fears to have her? That fear of losing the one you love.

He shook his head to clear it. He knew not whence the thought of love had come. He was drawn to Fellis, in fact captivated by her. But love? Nay, surely not that.

As was his custom of the past week, Stephen turned to go to Ebony's stall. He had made a point of paying some attention to the mare each day. He felt as if contact with her was almost like being with Fellis.

To his surprise the stall was empty.

He went back to the front of the building, locating Thad where he was brushing down a stallion. He pointed toward the vacant cubicle. "Where has Ebony gone?"

Thad looked up at the knight with eyes that glowed with pride for his lady. "Lady Fellis is riding her. It is a true wonder how well she is doing. What with her only learning since you came."

Stephen knew a flash of alarm. "She took no one with her?"

"Nay," Thad replied as he continued to rub down the stallion. "She said she would do well enough alone."

Stephen tried to appear unconcerned as he pushed at a pile of straw with his leather-shod foot. "How long has your lady been gone?"

Thad frowned. "Oh, these two hours or more."

Stephen scowled. Two hours. He gave much care to making his tone sound casual even as he reached for his saddle, which sat nearby. "Methinks I will join her. 'Tis still early."

He did not want Thad to see his concern for Fellis and misinterpret it for anything but what it was. The young woman was still very inexperienced a rider. He simply wished to be certain that no ill had befallen her.

For a brief moment he paused, wondering which direction she might have taken. Then inexplicably he knew that she had gone into the forest.

He was certain of it. He felt it was where she would go to find solitude.

Confidently he headed off in the direction of the wood. The same inexplicable power that drew him to her would help him to find her.

Even as he went, Stephen tried to convince himself that he was only worried that something had happened to her and that he had to be sure she was safe. Inside him a voice cried out that he was a liar.

Fellis had not been to the glade since Stephen came. It had not even entered her mind. It was as if Stephen, with his powerful presence, had made even the pull of her private place pall by comparison.

Unerringly she found the spot where the trees grew dense around the secluded place. There she tied Ebony to a sturdy limb and scrambled through the dense growth. The glade was as beautiful as ever. The moss hung as heavily from the trees, the breeze whispered delicately over her cheeks, and the water burbled as pleasantly as it spilled into the lily-dotted pond.

Yet everything seemed different. Today she felt no desire to pull off her clothing and dive naked into the gentle caress of the water. She found herself thinking of another caress, the velvet touch of Stephen's hands. If she closed her eyes, she could still feel the brush of his long fingers on her cheek.

With a groan of frustration she left, not looking back, nor knowing if she would ever return.

She remounted and rode back through the forest until she came to the river that wound its way around her father's lands. Fellis knew that if she followed the river she would come to the town at the base of hill on which the castle stood. But Fellis had no desire to go into the town, no desire to meet anyone.

Especially not Stephen Clayburn.

With a sigh she dismounted and led Ebony to the river for a drink. She then tied the mare so that she might graze on the new grass that dotted the riverbank.

That done, Fellis sat down at the edge of the water. After a time she began to notice the warmth of the sun on her heavy veil and reached up to pull it from her head. When she did so the thick braid of her hair rolled down her back to lay against the cool green grass.

She sighed again listlessly, leaning her chin on her hand. Even here Fellis could find no peace from her troubles. Her possible marriage to Wynn, her difficulties with Mother, her confused feelings for Stephen, all weighed heavily upon her mind.

Fellis had no idea how long she sat there, before she became aware of a soft sound behind her. A sound like that of a jangling bridle. But before she could even look about her, a voice called out from much closer than she would have expected.

"Lady Fellis."

She swung around with a soft gasp, knowing that deep voice from any other. Hurriedly Fellis gained her feet. "Sir Stephen."

He was indeed closer than she would have thought. His nearness, coupled with her own hasty motion caused her to stumble.

Stephen reacted without thinking, reaching out to catch Fellis before she could fall. As he pulled the maiden safely into his arms, he knew again that same rush of desire and possession he felt every time he touched her.

He looked down at Fellis, unable to take his gaze from the clear blue depths of her own. God, but she was lovely, her hair caught in a thick braid that lay across the back of his arm in a silken caress. He longed to free the silvery mass and run his eager fingers through it, even as he wished to once again kiss those soft lips that parted on her own quickened breath.

But he knew he must control his response to Fellis. He had come to see that all was well with her. And that was what he would do.

He made himself address her formally. "My lady, are you all right?"

Fellis took a moment to reply, her gaze clouded with surprise and other emotions Stephen dared not name for his own sake. To allow himself to see that she responded to him as he did to her could lead only to ruin for them both.

He loosened his hold on her, willing himself to do what was right.

As if she too had no wish to prolong any contact between them, Fellis pulled away. "I am well, Sir Stephen. Pray why would I come to harm?"

Stephen watched her averted profile, feeling more frustrated and helpless than at any time in his life. He knew that her coldness was only an attempt to cover her hurt at what had happened at Glenmarket.

Jesu help him, Stephen could not find it in him to blame her. His own hurt was near driving him mad.

If only there was some way to make Fellis understand that what they had done was wrong, so wrong that it must not happen again. No matter how badly he wanted it.

But how, when it felt so incredibly right?

She halted his chaotic thoughts by saying, "You need have no fear for me. I would not risk myself. I know how important it is for me to carry through with my duties, and will not disappoint you."

Stephen was surprised at the resentment in her tone. He tried to suppress his growing agitation. "Is that really what you believe? That I would come to find you simply because I want to keep you safe for your marriage to the Welshman?"

She raised haughty brows. "That is exactly as I believe."

Again he sensed resentment and wondered at the depth of it. Surely she could not blame him for what was happening. They had discussed her marriage and she seemed to understand that he had no choice in this matter. He was nothing more than the messenger of her fate. King Edward had decided the outcome.

He fought the desire to reach out to her. "Fellis, I wish there was aught I could do to make this easier for you. But I know not what it would be."

He saw then that though she kept her head high and her face averted, her chin trembled. Seeing her pain was more difficult than he would have imagined.

And this time the knight could not hold back. He placed a gentle hand on her arm. "Fellis."

She turned to him then, but still she refused to shed the tears that glistened in her lovely eyes. Her voice was barely audible as she spoke. "Wynn's people will never accept me."

He put his hand on her other arm and turned her to face him. "You must not think that way. Once they know you they can only...love you," he said. "I can conceive of nothing else."

She refused to meet his gaze. "But that day in Glenmarket. Those people who attacked you. Why would they do such a thing? They know you not."

He realized then that he should have told her about having seen Owain at Wynn's home, but there had been no opportunity. He'd been so busy trying to avoid Fellis for fear of a recurrence of what had happened between them that day that he'd unintentionally left her to fear this alone.

Quickly he explained, "Fellis, that man was no stranger to me. He was with Wynn the day we met. Do you remember what I told you about there being some resistance amongst his allies?" When she nodded, he said, "Owain was the very one who spoke out against me. He has no understanding of Wynn's position and the responsibility he carries. The man is a rabble-rouser. If it had not been for him there would have been no trouble that day. You must trust Wynn to keep him under control. He will not let such as Owain mistreat you." Stephen could not say aloud the next words that formed in his mind. That he personally would kill Owain himself if he acted against Fellis. The attack that day had been against him, and Owain had quickly backed down from striking her.

Oblivious to his thoughts, she looked up at him. "Why did you not tell me this before?" She bit her lip as a deep blush stole over her creamy cheeks and her gaze dropped to the ground.

Understanding that she knew the answer to that question, Stephen made no reply. They could not give voice to the truth of their attraction for each other. 'Twas impossible.

She glanced up at him again, appearing to forget her embarrassment in her need to speak her thoughts. "But, Stephen, there was a woman there with him. She was young and beautiful, with dark hair and eyes. I'm sure you saw her. I had seen her earlier in the day in the market and she was staring at us. It seemed as if she hated us, me. Why would she hate me? I have done her no ill."

Stephen was not about to tell Fellis the girl who had looked at her with such hatred was Wynn's doxy. It would serve no good purpose to anyone. He was sure that no harm would came to Fellis through her. Wynn was a man of honor and would not let his woman do aught to harm Fellis or his chances of making peace through a marriage to her. That much Stephen wanted to believe—had to believe.

The knight could only speak from his own heart. "My lady, you are beautiful. Too beautiful to concern yourself with the thoughts of any other woman. Many will look at you in your lifetime and know envy."

Heavens above, Fellis thought. He'd said she was beautiful again. And the intense look in his eyes as he stared down into hers had given weight to the words.

She felt drawn into their dark depths, prodded for a response to his hungry gaze. And it came, all of its own accord. Her heart thudded with the deep beat of a war drum in her chest, leaving her sure he could hear it, too.

She'd told herself this would not happen again, that she would not allow herself to be drawn to him in this wild, provocative way.

She wanted to think clearly, to question him further. Fellis sensed that Stephen was holding something back when he spoke of the woman she had seen at Glenmarket.

But nothing else mattered when he looked at her that way.

He was so undeniably handsome with his dark hair and eyes, and when he leaned close to her this way she was unaware of anything but Stephen. It was impossible to think about right and wrong and what his intentions toward her were.

Fellis could only feel.

Her pulse raced in her veins as she felt herself falling, down, down into him, Stephen. The man who had come to awaken her from the years of near sleep.

She could see that he too felt what was happening, for his dark eyes became hooded and his gaze dropped to her lips.

She raised her face to his, unable to do anything else in this moment out of time.

Then he found her and nothing existed but the two of them and their responses to each other. His mouth was warm and firm and sure on hers. This time she did not just follow his lead but opened her own mouth, urging him with her tongue to do the same.

When his hand found the back of her head, the other arm sliding down to encircle her waist in a band of tender steel, she moaned. A strange warmth built in her chest and traveled down, down to the depths of her stomach, causing a sweet sort of ache to grow there. Fellis melted like beeswax in the sun, pressing more tightly to him.

Now it was Stephen who groaned, his hips arching to hers and she felt the hardness of him against her belly. Felt it, and understood for the first time where these kisses might lead them.

Though she had little real knowledge of what went on betwixt a man and a woman, her vague imaginings were greatly solidified at the steely weight of him against her. Surely he must care for her to react this way to her nearness.

When his lips left hers to press heated kisses to her cheeks and the flutter of her lids, she whispered, "Oh, Stephen, Stephen, you do want me. And what have you done to me? For I want you, too."

Stephen stilled, burying his face in the curve of her neck as he fought for breath and sanity. His heart pounded like a battle drum in his chest.

Indeed what had he done?

There was no excuse for his actions. He had known not to do this, had vowed time upon time not to touch her. Stephen felt as helpless in the face of his desire for her as he had been only a short week ago.

He did not release her but whispered desperately as he tried to make her understand that this was wrong. "Fellis, this should not have happened." He felt her stiffen and try to draw back but refused to loosen his hold on her even though he knew he courted further disaster by holding her perfect form so closely to his.

She raised her hands to his chest, pushing against him. "Take your hands from me, sir."

He released her and could only watch when she looked up at him with bitter betrayal. "Why do you play this game with me? Do you think I am some addled maid, too simple to be hurt by what you do. I tell you I am not. My twisted ankle has not affected my mind."

Even as Stephen listened to the pain in her tone, he knew he could not help her. To even admit how he felt about her was to invite further hurt to her. If she knew how strongly his feelings ran, she might think they could continue on this reckless course of passion.

And that they could not do. Stephen was more certain of that than anything in his life.

They were each bound to do their own duty, his to see her married, hers to marry. There was no way around it. King Edward had decreed this and he was not likely to risk the peace of his borders for the wayward desires of one maiden and her lover. Even if that man was a trusted messenger.

To go on this way, to kiss Fellis and hold her as he had only made him want her more. Nay he could not allow it to continue. Stephen knew that he would only end in destroying Fellis, along with himself.

Fellis's attraction to him would pass, even if she must feel sorrow at this moment.

With that thought in mind, he turned from her. "As you will." The words were his own, but he felt as though they came from somewhere outside himself.

He could feel her watching him, willing him to meet her tormented gaze. For her sake alone, he found the strength to resist.

The effort cost him dear and when she turned and ran from him, he raised his hands to his face. He could not help wishing there was some other way.

He knew there was not.

Chapter Ten

Stephen was still dressing when he was summoned to attend Lord Grayson the next morning. Hurriedly he finished and followed the serf who had been sent to fetch him.

As he was led down the stairs and to a small chamber off the hall, he could not help but wonder at being beckoned by the baron. The man had of late been more cordial than when Stephen first arrived, but he'd not gone so far as to deliberately seek him out.

Lord Richard was waiting there for him, his handsome face set as if carved from stone. When Stephen entered, he did not rise from where he sat behind a heavy oak table that held a number of books and writing instruments.

The baron's expression told Stephen all he needed to know. There had been news from Wynn. And if he did not miss his mark, the outcome was not one that Lord Richard favored.

That could only mean that he had agreed to the treaty.

The realization came like an unexpected blow, and for a moment Stephen reeled. Fellis would most likely end in marrying the man. He tried to regain his composure, forcing himself to think coherently. This was what he had come here to accomplish.

Seemingly unaware of the younger man's distress, Richard Grayson wasted no time on niceties, gesturing to the parchment he held in his other hand. "A messenger arrived just a short while ago, and departed before I could speak with him. But it is all clearly laid out here. If I will sign the accompanying agreement of truce, the Welshman will meet her."

Concentrating on the fact that this was what must be, Stephen still found it hard to answer past the unwelcome lump of pain in his throat. "I see," he said at last. Unable to look the other man in the eyes, he added, "You will, of course, sign it."

When there was no immediate reply, Stephen looked up to study the other man. Surely Richard was not wavering in his resolve to do what he had agreed to.

But the knight could see that he was indeed torn.

Deep inside, Stephen could find no blame for the other man. Indeed he felt an unexpected sense of bonding with him.

Yet he would not allow himself to show his true feelings.

Calling on all his will to see him through this, no matter how difficult, Stephen sat down in the chair across the table from the Lord of Malvern. Carefully he began, "My lord, you must realize that there is little choice in this matter. We discussed this upon my first coming here. It was my understanding that you would go forward with this matter if Wynn was willing to agree to your terms."

Lord Richard continued to stare at him in silence.

Stephen indicated the roll of parchment, holding out his hand. "May I?"

With obvious reluctance, Richard placed the missive in his outstretched palm.

Quickly Stephen scanned the document. It was all there, laid out neatly in some cleric's hand. Wynn would agree to stop all acts of aggression against his enemy so that talks might go forward in the matter of a possible marriage between himself and the Lady Fellis of Malvern. Wynn also stated that he would personally see to the punishment of any of his folk who might break this agreement.

Relegating his personal feelings to the deepest part of his heart, Stephen set the missive on the desk and met the other man's gaze directly. "He has been most reasonable, even offering to punish any of his people who might disagree. It is all anyone can ask of him."

Richard looked away, his jaw tight. "'Twould seem so."

"Lord Richard, to have peace on your lands is of great import to you and yours, is it not? This is your opportunity to have that very thing which you most desire. Think on it. No more raiding, no more burning, nor terrorizing of your women and children. The possibility of a real peace is within sight. I understand that you do not trust this man, nor have you had reason. But he feels the same of you, and yet he has agreed to make a fresh start, to try to put the past behind you. This may not be the end of all the troubles between your two peoples, but it is a way to begin."

The older man looked from Stephen to the document with obvious indecision. Then he groaned, his expression becoming one of defeat. Taking a deep breath, he quickly reached forward and took up the roll. As if he feared giving himself any more time to think on what he was doing, Richard picked up a stick of wax. Holding it to the candle, he then set it to the bottom of the page and pressed his ring against the hot paste, setting his seal.

With that he stood, carelessly tossing the parchment to Stephen. Only then did he speak, studying the younger man with a dejected look in his blue eyes. "Understand that I bear you no malice, Sir Stephen. In the past days, after having come to know you somewhat, it is clear to me that you wish only to do your duty to the crown. But you must see that this situation is near untenable from my position. I feel as if I am finally coming to understand what I need do to be a father to Fellis. Now she will surely soon be lost to me. When you arrived at Malvern I made known to you that you must see this through by your own efforts. That holds true now more than ever. I will have no more to do with this other than to negotiate the exact terms of the marriage contract, should that take place. It is the least I can do to make sure my daughter is provided for.'' He paused, then went on. I only hope Fellis can forgive me for parlaying her future as the price of this peace, for never will I forgive myself.''

Richard wiped a hand over his face. ''The one thing I do feel obligated to do is inform Fellis of this news myself. That much you will be spared, Sir Stephen.'' He paused again, looking at the younger man intently. ''Somehow I do not believe doing so would be easy for you.''

There was no answer Stephen could give to the cryptic remark as he watched the other man depart. What had Stephen said or done to give away his true feelings?

Then he shook his head. Lord Richard had no notion of how difficult the situation had become for the knight.

And now he must take her to another man. But his pain was not only for himself, but for Fellis, as well.

His heart ached with the knowledge that he too had participated in the sacrifice of Fellis's future.

Fellis was being fitted for yet another new cotehardie and underdress when there was a scratching at the chamber door. Her mother, who was fitting the tight sleeve of the undertunic, called, ''Come.''

Fellis looked toward the door of the solar as it opened and was surprised to see her father standing there. Mary Grayson stood as her husband came into the room. "Richard," she greeted him cooly.

His tone was carefully polite. "Mary. Fellis."

Fellis knew there had been even more strain between them than usual. Not only because of his decision to treat with Wynn ap Dafydd, but also because he had thwarted her mother's wishes in buying cloth for Fellis's new clothing.

Her mother had told her repeatedly how displeased she was at being forced to fashion gowns for a wedding that would not take place. But she had not gone so far as to refuse to make the garments. It was as if she understood her husband would not be swayed in this.

As Fellis watched, his troubled gaze went from her to her mother. Instinctively she knew something was amiss.

Her mother seemed to sense the same thing, for she frowned. "What is it?" Her tone was sharp.

He drew himself up, his back rigid as he focused on his daughter. "Fellis, I have come to tell you something important. We have had news from Wynn ap Dafydd. He wishes to meet with you."

Mary gasped. "He will come here to Malvern?"

Her husband answered without meeting her angry gaze. "He will not. Wynn has asked that you meet him at an appointed place in the wood between here and his own lands. It is his desire that the meeting be an informal one on neutral ground. I see no problem in this. If you agree, Sir Stephen will escort you."

Fellis could barely think past the pounding of her heart. The moment had actually come. Wynn wished to see her.

The numbness that had kept any real anxiety at bay was finally broken. Her stomach churned with nervousness at the idea of meeting him.

What would he think of her, this Welsh lord? She knew from asking Stephen that the man was aware of her deformity. And Stephen had assured her that he would not care in the least. But even putting that aside, she wondered how he would react to her—Fellis.

Her mother's voice drew her attention away from her own fears. "You do not mean for this to happen?"

Richard Grayson's jaw flexed with suppressed emotions that Fellis could not even begin to name. He looked at his wife and Fellis saw the sorrow and regret in his eyes. "Mary, you must see that you do Fellis no service to carry on so. Can you not behave as a wife and mother ought in this matter if no other?"

Fellis spoke then, feeling proud that her voice did not quake with the fear and confusion inside her. "Father, I will meet with Wynn ap Dafydd. We all knew this time would come and I am prepared to do what I must."

"The meeting will take place on the morrow," he then informed them without even a hint of emotion in his voice.

Fellis nearly gasped aloud. So soon. But she made no comment, only nodding her acquiescence.

Mary Grayson stood as if carved from stone. Her back was so straight that she seemed near as tall as her much larger husband in that moment. She swung away from him, unable to bend in her attitude and beliefs.

Her husband could only shake his head as he turned to his daughter, his expression filled with regret. "I tell you now, Fellis, that I love you and wish that I had done better by you. You have put us all to shame with your courage in this situation."

With that he strode from the room, his hands clenched at his sides. It was as if the pain of facing them was too much for him.

Fellis turned to her mother, who had not said another word. She was surprised to find the older woman wiping at her eyes. As if feeling her daughter's attention on her, she swung around, hiding her feelings behind an emotionless expression and a stiffly held head.

Mary Grayson's gaze did not meet Fellis's as she spoke. "There is much to attend to. You will have need to wear something that will not give offense, as your father and Sir Stephen have termed it."

She began to fidget with the pile of cloth on the seat beside the window. "You must go to fetch Claire. We will have need of her steady hands to finish this sewing."

"Yes, Mother," Fellis replied softly. She left but not without a backward glance. It seemed that Lady Mary was not as indifferent to her husband as she had always appeared.

As she hurried down the corridor, Fellis could not help knowing that the changes in her life and those of her family had coincided with the arrival of one Sir Stephen Clayburn.

But as she realized this, Fellis could not help wondering if he had done more harm than good. For though their feelings had certainly come to light, it had brought much pain for all of them.

Now that the marriage was coming closer to being a reality, he would be going back to court and his own life, leaving them alone to face the knowledge of their misery.

For how could they know anything else? Her father could not make his wife see that he loved her. Her mother could not get past feeling that Fellis had been punished for the vow she broke as a young girl.

As for Fellis, she would marry a man she had always known as an enemy, yet found herself drawn to another as she had never thought possible.

* * *

When Fellis came down to the hall at the appointed hour the next morning, Stephen was waiting for her at the foot of the stone stairway.

He had to see her, to try to discern for himself how she was taking this turn of events. Since the day when Stephen had ridden out to find Fellis and again could not resist his attraction toward her, he had seen the maid only from a distance.

Stephen had never expected the sight that met his eyes.

The peach cotehardie she wore was slashed at the sides as fashion dictated, but much more modestly than the ladies at court would have worn. On her the less revealing cut was perfect, showing delectable glimpses of that perfectly formed figure in a close-fitting tunic of spring green. Over her glorious hair she wore a sheer veil of the same green, and the silvery fall had been braided through with peach and green ribbons then pulled over one slender shoulder. The delicate pastels were a lovely foil for her equally delicate beauty.

Stephen could not speak for fear of giving himself away. As he was unable to comment, the knight simply reached out to take her hand and place it over his sleeve.

Her searching gaze dropped at his silence. "Am I not fitting?"

He could not allow her to think so, and he whispered in a voice that was hoarse from the tight control he placed on himself. "Fellis, the sight of you takes my breath and leaves me struck dumb. Never have I beheld such a vision."

She raised her face, her eyes shining up at him. "Thank you, Sir Knight."

Lord, even now she had no idea of how beautiful she was, nor of the power she held over him. He knew he could never let her see. For her sake he need keep his desire a secret.

Stephen could only press her slim fingers more tightly against his side as he accompanied her forward.

As he led her into the hall, Richard Grayson was coming toward them. He too stopped and stared, as Stephen had, at the sight of her. He held out his arms, his eyes damp with pride and love. "Is this beautiful woman my daughter, my Fellis?"

Stephen felt his own throat constrict as he watched her go into those outstretched arms. He turned away as they held each other. This moment belonged to Fellis and her father. He went out into the courtyard where their horses awaited them.

Only a short time later Fellis and Lord Richard joined him. The Baron of Malvern helped his daughter to mount with careful attentiveness. He reached up and squeezed the hand she held out to him. "Go with God," he said softly.

She smiled at him and Stephen could see how her father's care had moved her, for her tear-filled eyes were bright. "Do not worry, Father. All will be well."

Stephen felt himself moved by her strength.

Lord Richard turned to Stephen. "Have a care for her."

"I will," Stephen replied, trying to keep his own rattled emotions from showing in his voice.

Suddenly there was nothing more to say and he looked at Fellis, his gaze questioning. "Are you ready?"

She took a deep breath and nodded for him to take the lead. She fell in behind him as they went across the courtyard, then exited the keep.

Fellis was silent as they rode along and Stephen did not attempt to break that silence. There was nothing he could say, for he might give away his own feelings. He could not help but be moved by Fellis's care for her father, especially after that man, however unmaliciously, had left her to the devices of a woman who could not face her own demons and thus put them upon her daughter.

Despite all the difficulties, Fellis had become the kind, loving woman she was meant to be.

He only hoped she would come to find some joy in this marriage, that much did she deserve without doubt.

This notion only caused more of an ache in his chest, so Stephen forced his attention back to locating the meeting place.

For her part Fellis did not even look up from her horse's neck, her hands tight on the reins.

Thinking to ease her nervousness, Stephen said gently, "Do not worry. All will be well."

She looked up at him as she rode alongside his chestnut stallion. Her eyes were dark pools of uneasiness. She swallowed hard before answering. "Dost you really believe that, Sir Stephen?"

He found it hard to form a reply. Did he really believe what he had told her? He gave himself a mental shake. It had to be. He would make it so himself.

He reached across the space that separated them and touched her sleeve, remembering all too well that he dared not clasp her hand. With great clarity he recalled what had happened the last time they actually touched—every time they touched. He smiled encouragingly, though his heart went out to her. "Aye. Do not worry. I will take care of everything."

Even as he said the words, Stephen knew that he had taken on more than any man should, but Fellis's happiness was more important than anything.

Fellis could not think of a reply. How could he take care of everything? 'Twas not in his hands alone. Then she reminded herself that Stephen's optimism had proved true thus far in the matter of Wynn ap Dafydd and what he would do. Mayhap he was right.

Nonetheless she could not prevent herself from peering around with trepidation as they left. Fellis felt a slight nervous tremor in her hands as they held Ebony's reins.

From his position slightly ahead of her on the forest trail, Stephen seemed to ride on unconcerned. She could not help admiring his nonchalance, especially after what had happened that day in Glenmarket. The incident had made her unhappily aware of the dislike of the man named Owain and many of his countrymen.

And women, she thought, remembering again the hatred in one particular woman's eyes. Not for the first time she wondered if Stephen had been holding something back when she'd asked him about that woman.

In her efforts to avoid the knight she had effectively prevented herself from having any opportunity to question him on the subject again.

Before long they came to a small clearing at the heart of the wood. It was bare of any other occupants, but Fellis knew they had arrived at their destination when Stephen drew his stallion to a halt.

She watched the knight as he looked around them with a thoughtful frown. "I believe this is the spot where he is to meet us. Your father was very clear in his instruction on how to find it." He indicated the downed tree at the northern edge of the clearing. "That is one of the landmarks he mentioned."

Stephen knew Wynn had written that he would be at the appointed place before them. Just then, Wynn stepped out of the forest across from where Fellis and Stephen had emerged.

The reason for his tardiness became apparent when he nodded toward Stephen and said, "Ahh, you come alone as I asked. Good."

Stephen watched then as the Welshman's curious gaze went to Fellis. He did not find fault with the woman sitting atop the black mare, if the appreciation in his hazel eyes was any indication.

Unexpectedly Stephen knew a gripping pang of anger in his guts. He felt as though Wynn were somehow trespassing. Immediately Stephen realized he could not allow himself to react this way and tried to dispel the feeling. Fellis did not belong to him.

It was Wynn who was to become her husband. But the sensation would not leave him and Stephen could not meet Wynn's gaze when it shifted back to him.

The Welshman turned to look at Fellis then came toward them. As he did so, Stephen hurriedly dismounted and assisted Fellis to the ground. Even though the other man had meant to do so, Stephen could not stop himself.

Wynn came to a halt just behind them. When Stephen turned to face him, still not moving from the maiden's side, the Welshman frowned but said nothing.

The expression remained as Stephen introduced them. "Lady Fellis Grayson, may I present Wynn ap Dafydd? And to you, sir, Lady Fellis."

Realizing that he would only make things more difficult for Fellis if he gave himself away, Stephen took a step back from her.

Only then did that frown fade somewhat, and Stephen's skills as a negotiator came to the fore. "I thank you for coming here this day."

Wynn nodded, looking at the taller man with a shrug. "I felt it was the best thing to do. For my people."

"Of course," Stephen replied. "But that does not negate the wisdom of your decision."

Wynn spoke then, his gaze direct on Stephen's. "There is something I have need to say to you, and Lady Fellis." He bowed to her before turning back to the knight. "I have heard of the events that took place in Glenmarket. Let me say that I am most aggrieved that you were attacked by one of my own people. Owain does not understand the importance of accepting what must be. He is cousin to my dead father and thinks to preserve the way of life he is accustomed to by living in the past. He has been disciplined for his actions.

"It was this incident that finally helped me decide to send the pact of truce to Lord Grayson. In truth some of my allies who opposed the idea came to see there was some merit in it. Glenmarket has been an island of peace for us heretofore. To have broken that peace was a mistake. Owain has no personal grudge against you, Sir Stephen. He simply resents you because of the message you brought to us. To attack you, a king's messenger, for no other reason, was untenable."

"There was no real harm done to me," Stephen answered, "but I am thankful that others could see the recklessness of his action."

Surely, Stephen told himself, it would help to ease Fellis's fear to know that many of Wynn's folk had condemned Owain's unaggravated act of aggression. He looked to find her watching the Welshman with a thoughtful expression.

For some reason this did not please Stephen as much as it should have. Even as his stomach twisted inside him, Stephen told himself this was what he wanted for her. She should come to see Wynn as something other than an enemy, and eventually care for him if she was to know any happiness in the future.

But the sensation of jealousy did not leave him. Knowing he must not allow them to see his true feelings, the knight said, "Excuse me for a moment. If you will attend Lady Fellis, Wynn, I will see to the horses." Before either could even answer, he took up the reins of both animals and led them away.

It took every ounce of Stephen's will to do that, to go to the other side of the clearing and turn his back on the two of them. He clenched his hands tightly on the reins he held as he fought to keep from turning around to look at them.

Fellis watched Stephen walk away with an unconscious expression of bewilderment. She felt an unexpected sensation of abandonment.

But this was why Stephen had brought her here. To meet Wynn, the man who might end in being her husband.

She turned her attention to Wynn ap Dafydd, studying him even as he did her. Fellis felt no sense of discomfort as he did so. His expression was one of curiosity, as she knew hers must be. For the first time she realized he might be as curious about her as she was about him. Did they wed, he too, would be marrying a virtual stranger.

She'd listened with great interest while he spoke of his regret at what had happened at Glenmarket. It seemed that Wynn was not as narrow in his attitudes toward the English as she'd feared he might be. He appeared to be as conscientious in trying to do what was best for his people as she was.

Knowing this made her feel as though she had something in common with him. It was so very little on which to hope for any kind of relationship.

Fellis looked down at her hands, feeling decidedly awkward. What did one say to the man one might marry? Even as the thought passed through her mind, she glanced toward Stephen's broad back, then wondered why she had done so.

At that moment Wynn laughed, drawing her attention back to him. "I am most happy to meet you, Lady Grayson," he said slowly.

She answered him honestly in her agitation. "And I you, sir. Though I must admit to having been somewhat apprehensive."

He nodded. "I appreciate your candor, my lady. I must ask your permission to be the same."

She gave him a pensive glance. "Of course you may do so."

He looked away from her, then back with a shrug. "I wish for you to know that though we have long been enemies, I will not hold that against you. For the purpose of these talks I would that you might forget that I have been yours. 'Tis the only hope we have of coming to know something of each other."

Fellis once again found her gaze straying to Stephen, who seemed to be ignoring them. For some unknown reason this perturbed her. She answered Wynn without meeting his gaze. "I am willing to try and do as you ask. It seems...strange that we should live so close and never meet. And now we have come together for the purpose of..." She flushed, unable to say the words.

Wynn spoke directly. "Though it may be difficult to do so, I think it best if we are honest with each other about our opinions on why we are here. Truly, what think you of the English king's decree?"

Fellis did not know how to reply. She looked up at him shyly.

"Come now," he asked, "have you nothing to say?" Obviously Wynn was not as reticent as Fellis, and for that she supposed she should be grateful. 'Twould only be all the more difficult if he was as reserved as she.

Still he waited for a reply and hesitantly she answered sincerely. "I think, my lord, that in the end we may have to do as King Edward desires. There seems little chance of finding a way out."

Wynn's body tightened with unconcealed arrogance and pride, reminding her of a wild cat she had once seen in the forest. The sighting had been brief but had left a lasting impression of untamed power in her mind.

Gazing up at him, she found herself thinking he was quite a handsome man with his dark curls, hazel eyes and athletic build. He was not nearly so tall as Stephen, but she had to tilt her head back to look into his face and he moved with a confident, manly grace.

When the Welshman answered, his words further assured her of his confidence in himself. "That may be as you believe, my lady. But I do not feel constrained to do what your king wishes, if it does not please me to do so. He cannot force me to have a bride I do not want. I choose what I will and will not take to myself."

"I...oh, of course," she answered, stung by his heat. She drew herself up to her full height. "I understand. If I am displeasing to you..."

"Nay," he interrupted impatiently, leaving her with no doubt of his sincerity. "'Tis naught to do with you. You are most pleasing to look upon. If one must have a woman of another's choosing you will be no trouble to accept. I but mean that I must see the good of this for my own clansmen before I am willing to agree. Their well-being must always come before even my own. And your king's. If 'twas not to the benefit of those I must have a care for, I would not have you were you the object of my devotion."

With a stiff nod, Fellis fixed her gaze on the open collar of his brown tunic. "I see."

His vehemence made her nervous. After all he was a stranger.

Seeming to sense her withdrawal, Wynn reached out and placed his hard hand over her clasped ones. "I am sorry. I did not mean to offend you. I but wish for you to understand that I make decisions that will affect many. If in the end I cannot comply with the order I do not wish for you to feel that it is aught to do with you."

As she felt his hand cover hers, Fellis knew a sense of comfort. But there was none of the fire that raced through her blood every time Stephen so much as touched her.

This gave her pause for thought. Obviously she was not the wanton she had told herself she was. There must be something about Stephen that caused her to react so, something that set him apart from other men and brought such passion rising to the surface when he was by.

At that moment, the hair prickled on the back of her neck and she felt compelled to look around. As Fellis did so, she found Stephen's dark gaze upon her and Wynn. His eyes seemed fixed on the Welshman's hand covering hers.

As if aware of her attention, Stephen looked up and their eyes met. She was scorched by the possession and heat in his gaze. Her field of vision narrowed until everything faded around them. Wynn might as well have been a shadow for all that she was aware of him and his hand on hers.

Fellis's chest tightened until she felt she couldn't breathe, and from her deepest depths, she yearned for Stephen. Her heart hammered inside her. Why could it not be the English knight who stood here beside her, who held the right to take her hand in his?

Just as she felt as if her heart must surely burst, a noise intruded on her consciousness. Fellis looked about, confusion making her slow to understand where the sound was coming from.

At that moment a slender woman with a fall of tousled dark hair burst from the forest to her right. A surprised Fellis realized that she had seen this woman twice before at Glenmarket.

What really shocked her was the expression on the dark beauty's face. Fellis had thought she'd seen hatred there before, but it was as nothing compared to the naked rage and loathing that burned in the brown eyes now.

Wynn reacted as though stung. He released Fellis's hand as if it were suddenly offensive and stepped back several paces.

Fellis watched, bewildered, while Wynn looked to the new arrival with complete surprise and something akin to guilt on his face. He opened his mouth, closed it, then cleared his throat and tried again. "Ardeth."

"Wynn," she answered, now centering all her attention on the Welshman. It was as if neither of them could spare a thought for the other two. Their complete concentration was focused on each other.

She spoke, her eyes growing damp. "Did you think I would not discover that you were coming here this day?"

He cleared his throat again, looking as miserable as any man could. "Nay, Ardeth, I did not."

The dark girl made an obvious effort to rally her dignity and failed, sounding more hurt than anything else. "My father does not approve of this meeting."

Wynn looked as though he'd been slapped. "Owain has no say in this. 'Tis my choosing as leader of my people."

Fellis near gasped aloud. So she was Owain's daughter. No wonder Owain was angry if he felt she might displace his daughter.

As if remembering they were not alone, the Welshman glanced toward Fellis, then Stephen and back to Ardeth. He drew himself up, taking a deep breath. "I did not give it any thought," he said more firmly. "You know I have my duty to see to and nothing will change that. Personal considerations have no place in these proceedings."

Fellis felt her heart sink.

This also explained Stephen's reticence in talking about the woman. He had known all along, and should have told her.

What was she to do? How could she face knowing she had taken Wynn from the woman who loved him? How could she allow herself to be the instrument of another's pain?

But as she looked at Wynn and saw his set jaw, Fellis recalled the way he had answered the woman just now. How much could she mean to him if he meant to set her aside to marry Fellis, even to do so in the interest of his people? How deeply could he care for her to treat her so?

Her mind was a morass of confusion.

Into that confusion came the calming comfort of Stephen's voice. "Fellis."

Fellis turned to him as he took her elbow in a steady but infinitely gentle grip, turned to him as a lily does to the sun. "We had best go and allow Wynn to deal with this problem in private."

He sent the other man a warning glance that not even Fellis in her unhappiness could fail to see. "I'm sure he will be able to take care of this matter so it will not interfere in his duty."

Wynn gazed back at him tight-lipped, then nodded. "I will do so."

When Ardeth opened her mouth as if to protest, the Welshman glared at her in warning. She subsided, though she took a step closer to him.

Fellis could only feel sympathy for the other woman as Stephen led her to her horse. It was impossible for her not to return the other's feelings even in part. For she could not help thinking that she might feel the same were their circumstances reversed.

Her unhappy gaze went to Stephen's face as he tenderly helped her to mount. She could see the suppressed anger in him. It was evidenced by the tight set of his jaw and the deliberately controlled way he moved. She could not help wondering how she would feel if someone else were to marry the man she loved.

The thought brought a lump to her throat and she had to look away, training her thoughts on finding her seat and leaving the clearing.

Stephen did not speak. He seemed bent on getting them both away as quickly as possible.

She allowed her gaze to move over that broad back, those arms, so strong yet tender. Never again would she know the taste of his lips, the touch of his hands.

Her horse came to a full stop on the trail and Fellis made no move to urge her forward once more.

She was only aware that Stephen had come back for her when he took the reins from her icy fingers.

Still without speaking, the knight dismounted and tied his horse and hers to a limb. Then he moved to her and reached up his arms in silent appeal.

Fellis went into them without hesitation, accepting the comfort of his embrace, uncaring in this moment as to the right of it. She only knew that she was cold and hurting and Stephen could warm her from the inside, that he would ease the ache as only he could.

When he drew back a bit to lead her to a fallen tree, she followed him without hesitation. At his silent urging, she sat on its moss-covered length.

Stephen came down beside her, taking her in his arms. Only then did he speak. "Fellis, I am sorry for what happened."

She buried her face in his shoulder, wishing she could get inside him somehow and hide from the pain of who she was. If she'd not been born with the accursed foot, if her mother had not seen it as a mark of God's displeasure, things might have been different for her. She would have been able to lead a more normal existence, to possibly meet a young man of noble birth, a young man who might have wanted her for herself. As it was, she had made no alliance and thus was available to act as pawn in King Edward's plans.

She sobbed aloud, uncaring that she bared her soul by her words. "Would that I were someone other than who I am. God rot that I was born with this foot, this deformity that has kept me prisoner in my own life."

Stephen held her away, willing her to look at him. "Fellis, do not speak so. There is naught wrong with you. You are perfect, beautiful beyond measure. Do not berate God for what he has made you."

His gaze was dark with frustration as he moved away from her to kneel at her feet. "Let me show you in the only way I can that there is no part of you that is not pleasing."

Before she knew what he was about, Stephen was lifting her cote and underdress. Then he raised her foot, the one she so hated, and slowly, his gaze never leaving hers, he removed her shoe. Only as he reached up to draw off her hose did Fellis realize what he was about to do.

Horrified, she tried to pull away. "Nay, please do not."

Stephen held her there in a determined grip. "I must make you see the truth and this is the only way it can be done."

She held her breath as he carefully but inexorably removed the stocking. As the fabric slid down her calf, Fellis had to close her eyes to block out the sight of the revulsion she would surely see in his face once her deformity was revealed.

Thus it came as an even greater shock to her when he raised that twisted ankle and pressed his lips to the pale, tender flesh. Her lids flew open of their own accord when a shaft of sweet pleasure so intense that it made her cry found its way from the spot where his lips touched to that most secret place betwixt her thighs. "Stephen."

He was watching her, his gaze dark fire as his mouth moved over her skin, caressing and tasting, and yes, adoring that so long unwanted part of her. And that flesh, which had lain withered and dormant, came to blazing life under his reverent ministrations. For with each touch the sweetness built until Fellis could feel a strange dampness grow in her.

Uncaring where this might lead, Fellis held out her arms. "Stephen."

He groaned, taking her in his arms and pressing sensuous lips to her own. She opened to him completely, offering him all the passion in her. And he responded in kind, his arm tightening around her back as his other hand moved to slide beneath the opening at the side of her cote. His warm hand found and cupped her breast and she felt it swell in his grasp. Gently he kneaded the aching flesh and her nipple hardened against his palm.

Fellis's mouth left his and she whispered, "Oh, please, Stephen, please. I know not what to do. This ache is driving me near mad."

He looked into her eyes, his dark with desire and tenderness. He took his hand from her breast and slid it down her side leaving a trail of fire in its wake.

Her cote and underdress were tangled around her knees, but Stephen found his way beneath them, stroking his hand over her knee, then her thighs as her legs parted. She moaned deep in her throat not knowing how it could possibly go on but feeling the pleasure build to an even tighter knot of tension inside her.

When he found and pressed his palm to the mound of her womanhood, she thought she would surely faint from the sweetness. But there was more, and as his fingers moved to caress that dark dampness, Fellis moved against him.

She was past thinking of anything beyond the rapture, the all-consuming ecstasy that rose up to wash over her in a tremendous flood of joy. Shuddering her bliss, she heard Stephen whisper "Fellis" against her hair.

Her eyes remained closed and she lay against him, basking in the warmth of a hundred suns. Every bone in her body felt as if it were made from the most pliant leather. Never had she imagined that such glory as she had just experienced existed in all the world.

Stephen had brought her to that glory.

A great well of emotion rose up inside her and Fellis turned within the circle of his arms. She wanted to kiss him, to tell him how much he and this moment meant to her.

But when her eyes met his a look of sadness stopped her. For a moment she was confused, not understanding what could be wrong, why he would be sad when the most glorious experience in her life had just occurred.

And then she knew. Stephen did not care for her. He had withdrawn as he had every time they'd shared an intimate moment. He had simply reacted to her own crazed response. And now that the heat had passed he was looking at her as if he were sorry it had happened.

What he'd just done to her, those things he'd made her feel meant nothing to Stephen.

Her face burned with a shame that went deep to the very core of her. It found its way to the lonely child she had been, with no one but her mother to care for and guide her.

Her mother had told her to do right, to be careful of the sin of passion because it could seduce one with the sheer pleasure of it. And she had refused to listen.

She was more sorry than she would ever be able to say that she had not listened to that advice. For only she knew how low her stubbornness had brought her.

Tearing herself from his arms, Fellis started off, then stumbled, realizing the fragile flesh of her twisted foot was bare.

"Fellis," Stephen said in an anguished tone. "You do not understand." He reached toward her.

She refused to look at him, trying with all her might to summon up some show of pride. Trying and failing, she whispered. "Do not touch me."

With a sob, she grabbed for her hose and dragged it on, then blinded by tears, forced her foot into the leather shoe. She hurried to her mare and gained the saddle without really knowing how she did so. Not bothering to see whether Stephen followed her or not, she rode for home, paying no heed to the branches that tore the delicate veil from her head and ripped at the clothing Stephen had told her she looked so lovely in only a few short hours ago.

Chapter Eleven

Stephen did not slow his stallion's thundering pace as they raced over the downhill slope of the hill they had just climbed. The sky was low and gray over the tops of the trees, and rain, which had begun to fall that very morning, poured down as if being wrung from the dark clouds over his head. The wind whipped about him wildly, tearing at his hair and clothing. But he paid it no heed, nor the rivulets of water that ran down his forehead and into his eyes.

Nothing could get through the sorrow and pain of his own self-torment. How could he have so forgotten himself that day after the meeting with Wynn?

Fellis. Her name was like a chant in his mind.

Since the day of the meeting with Wynn, Stephen had avoided her completely. The day he had stolen her innocence and very nearly her virginity. His shame over what he had done left him unable to face her.

Yet worse than coming close to taking what belonged to another man, he had also hurt Fellis by his action.

He knew that she was very susceptible to any personable man who might pay court to her. That all the years of solitude and her mother's plans for her to become a nun had made Fellis more naive than her years.

Which made what he had done even more inexcusable.

A young girl like Fellis was vulnerable to the man who could awaken her passion, show her what desire could truly be. As an experienced man, he knew this, understood the consequences. That was why in the past he had been careful to keep his own dalliances on an honest footing with women who would know what was happening.

He did not delude himself into thinking he was in any way special to Fellis. He had simply happened to meet her at a time when she was being thrown into a confused state by the drastic changes in her life.

He refused to acknowledge the regret at knowing the attraction she felt toward him was only an illusion.

Stephen prodded his mount onward through the downpour. Still he could not halt his self-recrimination. His actions toward Fellis had surely led her to believe he cared something for her.

God help him, it was true. Though even He could not name what form that caring might take.

He only hoped the Welshman was able to deal with the complication of Ardeth, as he had said he would—as he must.

Even if Stephen was of a mind to come forward and commit himself to Fellis, he could not. The negotiations with the Welshman had gone too far. Wynn was likely trying to convince his folk to accept the English maid as his future bride and their lady at this very moment.

And yet, in spite of all the things that made him know that Fellis was better off without him to complicate her life, Stephen could not get the image of her large blue eyes, dark with sadness and disillusion, from his mind.

Heaven help him but he hadn't meant to hurt her that day after they'd left Wynn to settle things with his woman. He'd simply been driven over the edge of his resistance. It had not started that way, when he'd first touched her, bared her foot and kissed it, he'd wanted only to show her in the best way he knew how that she was lovely. It pained him so much to have her think she was any less that perfect. But once he'd uncovered even that small part of her, placed his mouth to the fragile flesh, he'd been lost. The images of her beautiful form had ridden hard in his mind, driving him to forget all but how much he'd dreamed of holding her, tracing those perfect curves with his own hands. Her responses to him had only urged him on until he could not have denied her need, did it mean his life. Only the realization that he would wreak irreparable damage to her had kept Stephen from satisfying the flood of desire inside himself.

Stephen knew he would be further tested, that he must continue to keep that demon at bay, for his duty would force him to be near her again. He was the one who must take her to Wynn when the time came, even though seeing them together that first time had near ripped him apart.

From the moment Wynn had touched her hand, Stephen was forced to battle his own feelings of possession. Knowing that Wynn was to be Fellis's husband did nothing to quiet the resentment inside him.

He let out a growl of rage and self-hatred, leaning low over Gabriel's back. Not even here, battling the brutality of the elements could he forget what had happened, how he had hurt her.

Still he rode on.

Hours later, soaked and exhausted, Stephen returned to the keep. He did not go to the hall to sup with the other occupants of Malvern. In truth he felt even a morsel would sicken him.

Taking the back stairs to the upper level of the keep, Stephen hoped to meet no one. His wish was not answered.

In the corridor stood Lady Mary. She looked on the tall knight, her gaze taking in his soaked condition, the slump of his wide shoulders and the bleakness in his face. Stephen felt himself stiffen as he met her gaze. To his surprise, she did not seem displeased by his wretched condition, only thoughtful.

She said nothing as they stood there in the torch-lit corridor, each clearly awkward with the other.

At that moment, the door at the end of the hallway opened. Fellis's door.

Without conscious thought, Stephen found himself straining for a glimpse of her.

Lady Mary was forgotten.

His heart thudded as Fellis appeared in the opening. She seemed to hesitate when she saw who was in the passage.

Stephen could not prevent the longing that rose up inside him at seeing her there. His eager gaze took in her pale face surrounded by a curtain of hair the color of moonbeams. Fellis wore a gown of buttery yellow that made her creamy skin take on a luminous sheen. She was a candle in a dark night, beckoning him with her flickering warmth. Her gaze collided with his and his stomach contracted at the pain he saw there. He took a step toward her, completely unaware that he did so.

She reached out a trembling hand.

Stephen drew himself up. God help him, what was he doing? He could not let her see how he felt, how much he cared.

Shutting his eyes, he turned from her.

He sensed the closing of her door, for he felt the light of her presence leave the long, narrow hallway.

A voice intruded on his misery. "You will not take my daughter's virginity."

He swung around to face the woman and found her regarding him with dread. Not meeting her eyes, Stephen shook his head, hating himself for what he had already done. "Nay, I will not."

She asked, "I beg you not to hurt her."

His tormented gaze came to rest on Lady Mary's. "I would not do so for the world."

She continued to watch him with uncertainty, but something in his expression seemed to mollify her slightly. "You would do well to keep your word, Sir Knight. I know what path the sin of lust will take you on."

He frowned, puzzled by this statement. "If by lust you mean desire, there is no sin in that. There is only sin in taking what is not freely offered. Of taking from one who has not the ability to understand what they give. Fellis could not understand what she would give. That is why it would be wrong for me to take her. That and the fact that she is to marry another. Were we free to love, I would share my passion with her without guilt or sin. As any lover should."

Lady Mary looked up at him, her brow lined with tension. "But that is not right. Passion is a sin of the flesh, to be spurned and detested."

Stephen shook his head. "I know not whence these notions came to you, my lady, but I must tell you that I cannot believe this is true. God gave the gift of desire to a man and woman. It is to be shared with joy. How can any caring parent question the method of their offspring's very existence? To do so is to doubt God's wisdom in what is best for us."

She folded her hands tightly over her stomach. "But what if that child is not born whole? Then are we not to see that there was sin in its conception?"

Anger made his jaw flex as he formed a reply. "My lady. If you mean Fellis, I must stop you here. Would that I could make you see her as I do. Her infirmity is no sign of reprisal from God. 'Tis a challenge—" he shrugged "—that much is true, but when one thinks on all her other gifts, her beauty, her kind nature, her incredible strength, it seems as nothing. Do we not all have some imperfections? Fellis's small flaw pales beside all of my own. And those of most others.''

Lady Mary said nothing, only stared at him with obvious doubt, the words seeming to hang in the air between them.

Without another word, Stephen forced his numb limbs to work as he opened his door, passed through it, then closed the portal behind him with a sharp finality. All the while he fought an overwhelming urge to disregard everything he had convinced himself was right. He wanted to set Lady Mary and duty aside to go to Fellis, to tell her that he longed, above all things, to make her his. To talk of a man and woman sharing desire out of their love for each other only made his own plight all the more difficult to accept.

But he did not act on his desires.

Leaning against the door in weary resolve, he realized the significance of the scene he'd just had with Lady Mary. He had inadvertently ended in sharing more than his convictions about relationships, which was a clear waste of effort, for she was not likely to see any opinion besides her own as having merit. From her questions, it was obvious that the lady had guessed at his feelings for her daughter. What she might make of it he had no notion. Knowing her estimation of him, the knight had much doubt that the Lady of Malvern would tell Fellis what had passed between them. 'Twould not serve her purpose to do so. To tell her daughter of Stephen's feelings would only serve to make Fellis more attracted to the knight.

Stephen sighed, too tired to care what the Lady of Malvern might do, too filled with self-condemnation.

He knew that he had to pull himself together and put what had happened between himself and Fellis behind him.

If not for his own good, then hers. He had no wish to harm her further.

As he thought about the betrayal in her eyes, Stephen realized what he must do. He had to force himself to face her, to beg her forgiveness, then ask her if they might put it behind them. It was the only way.

She was still obligated to marry Wynn. And heaven help him, Stephen meant to make that as painless for her as it could possibly be.

It was up to him to help her.

Fellis looked up from her sewing to see Stephen standing in the entry of her mother's solar. A hot flush rose in her throat and face as she found herself drowning in the sight of him, so tall and strong and vital.

She could feel her mother's eyes upon her from where she sat near the table, which was covered with threads, cloth and all manner of trims. But Fellis did not look at her.

She could not take her gaze from the man. "I beg your leave to speak with you, Lady Fellis," he said formally.

Her cheeks paled at the remoteness in his expression. Since the day in the wood, he had not so much as spoken to her. Now he treated her with this coldness.

Fellis looked up when her mother stood. There was a certain thoughtfulness in the older woman's expression as she turned from her daughter to face the knight. Fellis also sensed a new but unmistakable hint of respect in her tone as she addressed him. "If you will excuse me I must see to something in the kitchens."

Before Fellis could even begin to think on this, the knight nodded with equal courtesy and she went from the room.

Alone now, with the tall, silent man, Fellis found herself focusing only on him.

Gazing down at the length of pale blue sendal in her hands, Fellis viewed it through a glaze of unshed tears.

Why was he here? Hadn't Stephen Clayburn done enough? What perturbed her even more was that he seemed so remote with her. What, pray, had she done to make him so?

With the thought came the realization that she could not let him see how much his rejection of her hurt. If what had passed between them was so distasteful to Stephen Clayburn that he must treat her so coldly she would at least retain some semblance of pride.

She held her head high, forcing herself to meet his eyes. "You wish to speak to me."

He came farther into the room, but only a few steps. "Let me first say, my lady, that I wish to beg your forgiveness for what occurred several days past. I am sorry for overstepping the very boundaries of honor which I had set. I accept full blame for all."

Blame, she thought. How very ironic that he would put it so. That the most wondrous and beautiful experience of her life could be reduced to such a word. It truly amazed and further saddened her that he could view what he had done to her as being blameful.

What could she then do but allow him to think as he would? It was the only way to salvage even a modicum of her self-respect, though it must be obvious even to Stephen that she had precious little of that where he was concerned.

She knew he was waiting for a reply.

Summing up courage she had no idea she possessed, Fellis raised her chin. "You need have no concern, Sir Knight. I have no more wish to discuss the matter than you. Suffice it to say that there was a mistake made, though not all of the responsibility is yours, some must be laid at my own feet."

She looked away. "I hope now, that you will not speak of it again. 'Tis best forgotten."

He looked confused for a moment, then nodded emphatically. "Very well then." The words seemed to express his relief well enough though his expression did not reflect that same emotion. If she had not known better she would have sworn he appeared disappointed.

Fellis watched closely as, taking a deep breath, he glanced away and back at her. "I have news to share with you."

Even before he went on, Fellis knew then what was making him uneasy.

Surely it must be about Wynn.

He spoke, confirming her thoughts. "Wynn has sent word that he wishes another meeting concerning the marriage."

There was a sinking sensation in her stomach. "He has decided."

The knight spoke without emotion, his long fingers, those same fingers that had moved her to utter his name against his lips, toyed with the hilt of his sword. "One would believe so."

Fellis shook her head to rid it of those intimate thoughts and forced herself to attend what the knight was saying. She made herself form a reply though her voice sounded hollow to her own ears. "I will trust you to hear his answer and bring news of it back to me."

Stephen looked to her with disappointment in his first unguarded show of emotion since coming into the solar. "Lady Fellis, I beg you to reconsider. I know that the previous meeting did not go as well as it might have. But could you not give it another chance? Wynn is good man and would not hurt you by intent. He has said he would deal with the problem of Ardeth. She can have no bearing on the course of events."

Fellis winced at hearing the other woman's name. She frowned at Stephen, not out of anger at Ardeth but at him. Had he no understanding that the other girl must be in pain at losing the man she loved?

Yet she gave away no hint of her feelings as she answered him. "I do not question that. As you say, he seems a good enough man and will surely do what he must. As far as I am concerned, there really is no need for me to attend this meeting." She shrugged. "I am simply a pawn in this."

He came toward her, reaching out a hand and then drawing it back before he actually touched her. "But there is need, my lady. Wynn will surely become your husband. It is for your good to know him better, to become familiar with him. 'Twill make the marriage more acceptable to you when the time comes."

She felt a rising ire. Did he think she would refuse the Welshman now, that he must still attempt to convince her? There was no need. "I have said I will comply. I am not so faint of heart that I would go back on my word at this late hour."

He replied, "At least come and speak with Wynn one more time. There is no need for you to go to him a stranger and I fear the marriage will be hard enough for you as it is. This may be your last opportunity to see him before the event takes place."

Fellis, looking at the earnestness on Stephen's face, could not doubt that he meant what he said. How could she tell him that it didn't matter how many times she might meet with Wynn? She would never love him.

Because she could only think of another, and that other was Stephen himself.

Fellis could not tell him that. She realized that because of this, she must make the pretense of meeting Wynn, of behaving as if her future were of some import to her. When in her heart she knew that nothing could really move her now.

She looked at Stephen with unknowing sorrow. "I will do as you ask."

He smiled, and Fellis thought she saw regret mixed with the relief in his eyes.

Quickly she glanced away, knowing she was mistaken. Stephen cared for nothing save seeing this wedding accomplished. When it was done, he was free to be on his way, to find his old life far from Malvern—and her.

As the first time, Fellis and Stephen went to the meeting without escort. Neither of them made any pretense at trying to talk. For that Fellis was grateful. She did not think that she could have continued to present such a calm facade if he spoke to her.

She neither thought of nor cared how she appeared in another new cote of azure blue sendal and an underdress of deeper cobalt damask. Her new clothing had come to mean very little over the past days.

She drew her light cloak closer about her shoulders to ward off the dampness left by the rains that had ceased to fall only the previous evening. Fellis was no more than peripherally conscious of the dank mustiness rising from the loam beneath the horses' hooves.

Wynn was waiting when they arrived at the clearing in the forest. Fellis could see by the determined set of his features that the Welsh nobleman had indeed come to some decision. Her stomach churned with apprehension.

The Welshman left his horse tied to the branch of a young oak at the far edge of the clearing, walking across the new-grown grass with obvious determination. Fellis heard the sharp crackle of twigs snapping beneath his leather-shod feet with an unexplainable sense of dread.

As he reached them, Fellis and Stephen dismounted without looking at each other. The knight simply took Ebony and secured her to the lower branch of a tall beech tree.

Wynn waited until he was finished, then greeted them briefly with a bow. "Lady Fellis, Sir Stephen." When they nodded he then spoke very formally to the knight. "I have resolved that I will do as your English king wishes."

Turning to Fellis, the Welshman addressed her in equally formal tones. "Lady Fellis Grayson, I ask, for the good of my people and yours, that you will do me the honor of becoming my wife?"

She had known that this would be what he had to tell them, yet hearing the words still came as something of a shock to her. This then was the moment that would decide her future. Once she committed herself formally there would be no going back, not without dire consequence.

Feeling Stephen's gaze on her but not allowing herself to look at him, Fellis took a deep breath. She needed every modicum of courage she had ever possessed to say the words that she knew she must. "I will wed with you, Wynn ap Dafydd, for the good of both our peoples."

The words fell into silence at the gravity of her acceptance.

Hopelessness made Fellis's knees weak. She looked at the ground, working to force back the tears that must remain unshed. Any dream of ever being with Stephen was lost to her now, for once and always.

Stephen was speaking then, and she made herself attend him. Fellis was surprised at the husky tone of his voice. "Your allies have agreed to this union?"

Wynn cast him a resigned glance. "There are dissenters among them. But I feel sure those few will come around. They will come to see that I do what is best for all, though some be hurt or angered by it."

There was a haunting note of regret in his voice that made
Fellis wonder what had caused it. Was he thinking of Ardeth and wishing he did not have to set her aside? For surely
this meeting indicated that he had.

Unexpectedly, the notion brought a feeling of kinship
with the man she would marry. It seemed that both of them
would give up much to follow their duty.

At least if they had no love for each other, there might be
a chance at respect.

With that thought in mind, she gave him her hand. Wynn
bent over in a surprisingly courtly gesture and kissed it. It
was as if he understood what was in her thoughts, for his
expression was pleased.

Stephen saw Fellis hold out her hand, saw Wynn take it.
As the first time it had happened, his mind flashed bright
hot resentment.

Doubling his fists at his sides, Stephen forced himself to
turn away, to block out the sight of them. He could not look
at Fellis in her new cote of pale blue that matched the color
of her eyes, eyes that he had watched grow hooded with the
intensity of her desire for him. Had he really thought he
could see them together and not want her for himself, that
he could stand by and witness the other man claim what he
wanted most in the world?

He'd known this moment would come, that Wynn would
accept her and that she would agree to take him. There had
never been any real doubt of it in his mind. What choice had
mere mortals against the wishes of a king?

But to be here, to see them this way was too much.

Even knowing that he was helping Fellis by bringing her
to see the man who would become her husband, Stephen
could barely hide his resentment.

He did not believe he could stand by and see them wed.
He had no wish to put himself through such torment.

What choice had he? King Edward had been very specific in telling Stephen he wished him to stay to the end, to make sure nothing went wrong. His obligation was to carry it out.

He squared his shoulders, and turning to face them, Stephen was relieved to see that Wynn was no longer holding Fellis's hand and the two seemed to have little or nothing to say to each other.

Going back to stand with them, Stephen addressed Wynn. "I congratulate you both and can only say that I will pray for your happiness."

Wynn nodded but said nothing, only glancing to where Fellis had moved to stand a few steps away looking decidedly uncomfortable.

Stephen drew the other man's attention back to himself. "My lord, there are some things I wish to discuss with you, if you do not mind."

Wynn nodded again. "As you will. Are we to begin discussions on the terms of the marriage contract?"

Stephen was aware of Fellis looking up then, her brows arching high in surprise.

The knight shook his head then watched her relax. "Nay, that Lady Fellis's father will attend to. You will have need to meet with him on that subject. I wish to ask you of your own situation. You did say there are those still opposed to the marriage?"

He answered. "Aye, but as I told you there is no need to worry."

Concern made Stephen frown. "They will not act against you?"

Wynn stared up into the taller man's face. "Nay, have no fear. They oppose the marriage, but the one who leads them is unquestioningly loyal to me."

At Stephen's obvious relief, he smiled. "I think, Englishman, that you actually care for my safety and not just the fact that I have promised to end the feuding."

Stephen looked at the other man, finding he felt a great deal of respect and even liking for the Welshman. "Methinks you are right," he said, then smiled, surprised to find himself doing so. "I find myself uncomfortable with the notion that you might be in danger from your own folk because of my actions."

Wynn waved a dismissive hand. "Do not worry over it, Stephen. My safety is not in doubt. The man who has objected the most strenuously would as soon harm his own son as myself, did he have one. To question his loyalty would be to question my own flesh and blood."

Without quite knowing why he did so, Stephen held out his hand in friendship. "May this union bring about the peace we all seek."

Wynn took it. Speaking softly so that only Stephen could hear him, he said, "I will not treat her cruelly."

Neither pretending he did not know what the other was saying or trying to deny the truth of what the Welshman had observed, Stephen said, "You have my thanks and my friendship, as well. If you would have it?"

"Gladly," Wynn replied.

Stephen glanced around to where Fellis waited nearby. She seemed distant, lost in her own thoughts.

Stephen knew a desire to go to her, to openly admit to Wynn how he felt about her. It seemed clear that Wynn had already guessed at the truth and still he accepted the knight's offer of friendship. If only he could just say the words, that he wished to have her for his own.

He did not, could not.

It was as Stephen turned back to Wynn that he was stunned to feel a quick rush of wind brush his cheek as a fast-moving object flew past his head. Reacting quickly, Stephen swung around to see the object land in the ground some few feet away. Immediately he recognized that it was an arrow. Thankfully it had passed between himself and Wynn without hitting either of them.

All this Stephen saw and assimilated in less time than it took a heart to beat.

He spun around, his horrified gaze going to Fellis. But though she stood there as if turned to stone, her face pale with shock, she was unscathed.

Then Stephen noticed a flash of color to his right just beyond Fellis's shoulder. He realized the assailant must still be lurking in the wood. This registered in his mind, and Stephen knew a nagging sense of confusion, he would have sworn the arrow had come from his left.

There was no time to waste in contemplating this.

He rushed forward into the edge of the forest, determined to see if he could catch whoever had shot the arrow.

Then he was upon them, grabbing at the back of a long dark cloak. It came loose in his hands and he was astonished to see that the assailant was a woman. Not just any woman but Wynn's leman, Ardeth.

Fellis had seen the arrow fly between the two men with a gasp of horror. Then as Stephen ran to one side of the clearing, Wynn had disappeared into the trees on the other side. A moment later Wynn emerged with a piece of string dangling from his hand.

Almost simultaneously, Stephen stepped out of the trees to her right. He was carrying a young woman before him, his strong arm clasped about her waist as she fought and screamed at him.

For a long moment Wynn stood perfectly still, his hazel eyes wide. Then somehow he managed to break through the shock that had obviously held him immobile. He came forward, worry and dismay lining his face as he called out to the woman. *"Cariad."*

Fellis watched as the beautiful Welsh woman held out her arms to him. Living so close to the border all her life, Fellis knew enough of the Welsh language to recognize the word *cariad* for the endearment that it was.

With sinking heart she saw Wynn hold out his arms. As Stephen released the girl, she went into them, crying on his shoulder as he held her close and whispered to her in their own tongue.

With lips thinned and brows raised high, Stephen interrupted them. "If you do not mind, there are several questions that have need of immediate answers."

They turned to the knight as if only then remembering his presence.

Stephen went on impassively, his green gaze fixed on Ardeth. "Your lack of weapon leads me to believe you are not the one who fired upon us."

"Nay." Wynn spoke for her. "Ardeth would not do such a thing."

"Really," Stephen replied. "From my own position it appears that she has some stake in the outcome of these proceedings. She might wish to end the negotiations by killing me and breaking the treaty with Lord Grayson."

Ardeth looked at Stephen with resentment as she replied. "I only followed Wynn. I knew why he was coming." She sent a hate-filled glance toward Fellis. "But I would not have shot at anyone." She glared at Stephen. "Do you really believe I would risk hitting my own dear love?"

Wynn shook his head and pulled her closer against him, his eyes on Stephen's. He held up one hand, showing them the piece of string. "This is a broken bowstring. I found it a few feet into the forest there.'' He nodded to indicate the direction.

Stephen took it. ''I take it then that the shooter is gone?''

Wynn replied with a glance toward the wood. ''I saw no sign of anyone. If the assailant broke his bow, he likely made haste to depart the vicinity.''

Stephen scowled at Ardeth. ''This is no proof that she was not involved.''

Wynn tightened his embrace. ''As you said, she has no weapon. Let me further reassure you of my own certainty that Ardeth would not try to stop this marriage from taking place, though she knows I must marry Lady Grayson to make peace between our people, she will not be displaced from my heart. Under Welsh tradition her children will suffer no stigma. I will treat them with the love and care they deserve because of the love I bear their mother.'' He was looking at Ardeth then, speaking from his soul as if nothing in the world mattered except that she believe what he said to her.

Ardeth only stared at him with her heart in her sorrowful brown eyes.

Fellis watched this scene unfolding with a sense of loneliness that near brought her to her knees. Wynn would not set Ardeth aside but keep her as his true love. Fellis was to be as nothing to him, would live without even the honored position as his real wife.

And even as she understood the years of solitude ahead of her, Fellis could not help seeing the way Ardeth and Wynn held each other. The deep and true love they shared was obvious. What, she wondered, would it be like to openly show her own love for a man?

Her gaze went to Stephen. God in heaven, he could have been killed just now. The arrow had missed him by a mere breath. And no one seemed to care very much about getting to the bottom of that. For her part she would rather deal with her hurt over Wynn's declaration toward his leman in her own time, not here before them all.

As Stephen spoke again, Fellis could see that even the knight seemed not to have a care for his safety, for his attention was centered on what Wynn had said. "Have you no care for Lady Fellis? She is to be your wife. How can you dismiss her feelings so easily?"

Wynn turned to her then. "Lady Grayson, I am sorry if what has occurred here this day has hurt you. I have not meant to do so. Ardeth and I have been in love since we were children. She carries my child even now. What manner of man would I be to forsake her?"

Fellis held her head high. It was becoming worse. She carried his child. How her heart ached for them, for herself. "There is nothing I can say on this other than I am sorry for the pain the situation has brought to your lives. As for myself, I know, as you do, what must be done."

She was pleased to hear the strength in her voice and went on to address the matter that was uppermost in her mind. "What troubles me is that Sir Stephen was just shot at. You say it was not this lady, but that does not tell us who is responsible and what they hoped to gain. When last we met you said you would keep your people under control. Who then has had the temerity to attack the king's own knight this time?"

"I have no answer to that," Wynn replied with furrowed brow. "I would be willing to stand my own life as warrant that 'twas not the same man as before."

Ardeth paled as he spoke and Fellis watched her recover herself with difficulty. Ardeth turned to Stephen and cried out in rage, "It is your fault that all of this has happened, knight. You came here and bewitched my love with talk of peace with your English king." She looked to Wynn who was watching her with a frown. "I would not betray you, *cariad,* and will do as you say. But you know there are those amongst us who do not want this. There are several men who might be driven to this act. We have no need of the English king's permission to do as we please. What is wrong with your own Welsh stronghold? We have no need of a castle. 'Tis their way, Wynn, not ours." She broke down in a heaving sob.

He pulled her close, his gaze tormented as he took a deep breath and tried to soothe her. "I know you speak and act from your heart, Ardeth. But you do not understand that I am not free to do so. I must think of the good of all my people. There is no room for obstinate pride. I must go forward to forge this peace with Lord Grayson. The English king is strong and has a powerful army. 'Twould be irresponsible of me to think I can defy him. I care not for myself, but many others would die needlessly. The benefits he has offered, license to a fortified castle and to hold a market, will do much to make our lands prosperous and our people happy. 'Tis a most unusual and generous overture. I would be thinking of nothing save myself if I refused it."

Wynn turned to Stephen then with a sweeping gesture. "'Twould be plain foolishness to kill this man. He would only be replaced by an army. I must discover who has tried to harm him." He raised Ardeth's face with a hand on her chin. "Do you know who shot that arrow?"

She swallowed hard as she met his eyes. "How would I know?" She looked away. "As I said, there are those who hate the Englishman and blame him for what has happened. They believe he has done some evil to convince you to forsake me and marry the cripple...."

Fellis could not withhold a gasp of shock. Never in her presence had she been referred to as such, though in the past she had suspected that it might be in many people's minds. This only confirmed her fear.

What amazed her was that, after the initial shock of hearing the words had abated, she was little affected by them. Over the past weeks, Stephen had helped her to see that she was not a cripple. Not by birth, nor in her life. It was the way she lived and behaved that determined who she was. One small defect did not make her less than others, unless she allowed it to do so. At this moment she felt that Ardeth was more defective than she, for the Welsh girl had used her pain as excuse to lash out at one who meant her no harm.

She felt her chest swell with the joy of her newfound fortitude.

Stephen turned to Fellis, unaware of her moment of self-discovery, his eyes telling her how sorry he was for this insult. Then he swung back to face Wynn, his voice hard with anger. "Such talk has no place in this. I have brought this lady to you in good faith as your intended bride, to bring about a peace that will satisfy King Edward's instructions. I will not have her insulted by this woman—" he motioned toward Ardeth disparagingly "—or any other person, no matter who they may be."

Fellis looked to the knight in surprise, then growing wonder.

Stephen was angrier than she had ever seen him. It was apparent in his voice, his rigid stance and the hands he clenched and unclenched at his sides while he fought visibly for control. Clearly his reaction was brought on by Ardeth's insult.

Fellis felt a rising sense of happiness. It began as a warm glow in her chest and radiated out to all parts of her.

This outrage of her behalf proved that she was more to him than a means to an end.

Hard on this feeling of amazed joy came equally strong feelings of regret. The emotion numbed her from the roots of her hair to the soles of her feet. She must marry Wynn. Never would she have an opportunity to explore this realization that Stephen actually cared something for her.

She knew she could not acknowledge even this, for Stephen was in obvious danger as long as he remained at Malvern. The Welshwoman had said herself that there were those among Wynn's followers who believed Stephen had somehow bewitched Wynn into going along with the king's plan. No matter how foolish such thinking might be, Stephen would still be a target.

Absently she looked at Wynn as he began to speak, gazing at his woman with censure. "You have no need to strike out at the Lady Fellis. She has done you no wrong, Ardeth, and is more victim in this than any of us. Have I not said you will remain the wife of my heart?"

Fellis stiffened at his words, watching as Ardeth blushed, seeming abashed at her own behavior.

Before she could speak, Fellis held up her hand. "If you do not mind, I have heard more of this than I care to at the moment. I am no one's victim here and will not be addressed as such. I freely do what I must to make peace, as you do."

Fellis felt she would surely explode if she stood here for much longer. Her emotions were raw and she strove with all her might to keep them from seeing it. She could not look at Stephen, fearing that she would give too much of herself away.

For Stephen's sake, she would marry Wynn as soon as possible. "As you have said, the wedding will go forward in a month's time. I trust that you will be able to assure us that you will make every effort to guard against another attack on Sir Clayburn."

Wynn nodded. "You have my guarantee that I will do aught in my power to keep anything untoward from happening to him."

Knowing that this would have to suffice, Fellis turned to go, then stopped, raising her head high. There was one thing she wished to make clear on her own behalf. She met the Welshman's eyes steadily with a show of bravado she had not known she possessed. "Let me say just one more thing. With your true feelings so clearly known, Wynn ap Dafydd, I trust you will not object that the marriage should be in name only."

Wynn blanched but inclined his head as agreement.

Fellis nodded stiffly. "Now, have you no objection, I will be on my way."

Stephen moved to block her path. "Fellis, please."

She held up her hand to stop him, still not able to meet his gaze for fear of giving away the riotous state of her feelings. "Nay. Do me the courtesy to allow me to go alone. I know the way and find I have a great need for solitude."

He kept his lips firmly closed, but she could feel the uncertainty in him. Only then did Fellis look at him, and her heart twisted in her breast, her gaze unknowingly yearning on his face. That handsome, most beloved face with its gentle green eyes.

As she looked at him and saw his concern for her, she knew that she loved him. Completely and irrevocably.

The truth of it rose up inside her like a wave crashing against the shore of her soul.

Never had she imagined that love could be so all consuming, filling her entire being with Stephen. Nor hurt so very much.

She tore her gaze away from his troubled one, realizing that she was risking everything in that moment. How could he look at her and not be aware of how deeply she cared for him? Fellis swung around, finding Ebony without even knowing how she did so. Only as Fellis mounted her mare and rode away was she able to relax the tight hold she had on herself.

Tears trickled from her eyes and she was glad they had remained unshed until she was no longer beneath the scrutiny of the others. She could not allow anyone to see how much Stephen meant to her, how bleak her future would be without him.

Fellis dashed the tears from her face with the back of her hand, doing her utmost to guide Ebony safely home. When Stephen was gone, the mare would be her only tie with the man who had come to change her life so completely.

Stephen watched Fellis ride away with a wave of longing so deep it near drove him to his knees.

He could see that she was hurt but did not know how to help. She had made her need to be away from them, away from him, most clear.

He would follow Fellis in a moment, but first he wished to say something to Wynn. How could he remain the man's friend after the way he had just treated Fellis?

Stephen turned to the other man with a growl that displayed his still-burning anger. "How dare you place Lady Fellis in such an untenable position. As your future wife, she is deserving of better treatment than that you should put your leman above her."

Ardeth gasped, but Stephen did not look at her.

Wynn frowned, his dark eyes narrowing as he replied with heat. "Sir Stephen, this situation was not of my choosing. In the name of your own king you offered the lady to me as a means to settle a dispute. I have agreed, though I have met with much resistance. Am I then also to put aside the woman I love?"

Wynn's tone grew more moderate. "It is only because I can see the way you desire Lady Fellis that I can have some tolerance for your attitude."

Stephen's eyes flew wide open at this. God, he had given himself away. "It is not as you think."

"It matters not to me, how it is," Wynn replied. "I have made my feelings on this matter known. As Lady Fellis has said, the marriage will be in name only. What happens betwixt you and the lady is no concern of mine. What is between us is only a political agreement."

Stephen could barely think past the throbbing in his head. It appeared as though Wynn had just given him free rein to have an affair with Fellis. Although he knew that he could not act on such folly, the words awakened desires Stephen was fighting hard to control. "I..." he began. "'Tis not an honorable thing you suggest."

Wynn watched him with something akin to pity, deliberately taking Ardeth's hand. "It seems you take your honor too seriously, Englishman, and think not enough on what might bring you at least a short-lived happiness."

Stephen could think of no reply.

Trying hard to block out the visions that Wynn's suggestion conjured up in his mind, the knight swung away and found his stallion. The fact that the Welshman could see nothing wrong with his having an affair with Fellis did not mean that Stephen could forget his own honor and knowledge of what was right.

He mounted and left the clearing without a backward glance.

Chapter Twelve

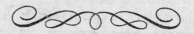

Fellis paused at the door of her grandmother's former chamber, the one now occupied by Stephen Clayburn. Her mother had assured her that the knight was out riding, as he had each day for the past three.

During that time, Fellis had caught only a glimpse of him about the castle and grounds. She had no wish for more. She fought down the flicker of self-derision the thought brought on.

It was true, she told herself. She had no wish for him to guess at what she had learned. That she loved him. Even if, as she now believed, Stephen did have some feeling for her beyond his obvious need to see her wed to Wynn ap Dafydd, he wouldst be put in an impossible position to discover that she loved him.

Fellis had no desire to see the pity that would surely come into his dark eyes if he learned the truth. Stephen had never professed anything more than friendship as far as she was concerned. It was true that there had been some evidence that he desired her, but she could not allow herself to think of that as meaning he felt more.

In spite of her mother's assurances that Stephen was gone from the keep, Fellis scratched at the door and waited with bated breath. When there was no reply, she let it out on a relieved sigh.

On entering the chamber, she went directly to the chest at the foot of the bed. Inside it lay her grandmother's clothing. Fellis had been surprised only a short while ago to discover that the elderly lady felt she was quite well enough to get up and sit in the solar for a time.

Though this made Fellis glad of heart, some of her pleasure had evaporated when her mother told her to run and fetch something for Myrian to wear.

At Fellis's look of shock, Mary Grayson had been quick to offer the information that Sir Stephen had gone out hours before and, if he followed his pattern of the past several days, would not return until well past nightfall.

Trying hard to hide her trepidation, Fellis had left her own chamber hurriedly, thinking to have the errand done in the event the man surprised them by returning in the early afternoon.

Looking down at her grandmother's chest, Fellis bit her lip. Stephen's cloak was tossed haphazardly across the chest. Gingerly she reached toward it, something inside her rising up in anticipation at touching something that had lain next to his warm body, another part of her dreading the simple act.

Telling herself she was being ridiculous, Fellis put out her hand and lifted the garment. The moment she raised it up, Stephen's scent came to her, redolent of leather, sandalwood and cool wind. Almost against her will she raised the cloak to her face, running the heavy green velvet over her cheek, and she took a deep breath, almost feeling Stephen there beside her.

So real was the sensation that she opened her eyes.

Opened her eyes and saw him standing there beside her, his dark hair tousled from riding, his eyes meeting hers with a heat that was scorching.

She flushed to the tips of her toes, realizing that she had been caught here like this in the most compromising of positions. So much for her pose of being distant and in total control of her feelings for him.

Lowering her arms, the cloak forgotten in her hand, she whispered, ''Stephen.''

To her surprise he did not speak, only reached out and gathered her to him. Although she'd resolved to keep him from guessing her secret at all costs, Fellis could no more resist Stephen than the sea might resist the tide.

Eagerly Fellis met his mouth, showing him how much she had missed him in the hurt and anxiety of the past days, how much she had wished that he loved her as she did him. Even though she knew there was no hope for them.

But as her passion rose up in answer to him, Fellis felt a growing sense of rebellion against the fate that must keep them apart.

Why should she simply accept that there could be nothing between them? All her life she'd been too ready to acquiesce to the wishes of others.

No matter that Fellis must marry Wynn to secure the future for her people, why could she not go to him knowing that she had experienced some small amount of happiness? She pressed herself closer into the knight's embrace. Why could she not have at least known the glory of this man's passion?

Even now, with his lips on hers, she did not delude herself into believing it was love Stephen felt for her. A man like Stephen would not have such feelings for her. He was free to love where he would without the complication that caring for her would entail.

Yet, as he kissed her, she knew he felt something for her.

Stephen's arms tightened around her and he drew her closer to him. The cloak slipped from Fellis's fingers as she raised her hands to his shoulders. Her fingers splayed across his broad back and she let herself drink in the essence of him, all cool, wild and hot at the same time.

"Oh, Stephen, Stephen, I want you so," she cried when he raised his mouth to press hot kisses to her lids and temples. "Hold me as you did that day in the forest. I long to know what it means to be a woman in truth."

His hold on her did not lessen, but she immediately sensed a difference in him and looked up. The dark green gaze that met hers was bleaker than she could have imagined. He leaned his forehead against hers, speaking gently. "Nothing will happen between us, Fellis. You must know that it cannot."

She wrenched away from him. "Are you telling me that you feel nothing?"

"Nay." He shook his head wildly. "But it cannot matter. You are not for me."

"You know Wynn ap Dafydd does not want me," she said in frustration, feeling anger rise like a noxious vapor inside her. "You all seem to know what is best for me?" She glared up at him, pressing her hand to her chest. "Have I not proven myself capable of doing what I should, of facing my responsibilities as a woman?"

He nodded. "Aye, and more bravely than any I have ever known."

"Then why do you persist in treating me as a child?" She wanted to strike out but she tried to control the impulse, wanting to make him understand. "That day in the wood when Ardeth called me the cripple, you thought that had upset me, didn't you?"

He shook his head as if confused. "She meant for it to hurt you. She spoke out of her own pain and jealousy..."

"Well, it did not, beyond a momentary twinge." She snapped her fingers. "I care not in the least what she thinks of me, because I know better. I have changed over the time you've been here. I have come to realize that I have some say in what happens to me and do not wish to use my deformity as an excuse to hide from making my own decisions."

Fellis looked up at him, her hands riding her slender hips. "Why, sir, must you persist in treating me the way you say that others should not?" Her tone grew more reasoning and she did not even stop to consider that what she was saying revealed her own secret. "Stephen, even now you decide for me. You wish to keep me from making a mistake because you will soon be gone from here. And that is not your right. I understand that you must leave and still I wish for us to be together."

Suddenly she knew why she was trying to convince him. There need not be anything for them beyond this moment. Fellis wanted Stephen to take her just this once, to accept her as a woman with a will and mind of her own. A woman who could choose what she would do in this instance. For the future was already settled for her. She said as much. "I want only what you would give at this moment and ask no more of you or myself than that."

He gasped. "Fellis, you know not what you are saying. I could not do such a thing. You deserve better than a night of illicit passion. What manner of man would I be to accept such a proposal? You would only end in hating me."

As he finished, there was a moment of silence as she tried to form the words she wanted to say next. How could she make him see that he was treating her as if she had no ability to reason for her own good? It was frustrating beyond measure.

Into the heavy silence intruded a sound, like the soft rasp of cloth over wood. It seemed to be coming from the doorway. Fellis looked up in fear that they had been discovered here together, possibly even overheard.

Stephen too must have taken note of the noise, for he went to the open doorway.

That seemed to break the grip of dismay that had held Fellis in its thrall. She realized how appalling this situation was. Here she was trying to convince Stephen to become her lover.

With a rush of shame she felt her face heat.

Stephen seemed not to even notice her change of demeanor as he turned back to her, his gaze dark with concern. "I can see no one." Running a hand over his face, he groaned, "What might someone have thought if they had come upon us?"

Fellis had no answer to that, nor anything else he might say. Already had she uttered too much of what she should have kept inside.

She started toward the door then realized she could not return to her own chamber without her grandmother's clothing. What would her mother say, for surely she had been gone far too long already?

With a soft cry of frustration, she reached for the lid of the chest. The latch proved unexpectedly stubborn and refused to work in her trembling hands.

She gave a start when she felt Stephen come close beside her. "Let me assist you." He raised the lid without trouble.

This only served to agitate Fellis further. It seemed as if Stephen never lost control of himself and his emotions as she did.

Not even bothering to pay any heed to what she took, Fellis quickly gathered all she could into her arms and ran from the room—from him.

* * *

Later that same evening, Fellis was surprised to receive a summons to her mother's solar.

Mary Grayson had not been in her chamber when Fellis returned from getting her grandmother's belongings. So glad was she not to have to face her mother's scrutiny after the humiliating scene with Stephen that she had not even questioned the reasons. She'd simply busied herself with first attending to the elderly woman's physical needs, then visiting with her while she got up for a short time.

To Fellis's even greater amazement her father was there in the solar when she arrived. He was seated in a cushioned chair beside the fire. His pose was a relaxed one, yet Fellis could not help thinking, as she entered, that he appeared ill at ease.

When he saw her, his expression changed to one of pleasure. "Fellis," he said in welcome.

She moved forward to bend and kiss his cheek. "Father." Since that day when she had gone to meet Wynn for the first time, her father had treated her with unwavering gentleness.

At that moment the inner door to her mother's sleeping chamber opened and Mary Grayson emerged from it. She stopped when she saw them there and took a deep breath before coming forward.

Fellis looked to her father, who seemed as confused as she by this strange behavior. He continued to watch his wife with a perplexed expression.

Mary Grayson was quick to see this and began with only a slight hesitation. "I am sure you are wondering why I have asked both of you to come here this evening." Though she spoke to both of them, her gaze was on her husband, and despite the obvious anxiety in her expression, there was also a hint of hopefulness there, as well.

Fellis watched her father nod.

Mary looked at her daughter then. "Fellis, let me begin by addressing you. I want you to know that I am sorry for all that I have put you through in these last years. I realize now that I have made many mistakes. I thought that your deformity at birth was a sign to me that I had allowed myself to love where I had no right. But I was wrong." Her gaze went to her husband's confused face.

He made as if to speak but she stopped him. "Please allow me to finish what I have to say. 'Tis hard enough done." She continued, "In the past few weeks I have come to see that I have been wrong. I am only sorry that it took a stranger's arrival to show me how very wrong. Sir Stephen Clayburn arrived with no preconceived notion of Fellis and what she was. From the beginning he treated her as any other young woman and questioned my inability to do so."

Mary looked on her daughter with the first open display of love and pride in Fellis's memory. "Fellis, he saw you for what you truly were, loving, strong and gentle. The only reason I could not see you as such was that my own insecurities and fears stood in my way. I had forsaken my own husband, and my duty to him."

She turned to Fellis's father. "I had forsaken you and my vows to you. Not because I did not want you or love you, but because I loved you too well. When our babe was born with a twisted ankle, I feared God had punished me for finding too much joy, too much happiness in your arms."

At this point Richard Grayson stood. "Mary, what are you saying? Do you mean . . . ?"

"I do," she told him. "I have been wrong, so very wrong. I believe now that Fellis's clubfoot was not some punishment from God but a test. A chance for me to learn how to show true strength and compassion. I failed that test miserably not only by marking our daughter's birth as a punishment but by turning away from the man I loved. Can you find it in your heart to forgive me?''

He rose and took her in his arms. "Mary."

They simply stood together like that, seeming too over-come at holding each other after such a long time to even speak.

Fellis could only stand in stunned surprise. What, she asked herself, could have brought this on? Her mother said that Stephen Clayburn had brought about this new under-standing of things. But the knight had been at Malvern for weeks and there had been no real change in her mother's behavior until this moment. Certainly, now that Fellis looked back, she could see that there had been signs that her attitude was becoming less harsh where Stephen was con-cerned. She had been surprisingly respectful of him that day when he had come to the solar to tell Fellis of Wynn's de-sire to meet with her a second time. But even that behavior was a far cry from the contrite woman they saw before them.

Fellis could not fathom what had been the catalyst that had brought about this wondrous yet astonishing transfor-mation.

She had to ask. "Mother?" Fellis found herself blushing as she intruded upon their silent communion. It was hard to think of exactly what she wished to say when her heart ached with happiness at seeing her father and mother embracing for the first time in her memory.

Mary Grayson turned to her, holding out her arms awk-wardly. "Fellis."

Hesitantly Fellis went to her. "Mother." She held back for a moment, looking into those eyes that had often viewed her with such censure and now were filled with a diffident but unmistakable glow of love. She felt compelled to try to un-derstand. "Why are you saying these things now?"

Mary Grayson blushed as she looked down at the floor, then back at her daughter. "I overheard you and Sir Stephen this afternoon in Lady Myrian's chamber. You were gone so long that I came to see if you had need of assistance to find what I had asked for." She put her hand on Fellis's shoulder. "I heard the way the knight refused you, putting your own well-being first, even at great cost to himself."

Fellis could feel the heat of embarrassment rising in her throat and face. Her wonder at her mother's changed demeanor was overshadowed by her own shame. She raised her hands to her cheeks. "Oh no."

That she had offered herself to Stephen like some wanton harlot was indeed bad enough, but to have had her own mother listening to the whole thing. 'Twas intolerable.

Gently her mother pulled Fellis's hands down from her cheeks, holding those icy fingers in her own. "Do not feel shamed by what happened. You care for the man. And I must admit that were things different it would be him I would see you with. He is a good man, Fellis, able to set aside his own desires for the good of another. It was learning this that made me finally see that the other things he had said to me had merit. He could have taken you this very day in that very chamber. He would not have any need to force. You made clear your desire for him, but he denied himself something he wanted, for your good."

Fellis backed away. "Oh, Mother, you heard all that. What you must think of me now?"

"I think only well of you, daughter. 'Tis clear to me your heart is given to the knight. And he is worthy, if any man can be, of that gift. If only it were in my power to give you your heart's desire. But I cannot. The path of your future has now been set. Stephen Clayburn must go, but it will not be without my deepest regret and thanks for all he has done for us.''

"And mine," Richard Grayson echoed, placing his hands on his wife's shoulders from where he stood behind her. That her father was dazed by this change in his wife was readily apparent as he looked at Fellis, but she could also see the happiness in him. "I cannot say that I am pleased that the man's will was so sorely tested where you are concerned, Fellis. Yet I, like your mother, am grateful that his care for your good was more important to him than his own desire. Given the turn this day has taken, I find I am inclined to be tolerant."

Fellis could not take it all in. Not only was her mother forgiving of what she had overheard, but it seemed her father would not reprimand her. Nor did it look as if either of them was angry with Stephen. This made her mother's metamorphosis all the more apparent, considering the way she had always spoken of the sins of passion in the past.

Albeit this seemed a good thing, Fellis could not accept so much so quickly. Despite their leniency in this matter she found it unbearable to face her parents, knowing they were aware of her deepest secret.

She backed away from them. "I must go."

Her father held out his hand to her. "Nay, let us help you. Too much have you undergone alone already."

Mary Grayson seemed to understand some of what her daughter was going through. "Let her go, Richard. 'Tis only fair to give Fellis some time to herself. Unfortunately, I have been very thorough in my teachings."

Looking at them standing there, Fellis knew her mother was indeed correct. This change would take more than a little bit of adjustment. She must now reconsider all her mother had ever said to her about what she must and must not do.

She turned and hurried from the solar.

As she did so, Fellis realized that part of her shock came not just from seeing her mother behaving and speaking so differently. It also came from realizing that the change had come too late for herself.

Her parents at least had a future—together.

Fellis had no such hope. She was to marry Wynn ap Dafydd.

Stephen was lost to her. And even if he had not been, he would not have her. She knew her mother believed Stephen had been noble in sending her away.

Fellis was not so certain. He admitted to wanting her, but it was not the same deep, aching need she felt for him. He refused to forget that he had come here out of duty. And that duty would not be denied, even when she had come near to pleading with him to disregard it.

For Fellis knew Stephen felt as her parents did, that she had need of protection. They had come to approve of the knight, because he continued to treat her as a child without the power to make decisions about what was best for her. After all that had passed between them, he could not see that she was a woman, with a woman's wants and needs. That was the way she wanted Stephen and her parents to view her, not as some helpless infant.

Stephen would soon leave Malvern for good. He would leave her with scant memories of his loving to see her through the long years ahead.

She had told Wynn that theirs would be a marriage in name only. It was surely ironic that she was to live the rest of her life in the same state of purity that she would have if she had taken her vows.

It seemed that in the end, her future existence would not be so very different from what it would have been before the knight came into her world.

Only the newfound pain of her broken heart would mark the fact that he had come into and would soon be gone from her life.

Fellis spent a restless and miserable night. The hours between blowing out the candle, as she climbed numbly into bed, and dawn seemed to stretch on interminably.

In spite of her fog of despair, Fellis did her very utmost to lie still and silent so as not to waken her grandmother. The elderly woman needed her sleep to help her fully recover from the illness that had ravaged her already delicate health.

Yet there were a few times lying there that Fellis was sure she sensed a change in the older woman's breathing. But Grandmother never spoke or made any overt sign that she was awake and Fellis told herself that she was simply mistaken.

Morning did finally arrive and with it no answers to the problems that plagued Fellis's heart and mind. She went about getting her grandmother's breakfast and readying her for the day with a heavy burden of sorrow weighing her down.

As she was setting aside the bowl she had held for the elderly woman, her grandmother broke the silence. "Fellis," she asked, her blue eyes troubled, "is there aught I can do to help you?"

The young woman blanched, then felt herself flush, though she tried to speak with an even tone. "I do not know what you mean, Grandmother."

The older woman refused to be put off. "I can see that you are troubled, child. And I know that you slept no more than I."

Fellis reached out to cover the blue-veined hand. "I am sorry, Grandmother. I had no wish to disturb your rest."

The elderly lady made a sound of dismissal. "There is no need to apologize. You did not keep me awake. 'Tis a complication of living with these old bones of mine. Many nights do the aches and pains keep me from my rest. But I know it is not the same with you. Methinks your hurt lies more in the region of your heart." She watched Fellis directly.

Trying to hide the truth by looking away, Fellis turned to busy herself with rearranging the items on the tray, but she could not hide her embarrassment from herself. Was she to have no privacy in this matter? Did every member of her family see how hopelessly in love with Stephen she was?

If they did, did he too know the truth?

The thought was mortifying. It was one thing for Stephen to believe she was wanton enough to throw herself at him. And quite another for him to know that her actions were not simply motivated by a physical need but by the love she bore him. She did not want the worldly knight to know she had been so foolish as to fall in love with a man she could never have.

She felt her grandmother's hand on her sleeve and turned back to face her, trying to mask the sadness in her eyes.

"Fellis." The older woman's gaze was full of compassion and understanding. "Don't hold yourself from me, dearling. I wish you only well. Too long have you had to be strong with no one to care for you."

Fellis looked at her for a long moment in which she fought hard for control of her emotions, fought hard and lost. She laid her head on the old woman's lap with a cry of misery. "Oh, Grandmother, what am I to do?"

"There, there, love."

Fellis felt the old woman's hand on her hair and looked up, her expression bleak. "You don't understand, Grandmother. Mother and Father have decided to reconcile. And even more unbelievable than that, they know of my feelings for Sir Stephen. Instead of being angry, they treated me kindly.'' She smiled bitterly through the sheen of unshed tears in her eyes. ''You see they think that Stephen is too noble to defile me.''

''But that is a good thing, dear,'' her grandmother answered with a bemused expression, then shook her head. ''Obviously Sir Stephen's presence has been able to break through the wall your mother had erected to keep us all out. For that we can only thank him. Sir Stephen seems a man of great honor and integrity.''

''Rot his integrity,'' Fellis cried in frustration. ''I am in love with him and he turns me away.''

Grandmother answered softly. ''Have you told him?''

''Nay.'' She put her face in her hands. ''How can I tell him when there are so many problems between us, not the least of which is his life is in danger? It is all so confusing.''

The older woman sighed deeply. ''Never were truer words spoken.'' She reached up to gently take her granddaughter's hand from her face. ''Now please, child, tell me what you are talking about when you say Sir Stephen is in danger.''

Fellis looked at her wondering if she could possibly unburden herself. What if Grandmother went to her father and told him of the attempt on Stephen's life? Would Lord Richard then refuse to go forward with the wedding? He had made his own displeasure with the arrangement known since the beginning. Only because Wynn had appeared to live up to the truce they had both signed had he felt obligated to go along with the king's directive. Surely any hint that the Welsh had broken their word would be sufficient reason for him to renege.

She could not let that happen. Fellis longed for peace. Over the course of the weeks since the truce was signed, there had been much less mayhem and strife amongst their people. Not since the day the crofter had come to report the fire in his outbuilding had any untoward incidents occurred.

Grandmother interrupted her thoughts. "Well."

Fellis frowned, unsure as to what she should do. "You will not tell Father what I tell you?"

The other woman gave her a long, assessing look. "You have my word. Though I may end in advising you to do so."

Ignoring the last remark, Fellis began. As she did, it was as if the words flowed of their own accord, as if they had been too long bottled up inside her. She explained everything, starting with the first threat to Stephen at Glenmarket and all that happened since. Fellis even told of Wynn and Ardeth's relationship, though it pained her to do so. Through it all, Grandmother did not interrupt or make any sound until Fellis spoke of the attack on Stephen in the forest.

Here the older woman brought her up short with a curt question. "Why did you all assume Stephen was the target?"

Fellis looked at her. "Who else would it be? Stephen had been threatened by Wynn's man, Owain, in Glenmarket." She put her hand to her breast. "Are you saying they mean me harm? It does not serve. I was standing away from Wynn and Stephen when it happened."

Lady Myrian shook her head. "Pray listen while I tell you something, then we shall see if you too grasp what I suspect is the truth."

Her eyes took on a faraway cast. "When we first came here and you were a babe, your father had the best of intentions. He had been awarded the honor for service to the crown in France. He meant to try living in harmony with his neighbors. To that end he did contact Wynn's father, Dafydd. Dafydd was mistrustful, but he agreed to come to the castle and talk. He came once and never again. Your father learned afterward that the man had been poisoned, and that Dafydd lay desperately ill for some time afterward. After a time we learned that Dafydd's cousin had blamed Richard for the attempt on Dafydd's life." Myrian gave Fellis a long look. "He took no poison here. Your father would not have lied on that. Sometime later a Welshman came begging entrance to the keep. He asked for positions for himself and his family. He was questioned as to why. The tale he told was one that gained his entry and your father's trust. That man was Walter, the same Walter who manages the granary to this very day."

Fellis could not help being drawn into what her grandmother was saying. "What was it he told?"

"He said that he knew who had tried to assassinate Dafydd, and that it had been his very own cousin, Owain."

Fellis gasped, the older woman's reasoning beginning to become clear to her.

Myrian went on. "Owain did not want to make peace with the English, hated them with every fiber of his being and would do anything to stop Dafydd from treating with them. But, you see, after Dafydd believed he had been poisoned by your father there was no more need to harm him. When he was finally recovered he went on a spree of vengeance that lasted for years and wreaked havoc on both sides. Which I might add seemed to thrill Owain." She ended with a heavy silence.

Fellis was seeing just where her grandmother was leading. The thought was a disquieting one. She said slowly, "Owain."

Grandmother nodded. "You do see. 'Tis only logical. Why at this point would they bother with Sir Stephen? Surely Wynn had discussed his decision to marry you with his folk. With that choice made, Stephen is no longer the object of threat. His part in it is done.''

Fellis's mind was numb. ''But, Grandmother, it is too much. Wynn would never believe this. He professes to trust the man completely.'' She shook her head trying to think clearly. ''Can you actually suppose that Wynn was the target of Owain's arrow?''

''Aye, I do, as do you,'' she replied, and there was no satisfaction in her blue eyes. ''It is obvious when one knows how far he has already gone to keep from making peace with his enemies.''

''But,'' Fellis said, ''Ardeth would recognize her own father. She told Wynn that she did not know who it was.''

''And mayhap she did not,'' Myrian reasoned. ''And even if she did, would she give him away? Think on it. How easy could it be to choose between your father and your lover?''

Fellis knew not what to say to that. ''What am I to do?''

''You must tell someone. Wynn could be in terrible danger.''

Fellis pressed her hands together tightly. ''I cannot tell Father, not now with the marriage contract still unsigned. He looks for any reason to cry a halt to the proceedings. Besides, Wynn would not even listen to him.''

''Then you must go to Sir Stephen. You said he and Wynn ap Dafydd are on good terms. Mayhap he can convince the Welshman of the truth before it is too late.''

Fellis stood, biting her lips. Of course she must go to Stephen. He was the only one who had any hope of rectifying the situation. Surely, with his ability to reason and handle difficulties with aplomb, he would be able to make it aright.

She did not even question her unshakable faith in the knight. She believed in Stephen utterly and without reservation.

Fellis knew that she would have to meet with him in secret. She wanted her father to get no wind of this.

She would have to go to his chamber after everyone else had found their rest. She realized, as she thought this, that Stephen might misinterpret her actions and refuse to speak with her. She would simply have to chance that possibility.

Pray God, he would not turn her away before she had an opportunity to explain.

Chapter Thirteen

Lying in her bed, Fellis knew what she had to do. All that delayed her now was listening for the castle to settle for the night.

She only wished that Wynn was not the catalyst for her nocturnal visit to Stephen's chamber. Fellis would rather have been going there for more personal reasons.

When all was quiet, Fellis rose from her bed, trying not to waken her sleeping grandmother, and reached for the black velvet robe that lay across the end of the bed.

With silent deliberation she went to the door of her chamber and opened it. It made not a sound.

From the bed she heard her grandmother's voice. "Go with God, child."

Fellis paused without looking around. "Thank you, Grandmother." Then she let herself out, closing the portal gently behind her.

Fellis made no effort to hide her presence in the hallway. She did not hesitate at the entrance of Stephen's chamber but simply pushed it open.

The sight that met her eyes fair took her breath away.

Stephen sat before a softly glowing fire, seeming as if his mind were far away from this place. Her gaze dropped to the bare expanse of his golden chest and she knew a tightening in her lower belly. He wore nothing save his drawers, and her eager gaze roved over his flat stomach and narrow hips, then sought out the smoothly muscled curves of his long, powerful legs, one of which was drawn up so that he might rest his elbow upon his knee. The firelight played on his hair and the golden skin that she so longed to touch.

But she lowered her gaze, knowing she had no right to touch him. Her fingers tangled in the velvet of her robe.

As he looked up, she raised her chin, knowing she must get her traitorous thoughts under control.

As it had all the nights since Wynn had officially agreed to wed Fellis, sleep eluded Stephen.

He was startled by the opening of the door.

Joy, mixed with horror, exploded inside the knight as he saw Fellis there, her glorious hair swirling about her in a silken curtain. He rose, clenching his hands at his sides as he fought the chaotic emotions. "What do you here?"

But even as he spoke, his belly tightened at the sight of her beauty. As she took a step forward, his gaze was drawn to the open neck of her velvet robe, the motion causing the curve of her high firm breasts, just visible above the neck of her night rail, to be thrown into the firelight. His manhood throbbed and swelled and Stephen wished he was wearing more than just his drawers, for he knew his arousal must be evident to her.

She held out a delicate white hand. "Do not send me away. I must speak with you."

Stephen could think of no reply, for the truth was that he knew he loved her as darkness loved the light. She was everything to him and since the day when he had come into this very room and kissed her, the day she had offered herself so sweetly, he had thought of nothing else but having her. Not just for one night but for always. Stephen wanted to beg her to go away with him, somewhere, anywhere that they could be together to share their love openly.

He found his mind dwelling on the fact that he had distant relations in Scotland who would surely take them in and give him a position.

But he knew such thinking was nothing short of sheer madness. Fellis was a gentlewoman, and the idea of asking such a thing of her was unworthy. She deserved so much better than he would be able to give her as a rebel to the crown. He was sure then even the moneys left to him by his grandmother would be forfeit.

Nay, he could not even think it.

But here she was, looking so lovely that he was robbed of his ability to think. He raised his gaze to her face and found that she was indeed aware of his arousal, for her blue eyes had darkened to cobalt and, as she looked up to meet his gaze, her lids were heavy with unmistakable desire.

She came forward. "Stephen...I..." But her hungry eyes had dropped to rove over his chest. She stopped mere inches from him.

Fellis, swallowed, and ran her tongue over her lips. "I..." She began again, then paused as if having some difficulty with her train of thought. Her gaze dipped lower still. "Oh...Stephen," she whispered.

Stephen groaned aloud, reaching for her even as he felt himself stiffen further. His hot mouth found hers and her lips parted beneath his as she kissed him with a fierceness that surprised him even as the intensity of her response played further havoc on his control.

Fellis was lost completely. Everything but this man and this moment was forgotten. There was no way for Stephen to hide his desire for her now. She was achingly aware of the fact that he wanted her as she did him. Why should they not do what they both wanted so desperately?

Her breasts swelled against the hard, smooth expanse of his chest. Fellis knew a growing need to free them so that there was no barrier between her aching flesh and his.

She raised one hand and tore at the front of her robe, pulling it aside, then groaned in frustration when her fingers met the barrier of her thin night rail. Fragile though the fabric might be, it was too much to lie betwixt them.

Realizing what she was about, Stephen tore his mouth from hers. "Nay," he said, "It is wrong. We cannot."

She looked up at him, her eyes dark with passion, making no effort to cover her near nakedness. Cocking her head to one side, her silver hair gliding like liquid silk over the black velvet robe she wore, she slowly slid it back off her delicate shoulders. "Why is it wrong, Stephen? Who would we harm?"

Stephen's hot gaze scorched her as it found her breasts, and her nipples hardened in response. He made a hoarse sound in the back of his throat and she let the robe drop to the floor.

His response made her bold. "I do not believe it is because you do not want me. After that day in the wood..." She did blush now as she spoke of the time he had caressed her so intimately in the wood. "Well...the way you touched my ankle and then . . . I thought that you might actually be the one person who was not repulsed by my deformity. Mayhap I was wrong in thinking that."

Stephen raised his eyes to her face. Fiercely he shook his head to stop her from going on. "Repulsed by you. That is as far from the truth as anything could be."

Fellis looked at him closely, then as if what she saw encouraged her, she raised her slender fingers to place them on his chest. "Then pray tell me," she asked with a smile as seductive as any courtesan's, "why should we be denied this?"

Her cool fingers fair burned him where they lay against his flesh. Stephen ached to take the lushly curved mouth with his own. This Fellis was not one that he had known before, but a woman who knew what she desired, a woman who could openly make her desires known to a man. She was not the child they'd all taken her to be.

Every vibrating nerve in his body told Stephen he had been a fool to decide Fellis was not woman enough to know that she truly wanted him. He'd been mad to keep himself apart from her because he had judged her too innocent to make a rational choice about being with him.

Or had he been wrong to think her too innocent? Trying desperately to think clearly, Stephen wiped a hand over his face.

He knew he had to try to make her understand some of what was in his mind. "I know not what is right, Fellis. I only know that I want you, have wanted you from the moment I saw you. 'Tis all I think of night after night, you, and having you here in this bed. I have thought of precious little else since the first day I came here."

He looked at her, his eyes pleading with her to understand what he was about to tell her. "When I was looking for the castle, I took a shortcut through the wood. I became lost." He watched as uncertainty crept into her face. "I had no intent to spy on you. It is just that when I saw you there in the water, I could not think, could not reason enough to simply turn and go as honor dictated." He spread his hands. "I have been mad with longing for you from that first moment. I had seen you, beautiful, perfect, and compelling enough to fill my thoughts both day and night with your image and no other."

Even as he watched, Fellis's eyes darkened to a startling shade of blue that was near purple. She reached out and took his hand, bringing it to her breast. "Then pray do not hold yourself from me another moment."

Stephen could not breathe, his heart was pounding so hard, and he closed his eyes as she pressed his hand to the fullness of that perfect breast. Then he felt the nipple pucker and harden beneath his palm and he was lost.

Still not opening his eyes, Stephen molded her supple flesh with his fingers, reaching out to take the other in an equally firm but gentle caress. Her skin was smooth as cream and cool in his hands, making his own body heat in reaction to the feel of her.

He heard Fellis sigh and opened his lids. Her eyes had drifted closed and her head was tilted back to expose the tender white flesh of her throat. Her pink lips were slightly parted as her breathing quickened.

Stephen could not resist this invitation, nor did he even wish to try anymore. For good or ill, this moment was theirs and theirs alone. Heaven help him, he meant to live it as if it were his last.

Which, a voice whispered in the back of his mind, it might as well be.

There were no words to relay what was inside him, the pain and the joy of this moment. So he told her nothing of how desperately he wished above all else that she was his and not another man's. Stephen simply took her into his arms, allowing his lips to say all that was in his heart.

She responded by melding herself to the length of him, pressing those perfect, soft curves to his hard planes and muscles. Everywhere her body touched him he felt the tingling awareness of desire.

Fellis moaned, opening her mouth as Stephen's tongue sought entry to her softness. She was all sweet and moist and tasted of mint. He deepened the kiss, allowing his hands to slide down her back, her skin warm and inviting through the delicate fabric of her gown. Gently but inexorably he pulled her against his rising need.

She pressed back, her hips molding to him without hesitation, as if she welcomed the feel of him against her. Stephen knew a building heat inside him, a heat that threatened to engulf him, firing his blood and making his heart pound in his chest.

Fellis was achingly aware of the hard-muscled length of the man who held her in his arms. She kissed him with every bit of pent-up longing inside her.

When Stephen's strong hands found her bottom and lifted her against him, she raised her own fingers to tangle in his auburn hair, so filled with life and heat in the light from the fire. She could only think of him, Stephen, and how very much she had wanted him.

She rocked against him, feeling a pooling velvety heat at the juncture of her thighs. Fellis wrapped her legs around his hips, sobbing her pleasure as that aching part of her came into closer contact with his maleness.

But though Stephen reveled in her responses to him, he was frustrated by the barrier of their clothing. The drawers and gossamer-thin gown that had seemed as naught when he was trying to resist her now prevented him from finding a home for the desire that raged inside him.

When she grasped his shoulders and moved her hips against his, Stephen understood that Fellis too felt his frustration. He wanted above all else to soothe that craving.

Fellis was weak with the hot pulse of passion inside her and she was grateful that she could trust Stephen's strong arms to support her. She could not have relied on her own legs to do so for they quivered uncontrollably.

When he moved she cried out, "Nay," holding him to her in her fear that he would put her aside.

She need not have feared. He whispered hoarsely, "The bed, Fellis."

"Yes." She nodded, kissing him wildly as he took her there.

He laid her down gently despite the torrent that drove him to satisfy his own need without delay. Drawing back, he removed his drawers, the simple task proving more difficult than he would have imagined, due to the unsteadiness of his hands.

He at last freed himself and, after dropping the garment to the floor, he looked up to see her eyes upon him, heavy lidded and damp with desire.

She held out her arms and he came into them.

He kissed her slowly, lingeringly, wishing to make this moment perfect for her.

Fellis felt herself slipping down into a void of heat and fire, knowing only longing that continued to build inside her. When Stephen reached to take her gown over her head, Fellis could not even assist him. She was only impatient for him to come back to her. When he did, as his mouth found the peak of her breast, she rocked toward him and cried, "Nay, no more. Make me feel the way you did before. Please, I can stand no more of this, for surely I shall die of the pleasure."

And neither could he wait another moment. Positioning himself over her, Stephen prodded at that silken gateway betwixt her legs. He held back, biting the inside of his cheek with the strain of it. He had no wish to hurt her, for no matter how eager, Fellis was a virgin.

As if impatient with his hesitation, Fellis rose up to meet him, pulling him down to her. "Stephen."

He closed his eyes, drawing on his will, as he allowed himself only a minute movement. "I do not wish to hurt you more than I must."

With a cry of frustration, she lifted her hips, impaling herself upon him. Her lids flew open at the burning sensation as her maidenhood tore. The discomfort quickly became a far distant memory as she felt the sheer joy of being filled by him, Stephen, the man she loved.

He brushed a lock of hair from her eyes, forgetting his own need in seeing her scowl of pain. "I have hurt you."

She raised up to kiss his lips. "The pain is gone now. And gladly. 'Twas a gift that I wished to give you and no other." She pushed back into the bed to look at him then and he saw that the passion had not left her gaze. "Now will you love me?"

He groaned, his tight hold on himself breaking. Closing his eyes, he began to move inside her, each stroke bringing them closer to the fulfillment they sought.

Her breathing became shallower, and her head was thrown back with abandon as she found the rhythm without coaxing. She made no effort to hide the depth of her pleasure and that made his own all the more intense. Then she was crying out his name, "Stephen, Stephen, Stephen." And he could no longer hold back the tide of his own ecstasy. He felt himself explode inside her as wave after pulsing wave took him to the sky and beyond.

Stephen felt the contractions of her fulfillment ease even as he became aware of himself and where he was once more.

But when he opened his eyes and looked down at Fellis he found that, unlike the other times when he had lain with a woman, he felt no immediate disconnection to her. There was no feeling of sliding back into himself.

With Fellis, he felt joined in a way that went far beyond the physical. Gazing into her eyes, it was as if there was no separation of bone and flesh. There were only their eyes, their souls entwined and enmeshed as no other lovers before or after them.

Even when he moved to lie beside her, the connection remained. He reached to pull her against him, cradling her head on his shoulder.

She gave a sigh of unadulterated sensuality, snuggled against him and closed her eyes. She yawned. "I feel so good, so happy," she murmured. Her head tilted to the side and she was asleep.

It was at that moment that Stephen knew he could not let her go. Not even for the wishes of a king.

Come what may, Stephen wanted this woman for his own, for now and all time to come. He could not stand by and watch her marry another man. She would never marry any man but himself.

He had once thought that he could not allow himself to love because that love might bring him pain, now he knew he could not keep from loving. To do so would be to deprive himself of Fellis, of every moment he was blessed to spend with her.

Having made that determination within himself, how was he to solve their other problems? The most difficult being that of her proposed marriage to Wynn. King Edward had decreed the union take place, but he had done so because of the strife in the region.

If Stephen was to come up with another solution to the problem, would King Edward's desires be satisfied? Stephen's jaw flexed. He must. Stephen knew that Wynn had come to trust him to some extent and that that trust would continue to build if given time. He also knew that such a state did not exist between Lord Richard and the Welshman.

What then, if Stephen was to treat with Wynn directly? As Fellis's husband and Lord Richard's heir, Stephen could do so. He frowned wondering how the baron would accept such a proposal. Unconsciously he raised his brows arrogantly.

He was of a fine and noble family. It was true he was a second son, but he was not impoverished, and Lord Richard had need of a son-in-law who would be able to give all of his alliance to Malvern and its problems. Then the knight smiled mockingly. Surely he would be preferable to Wynn ap Dafydd, whom Lord Grayson had never made any pretext of accepting for any reason other than that he must.

The more he considered the more reasonable the notions that were teeming in his head appeared. Wynn did not want Fellis, and she did not want him. Lord Richard did not welcome Wynn, but seemed to have some tolerance for Stephen. As did Wynn.

Surely his plan would succeed. All he need do was set it in motion. 'Twas not as if telling Wynn of his feelings for Fellis would come as any surprise. The other man had given Stephen leave to do as he would where she was concerned.

So excited was he by the notion that he might actually find a way to obtain his heart's desire that he squeezed the woman in his arms with excitement.

She woke with a start, her eyes flying open. When she saw his face, she smiled with contentment. "I knew you wanted me."

"Wanted you?" He raised her slender hand to his mouth to press a hot kiss upon her palm. "Tell me you will marry me, Fellis. I cannot rest until you are mine."

For a long moment there was only silence, then her eyes widened in horror and she pushed away from him. Stephen was so startled by her actions that he did not try to hold her to him but released her immediately.

Fellis sat up, pulling the bed cover to hide her breasts, as if suddenly realizing her nakedness. She turned away from him, shaking her head. "Marry you. Nay I will not marry you, Stephen. Have you gone mad that you would even suggest such a thing?"

He rose to go and stand beside the bed facing her, making no effort to hide his own nakedness. He no longer had any secrets from Fellis, she was the other half of him. And he meant for her to understand that he could not go on without her.

But before he could say any of what was in his heart, she leapt from the bed. "Wynn, dear Lord, how could I have forgotten. I am surely the most selfish female that ever took breath."

"You are not..." he began.

She stopped him with the look of anguish in her eyes. "Stephen, I came here to tell that I believe Wynn is in danger. We may be too late to help him already and it is my fault." She was shaking so badly that it was difficult to think and she did not seem to be able to find her clothes. "What have I done?" she cried, finally locating her robe across the room on the floor before the fire. She moved to take it up in her trembling hands.

He shook his head in confusion. "What is this about, Fellis? You make no sense."

She rounded on him in utter frustration. "Stephen, can you not understand? It was Wynn who was the object of the attack in the wood, not you."

Stephen frowned and came forward to grasp her shoulders in his hands. "Fellis, what do you mean that it was Wynn?"

"I talked with Grandmother about it and she helped me to see the truth," she answered, trying to calm herself enough to explain. But her guilt at having forgotten in the heat of making love to Stephen was great. She took a deep breath. "Wynn is the one they must rid themselves of in order to stop this wedding. He has already agreed to go forward. By killing you they only risk angering King Edward further. In order to live up to his agreement, Wynn would be forced to punish them himself. You saw him that day, the way he spoke to Ardeth. He is bent on seeing this done.''

Stephen stood every still. "Yes, I can see that this notion has merit, but how can we help? We have no idea who might be at fault. Wynn would not believe us. Part of the reason I never thought any further than I did on the matter was that both he and Ardeth were so adamant that I was the target.''

"How could she do anything else?" Fellis said. "She could not tell Wynn the truth. It is very likely that her own father is part of the plot.''

"Her father?" Stephen replied with growing confusion. "Owain? Fellis, this cannot be. Wynn trusts him completely. Why do you think this?''

Quickly, and with growing anxiety, she related the story her grandmother had told her about Owain's having poisoned his own cousin.

"Dear Lord," Stephen answered. He shook his head from side to side. "How am I to convince Wynn of this? He will never believe me over Owain. You have said yourself that they believe your father was responsible for the poisoning.''

"You must try, Stephen," she pleaded. "I know that if anyone can convince him of the truth it would be you.''

Stephen wiped a weary hand over his face. "I wish I felt your faith in me was justified, Fellis. I am afraid that this time I may not be able to make this aright.''

"But you must!" she cried. "If Wynn dies, the fighting will resume and that cannot happen.''

He reached for his discarded clothing. "I had best act quickly then, for your father has set up the first meeting to discuss the terms of the marriage contract on the morrow. If they are going to act against Wynn again, it might very well be as he is coming here. 'Twould be easier for Owain and his followers to blame your father for his death.''

Fellis dropped the blanket, her shyness forgotten as she pulled on the robe. "You must wait for a moment while I dress."

He stopped in the act of pulling on his tunic. "Nay, Fellis, you are not coming. It is too dangerous."

Her lips set in a mutinous line as she pulled the robe about her. "I am coming. And let me tell you that if you leave without me I shall only follow on my own."

He looked down at her, finding himself stimulated by her spirit and beauty. Her lips were still swollen from his kisses, her cheeks flushed not only with anger but with his loving. He could not restrain a grin. "Are we having our first quarrel?"

She flipped her tousled locks back over her shoulder as she eyed him with distrust at this abrupt change in attitude. "Hardly."

He could not prevent himself from kissing her then, quickly but fiercely. "Knowing your ill nature, I'm sure there will be many once we are wed."

Her lips thinned, but she withheld the retort that sprang to her mind. Stephen was so handsome in the firelight, and she could still feel the lingering evidence of his loving in her heavy limbs, despite her anxiety for Wynn ap Dafydd. She knew there would be no marriage between them. Yet she could not argue with Stephen on that now.

She had come to realize that love did not work the way she had supposed. Far from abating with each bit of Stephen she shared, it seemed to grow until she knew that being without him would be as losing all her senses—sight, hearing, taste, touch, smell. Naught would reach her once he was gone, not the warmth of the sun nor the chill of the darkness.

And go he must, especially now when he was so bent on having her for himself, not only as a lover but as his wife.

Fellis did not delude herself into thinking Stephen's proposal meant they could actually marry. She knew his words were brought on by the incredible desire that drove them together like a tangible force.

She must marry Wynn. It was her duty to do so. She must make peace for her people.

Stephen knew this. Once away from Malvern, and her, he would realize how mad he was for suggesting such a thing as marriage.

She knew how deeply a part of him his honor was. Marrying her would mean forsaking his own moral code and his duty to the king. Fellis knew this would only make him hate her in the end. Thus, even if the knight was genuine in his desire to wed her, she could not allow him to do so.

No matter how badly she longed to be his, not for one night but for always, Fellis could not allow their passion for each other to destroy them.

Turning so that Stephen would not see the truth on her face, Fellis said, "I will be back in a moment. And make no mistake that if you leave me I will follow you." She then hurried from the chamber.

Chapter Fourteen

Fellis hurried down the corridor and into her room.

She barely made a sound as she went to the trunk against the wall and removed several garments. The fire had burned low in the grate and it was difficult to see exactly what she was putting on.

To her relief her grandmother remained sleeping.

Grabbing her leather shoes from beneath the edge of the bed, Fellis then made a hasty exit.

Stephen was waiting in the hallway.

He seemed impatient to be off and she passed him without slowing down as she made her way to the tower stairs that led to the outside of the keep, rather than taking the ones that would lead them through the hall.

The knight followed her without speaking.

Once they gained the courtyard, Stephen halted her with a hand on her arm. "Fellis, I do not have any specific plan for what to do once we arrive. I do not wish to bring your father into this before we speak with Wynn himself." He looked at her closely. "Is there no way for me to convince you that you should remain here? There could be great risk for you in going there with me tonight. If what we believe is true it seems likely that someone will try to stop us."

Her lips thinned. "Nay, Stephen. Have I not made clear that I will not remain behind? I understand what you say but I am not afraid. We shall do this together."

With a resigned nod, he said, "So be it. We shall do this together." Stephen then started toward the stable. It took only a few minutes for him to saddle each of their horses. Stephen then drew them out into the deserted courtyard.

All of this was accomplished in relative silence, for they did not wish to draw the attention of the guard posted at the castle gates.

Once Fellis was mounted, Ebony danced beneath her restively. It was as if the mare somehow sensed her mistress's own agitation. Reaching out, she ran a soothing hand over the mare's neck. The horse calmed and Fellis whispered, "There's a good girl."

Stephen swung up into the saddle and looked toward the portcullis with a pensive frown. He turned to Fellis. "I have no doubt that the guard will allow me to exit without incident, but I am not so certain as to whether he will do so if I take you with me."

She motioned him closer to her, for though he had spoken softly Fellis was fearful of the sound carrying farther in the stillness. "Shh." She then pointed off in the other direction. "There is another gate. It is not tall enough for us to pass through while mounted but we can go that way."

He nodded, motioning for her to lead the way.

Only a few minutes later they had gained the outside of the castle wall and, so it seemed, with none the wiser.

Stephen prodded his mount to a gallop and Fellis followed suit. Though she was not quite comfortable with the pace, she made no complaint but simply held on to the reins tightly.

They raced down the hill and into the enveloping darkness. Looking about them, Fellis realized that night seemed so much darker from outside the protective walls of the keep. She could make out very little of what was around her and could only trust in Stephen to lead the way. Fellis was thankful for Ebony's surefootedness. One wrong step could mean disaster.

They skirted the village without slowing, and soon the forest on the other side of it loomed before her eyes.

Once inside the trees, it was near impossible to see anything. Fellis could only keep her gaze focused on Stephen's back ahead of her, even as she listened intently for any unusual sounds around them.

The other times Fellis had followed Stephen across her father's land and onto Wynn's, they had only traveled for a short time. Now, riding along behind him, she felt as if the ride were interminable.

Telling herself that it was only the darkness and her own anxiety over what would happen when they did reach Wynn's stronghold, Fellis refused to give in to the feelings of fearfulness. She herself had insisted upon coming and she would not delay Stephen any more than she already had.

Though he had admitted that he had no real plan in mind, Fellis was confident that Stephen would find a way to see Wynn. It was their only hope of helping him and thus securing the peace their people so desperately needed.

Stephen knew that Fellis would be having a difficult time following him, and tried to adjust his pace as far as possible in order to accommodate her. Though she had insisted on accompanying him, he did not feel right about pushing her too far. She was still a fairly inexperienced rider.

As they rode on, Stephen was beginning to form a plan for warning the Welshman. He had not wanted to wake Lord Richard, firstly because of being delayed, and secondly, because he was not sure how Wynn's men would react if he was to arrive with the baron and his men. Stephen did not wish to inadvertently create more problems. He only hoped that Wynn's men would be willing to allow him to see their master at this hour. The knight was aware of a growing sense of urgency in telling the Welshman what they suspected.

As they drew closer to Wynn's stronghold, Stephen recalled the first time he had met with Wynn and how he had been stopped by his men in the forest. Stephen slowed his pace, not wishing to appear threatening to anyone who might be on watch.

Fellis did the same behind him, calling out softly, "Is aught wrong?"

Stephen turned, raising his hand for silence. He whispered, "Nay, but go quietly. We simply do not want our purpose to be misinterpreted."

She made no reply and Stephen turned his attention back to the path. He went along cautiously, his gaze searching the blanketing darkness around them. Stephen was barely able to see more than a few feet in front of him, but he was not overly concerned with this as he trusted Gabriel to find the way. This was not the first nighttime adventure they had undertaken together.

What was different was that this time Fellis was with him, distracting him with worries for her safety. He also knew that a man's life could very well be at stake if he made a wrong decision now.

It was only a short time later that Gabriel snorted and tossed his head as if sensing something ahead of them on the path. Thinking that it must be Wynn's guards hiding in the trees up ahead, Stephen prodded the horse forward.

Before they could progress another step, several horses and riders emerged from the trees. Not being taken off guard as he had been the first time, Stephen hailed them immediately. "I wish to be taken to Wynn ap Dafydd."

There was no reply as one of the fellows took out his knife and leapt upon him. Surprise did not hold Stephen captive for long. He grappled with the assailant, who grunted and tried to force him sideways off the stallion. "Stay your hand," Stephen called out.

From the thud behind him, Stephen thought Fellis had not been so fortunate as to remain seated. His suspicions were further confirmed when he heard her gasp as the wind was knocked from her. She cried, "Get off me, you great beast."

Panic raced through his veins at the sound of her muffled voice. Without further ado, he pushed the other man away from him and heard him hit the ground.

Stephen could only think of his beloved. But at the back of his mind was a growing anger that Wynn's men would treat them this way.

Before anyone could even think to stop him, he had jerked the fellow from atop her and thrown him aside.

She held out her arms. "Stephen."

He took her to him. "Are you well?"

She took a deep breath and moved a hand to her backside gingerly. "I think so, yes."

By now the attackers had recovered their equilibrium and they moved to circle the embracing couple.

Stephen looked around, not able to make out any faces in the darkness but hoping someone would recognize him. "I am Stephen Clayburn. You are Wynn ap Dafydd's men, I take it? I wish to speak with him."

The answer came from a voice with a thick throaty accent. "You make mistake, *Sais*."

Stephen stared in the direction of this voice. Something about the tone, some sense of threat, told him that all was not as it should be. "Are you Wynn's men?"

There was a long silence. Then something was said in Welsh and they were set upon. Thinking only that he must protect Fellis, Stephen tried to push her behind him. But there were too many for him to fight at the same time. He became separated from her as he was beset from all sides. There was no time to draw his weapon as they jumped on him, and he fought them with his fists, punching and jabbing ferociously. In spite of the fact that he managed to injure several of the men in the struggle, Stephen was finally taken.

He was plagued by fear of what might be happening to Fellis and strained to free himself from the men who held him captive. His arms were wrenched up from behind and he could only call out to her as he felt his wrists being tied together. "Fellis."

She answered immediately. "I am well. I did not struggle and they have not hurt me."

Despite her assurances, Stephen was filled with rage. He growled in frustration. "Look at us. We are one knight and a girl. We offer no threat to you. What is this about?"

No reply was forthcoming.

There was an exchange of words in Welsh and a moment later the flare of a torch lit the night, creating a small circle of light in the darkness. Several sets of suspicious eyes studied Stephen and Fellis where they stood. He recognized none of the faces around him.

Stephen looked to Fellis and saw that she too was bound. She lurched away from the man who held her and the fellow allowed her to move to stand beside him. She shrank back against him. Stephen could hardly fault her on that, for the men did look somewhat fearsome with the light flickering over their sharp, lean features.

One man seemed to be wearing an expression of deep concentration. He was silent for a long moment, studying Stephen in the light of the torch. He turned to one of the other men and spoke in his own tongue. From his attitude and tone of voice, Stephen surmised that he was their leader. There was a heated exchange in which the men seemed to be arguing about something. The only words Stephen understood were *Wynn, Owain,* and *Ardeth.* Not much to go on.

After a time, Stephen saw two of them nod, though they did not seem pleased with whatever they were agreeing to. Those two then departed into the darkness.

When the argument broke out amongst their captors, Fellis had been unable to comprehend what had caused it. She understood so little Welsh and they spoke very quickly in their heat. But she did know that it had something to do with Wynn, Ardeth and Ardeth's father. After the two men left, there was a long silence, then she and Stephen were led to tiny clearing some distance from the trail.

While they waited for Fellis knew not what, she and Stephen were allowed to sit upon a fallen tree trunk. Obviously they did not see the knight as a possible threat, bound and outnumbered as he was. While one of the men set about building a fire, their leader began to pace nervously.

Fellis was grateful for the tiny blaze. It did help to dispel some of her nervousness and she held her trembling fingers out to it even though the night was fairly warm.

Seeming to understand her feelings, Stephen gave her a look of encouragement. He said very softly, "We will find a way."

She made no reply as they were cast a glance of warning from the man closest to them.

There was no hint of blame in Stephen's eyes. But Fellis knew there should have been. It was her fault they had gotten into this situation. Without her, he would not have been taken. She was certain of that.

Stephen's care and consideration made her love him all the more and wish desperately that they were free to be together.

He seemed to sense her thoughts, for he smiled into her eyes. It was obvious that Stephen had not given up the notion that he was going to have her for his own. She could see the truth of that shining in his gaze. There was no point in even trying to remind him that this could not be, not considering the circumstances.

Silently Fellis sat there, drawing unconscious strength from his nearness as they waited for what seemed an interminable amount of time. Then finally out of the darkness around them came the sounds of someone approaching. Someone who was making no effort to remain quiet.

Fellis's eyes grew wide as Wynn, escorted closely by two of the men, stepped into the glow of the firelight. What caused her surprise was the fact that he too was bound, as she and Stephen were. She felt Stephen start forward beside her. He subsided and when Fellis looked to him, she saw that one of their captors had placed a heavy hand on his shoulder.

Wynn's expression was dark with anger. He glared at the man Fellis had thought must be the leader of the group as he was led forward. She heard him speak furiously in his own language, but the one word she could make out was "Lloyd," and she could only assume that was the fellow's name.

The two men became involved in heated exchange. The one called Lloyd seemed to become more upset as they went on. Finally he swung around, turning his back to Wynn. He made a motion with his hand and Wynn was dragged to where Stephen and Fellis sat. The three of them were taken to separate trees and tied just out of reach from each other.

Their captors then became involved in another heated discussion amongst themselves.

Stephen asked of Wynn, "What is going on?"

Wynn frowned, speaking softly. "I was woken from my bed by two of Owain's men. They told me that Ardeth was ill and needed me." He grimaced bitterly. "'Tis obvious that was not the truth."

Stephen asked, "You say these are Owain's men."

His expression filled with confusion, Wynn said, "Aye, but I do not understand why they would do this. Why have they taken me and both of you?"

Stephen spoke up. "Fellis and I were on our way to see you when we were set upon."

"You were coming to see me. Why? I wish someone would explain something soon. I feel like I am going mad."

Stephen answered, "I can explain some of what is happening, but I can guarantee that you will not like what I have to impart."

"Try me," he replied cryptically.

Stephen began by cautioning Wynn briefly. "I beg you to allow me to finish what I have to say before you interrupt."

Wynn nodded by way of agreement.

Without further preamble, but taking care to speak quietly, Stephen launched into the tale that Fellis had told him some two hours gone by. The Welshman did as Stephen had asked and remained silent through the entire narrative though his expression became grimmer and grimmer as the knight went on.

When finally Stephen took a deep breath and named Owain as the man who he believed was at the heart of not only the attempt on Wynn's father's life but who also wished to harm Wynn himself, the smaller man cried, "No. I will not listen to this."

"But you must." Stephen's tone was hard. "Your very life may depend on it."

The Welshman shook his head in denial. "I will not heed you in this. Owain has been like a father to me since my own father died some three years ago. He would not harm me."

Fellis felt anger and blighted hope boiling up in her chest. Finally she could not hold back any longer. She interjected with a gasp of exasperation. "This tale is true, sir, whether you believe it or no is your own choice. But ask yourself why we would come to you this way if 'twas a falsehood? What could we hope to gain? We have indeed placed ourselves in danger to assist you and you refuse to see the truth. And why then have we been detained and bound by Owain's own men?"

She turned her face away. "Pray leave go, Stephen. We can do naught for him if he refuses to see the truth." Still without facing him, she said to Wynn, "My greatest regret in this is that we have lost our hope of peace. For even if we are able to escape our current predicament, Owain will eventually rid himself of you. When you die, the fighting will begin anew. Know, sir, that that is why we bothered to come here this night. For the good of your folk and mine. As for myself, your demise will only save me from a marriage that was not amenable to me from the onset."

Wynn halted her gruffly. "Wait."

She turned back to him to find him studying not her but Stephen with haunted eyes. "Can this really be true? Has he done these things?"

Stephen nodded. "We believe he has."

Wynn shook his head with pain rather than denial. "There is something else you must know, something that makes me think you could be right, no matter how it hurts me." He looked away, his jaw flexing. "He has taken Ardeth away to his own holding some miles from here. Since he learned that a date had been set for the wedding, he has forbidden us to see each other."

Stephen spoke, drawing Fellis's attention. "There is something more I must say to you on that subject, my lord." His eyes locked with hers, and she felt a sinking sensation in her stomach.

"Nay, Stephen, do not," she said.

"Aye, I will," he said, looking at the Welshman, his face set with resolution. "I intend to marry this lady myself, so Owain can rest easy on that measure at least."

She cried out in exasperation, nearly forgetting the need for quiet. "You are a madman, completely. Have you no sense whatsoever?" She turned to the smaller man. There might still be some hope of salvaging the peace between their two peoples. "Do not pay him any heed. He knows naught of what he speaks."

When she looked to Wynn, he was watching Stephen with assessing eyes. "What do you mean?"

"I mean that I have a proposition to set before you."

Before Wynn could make any reply to this or Fellis could further try to persuade him of Stephen's idiocy, they were interrupted.

Several of the men had come forward to take them from the trees. Wynn was untied first and when he lunged to get away, he was hit over the head from behind. He crumpled to the ground.

Fellis was taken next. She felt herself grabbed and held against the hard wall of a male chest. The fellow who held her made no pretext at gentleness, for his hands squeezed her arms so tightly that she cried out.

Stephen had been released by now and leapt to assist her in spite of his bonds. He was set upon by two men who jumped at him from behind. He shrugged them off and continued to come forward. Only when her captor pressed his dirk against her throat did Stephen come to a halt with a cry of despair. "Fellis."

Her own soul was in her eyes as she turned to Stephen. The blade pressed to her throat kept her from answering. It was clear that their captors had come to some sort of decision concerning them and this might very well be the end for the three of them. Only when Stephen and Wynn were both bound at the feet and gagged did the assailant take the knife from her throat. With a gasp, she raised her hands to rub her neck and, feeling dampness, brought them down to see a spot of blood on her fingers.

The man who had held her watched without any show of emotion. In barely intelligible English, he said, "You will no scream."

She shook her head, even as her gaze went to Stephen where he now lay trussed on the ground some feet away, his eyes telling her how terrified for her he was. Seeing beyond the fear, she recognized the burning rage inside him, as well.

As Fellis's feet were tied, she could only hope that they were not to die. Judging by the actions of these men thus far, she held out little hope that their lives would be spared.

Fellis and Stephen were set atop their own horses, with the reins being held by two of the men. Wynn was tied face-down to the back of another man's mount. The others closed in around them.

Fellis did her best to retain her balance with her hands tied behind her. It took some effort to do so.

Once she was settled, it became easier and she began to take note of their circumstances. To her chagrin she could not see any way for them to even hope to escape. Each of them was kept separate from the others, and was well guarded by at least four men armed with swords. As they started off for she knew not where, Fellis attempted not to think how badly things appeared to be.

Stephen worked furtively at the knots that bound him and tried to think of some way, any way, to get them out of this. His gaze went to Fellis where she rode ahead of him. She was surrounded by four men, and Stephen knew that even if he could free himself he would not be able to reach her before one of them might do her harm.

That these men meant business he had no doubt.

He could not risk it. He was not prepared to lose her now when it looked as if there was some hope for them. All he had to do was get free. But how?

Stephen knew he had to devise a plan. He was positive that these men were acting on Owain's wishes. Their behavior and the dissent and uncertainty among them marked the men as common soldiers. They were not the masterminds of complicated plots. He wondered if he could use that against them. As yet he had seen no way to even hope to escape that would not mean leaving Fellis to their tender mercy. That he was not prepared to do.

Nor did he wish to leave Wynn to suffer Owain's betrayal.

As he thought of the Welshman, Stephen could not help wishing that he had been presented with enough time to explain himself in regards to his own marriage to Fellis. There was no telling what impression the Welshman had gained from what Stephen said about marrying her. He must surely believe the knight mad as Fellis had accused him of being. He had not even told her of his plan to make his own peace with Wynn. Had not even told her he loved her.

He clamped his jaw tightly as he resolved that they would find a way out of this. He raised his head, determined to watch for any mistakes the men might make. He was going to say those words and many more.

It was quite some time later that they came out of the wood and crossed over a stretch of well-tended farmland. It was just moments after that when Stephen saw a long house very similar to the dwelling Wynn lived in loom up out of the darkness. There also appeared to be several other buildings of stone and wood clustered about it.

A dog barked in the predawn night and another took up the call. The sounds ended sharply a moment later.

One of the men dismounted and went into the dwelling. He returned some minutes later with Owain who was still fastening the belt over his tunic.

Stephen did not even try to hide the disdain in his eyes. He watched as Owain came forward. As he saw the captives, his eyes grew wide with what could only be described as horror.

He barked out a question in Welsh that made the men grimace. One of them moved to where Wynn was draped over the back of the horse, unconscious.

He then turned his displeasure directly on the one Wynn had called Lloyd. His voice was sharp with disapproval.

Lloyd answered at length, obviously telling his master everything that had taken place as he gestured first to Fellis and Stephen, then to Wynn. There was more than a hint of pleading in his voice.

Owain finally made a cutting motion with his hand, effectively ending the conversation. Lloyd subsided, though he could not have failed to see the rage in Owain as he turned from him.

Owain came to stand a few feet from Stephen. After a long moment in which he studied the Englishman with obvious hatred, Owain rasped out another order. One of the men prodded his horse forward and removed Stephen's gag.

Owain addressed him in English. "Well, *Sais,* I had not expected to see you again. I cannot say I am glad that my orders have been so badly bungled. I know not how you came to be in the right place for my men to take you, but they have."

Stephen showed no fear as he answered, "Why have they taken us?"

"Why, because they assumed I would want you dead, of course." Owain raised his hands as he shrugged. He waved toward Wynn. "What were you doing on Wynn's lands? It is by your own foolishness that you were taken. I had set my men to watching him for days. They waited only to find the right opportunity to catch him alone and kill him. You, *Sais,* were to be blamed for his death. These fools—" he looked around him and several of his men shifted uncomfortably "—made the mistake of saying that Wynn was to come to Ardeth." He shrugged again, but the rage in his eyes belied the offhanded gesture. "Now I shall have to kill you all." His eyes grazed Fellis, where she sat in white-faced silence. "I will also be forced to explain how Wynn was safe when he arrived and left here."

Stephen felt like banging his fist against something hard. He now realized that he had played directly into the maniac's hands.

Owain was speaking again. "I could not allow him to simply go about his business, not after he had agreed to treat with our enemies and dishonor my daughter so he could marry this English bitch."

Stephen saw Fellis raise her chin at hearing the insult, and he had to bite the inside of his own mouth to keep from telling the whoreson what he thought of the remark. He knew he had to go carefully here. He must get Fellis and Wynn out of this situation alive.

Stephen forced himself to answer calmly. "I can only think, sir, that you have forgotten I was sent here by King Edward himself. You may be able to kill your own kind without fear of retribution, but I will be missed. As will this lady. Her father knows where we are and that we had discovered your plans to murder Wynn ap Dafydd."

In the early dawn Stephen could see Owain pale at what he said. Yet the Welshman was not ready to back down and made to bluster his way through. "How would you have told Lord Grayson when you could not have known until this very night?"

Stephen raised dark brows. "We know of your attempts to kill his father years ago because he was willing to treat with his enemies."

Owain let out an angry retort, but his expression was troubled to say the least. "How could you know?"

"That is none of your concern, suffice it to say that we do. I must tell you again that you cannot kill us without facing the consequences. King Edward has had enough of this feud and will end it by force if he deems necessary. Murdering his own messenger will certainly drive him to do so."

Owain backed away from them, his brow creasing with a frown. "Put them in the lambing hut." He started to turn away then stopped, glaring up at Stephen where he sat atop the stallion. "Make no mistake, English knight. You have given me some cause to contemplate the method. But believe me, kill you I will."

Chapter Fifteen

Fellis watched the gray-haired man and the knight with no small amount of trepidation. As Stephen had just told him, they could not be killed without fear of retribution. It was not true that her father knew where they were, but her grandmother would surely guess.

Fellis could hardly think what her parents would think when they awoke to find her and the knight gone from the keep. She gave herself a mental shake. This was not the time to worry about such a thing. Survival must be the first thing on her mind now.

Even in the poor light of this early hour, Fellis could see the rage and resentment on the older man's face as he looked up at Stephen. There seemed no hint of tolerance or compassion in him. Could he but think of a way to dispose of them without bringing down the king's wrath, he would do so.

With an angry wave of his hand, Owain barked out an order in his own language and stalked into the long house.

The man closest to Fellis dismounted and reached up to lift her from Ebony's back. He made no effort to speak to her or handle her gently as he tossed her over his shoulder. She moaned as his hard shoulder dug into her stomach.

Stephen's voice echoed across the space that separated them. "Have a care, you bastard!"

Fellis did not know if the man understood exactly what Stephen had said, but the tone had been quite plain. Her captor only laughed, calling out to his fellows and she heard the sound of a fist striking flesh.

Desperately Fellis tilted her head, trying to see what had happened. She barely had time to note that a trickle of blood fell from the side of her beloved's mouth. She grunted with outrage behind her gag as she was carried away.

Yet in spite of all that was happening to him, to them, Fellis could not help a feeling of pride in the man she loved. Even now there was no hint of submission in the angle of his proudly held head, nor in the defiance in his dark green gaze.

She was taken a short distance around the side of the main dwelling. When they came to a halt, she heard the sound of a bolt being drawn back, then a heavy door opening on rusty hinges.

A moment later, she was unceremoniously dumped, faceup, onto a pile of straw.

The man then left without a backward glance.

Fellis tried to shift to take some of her weight off her arms, which were pinned beneath her, but could not. With her feet bound so tightly, she could get no leverage. She wanted to cry with desperation. She made herself breathe slowly and deeply, for with the gag over her mouth it was difficult to get enough air unless she stayed calm.

What, Fellis wondered, had they done with Stephen and Wynn?

Her question was answered only a moment later when Wynn was brought in by two men. He roused enough to groan as they laid him none too gently on the hard-packed dirt floor. Even if he had been awake his gag would have prevented him from speaking. From the angle at which he had been placed across the shack from her, she could not see if his eyes were open.

Directly behind them came four more men carrying Stephen. His gaze sought hers for a brief moment as he was brought in, and she felt his relief at seeing her there. He did not speak, for he was gagged again. A shiver of misery ran through her as she saw his face was marked by several cuts and darkening bruises.

She looked toward his captors with silent fury. Each of the four were sporting lacerations and bruises of their own. Her eyes narrowed in unapologetic approval.

It appeared Stephen had given at least as well as he got.

The knight was near thrown to the hard floor, before the men swung away and closed the door behind them. As they left the proximity of the makeshift prison, Fellis could hear the fellows heaving sighs of what sounded like relief.

Then there was only silence.

Fellis felt totally helpless lying there on her back, unable to turn right or left because of the way her hands and arms were crushed beneath her. What was she to do?

Just moments later, she became aware of movement on the far side of the structure. It was a strange scraping, scuffling noise, but she could not raise her head high enough to see what was causing it.

The noise went on for some time, and Fellis grew accustomed to it. Other sounds began drifting to her as the occupants of the holding awoke.

She heard the sounds of people talking, doors closing, water being thrown out. Concentrating on the homey noises began to lull her in spite of her fear and anger. The night had been a long and exhausting one. In spite of her physical discomfort and fear, her lids began to grow heavy.

Thus it was with no small start that she saw a face appear above hers. Stephen's face, recognized instantly even from her odd perspective. She cried out behind the gag, choking herself in her startlement.

Hurriedly he reached out to tear the rough cloth from her mouth. "Shh," he whispered, reaching to take her up against him, holding her head to his chest as he gripped her tightly in his arms. "Shh, love, do not make a sound."

She fought hard to take in breath without making any noise, but it was difficult. Finally her breathing calmed and she pressed her head against his shoulder in silent thanks and the pure joy of being close to him again.

"You managed to untie us...." She gasped then as her arms were freed and started to tingle as if being bitten by thousands of ants when she moved them.

Stephen nodded, the bruise beneath one eye making him appear slightly rakish. "I simply found a sharp edge on the stone wall near the floor and used it to cut the ropes."

He gave her a quick kiss. "And now," he said, as he freed her feet, "I must untie Wynn."

He moved to where the other man lay, his legs stretched before him, in the center of the room.

The moment Stephen removed the gag from his mouth, Wynn said, "You were right. Even though I knew in my mind that you must be, I still felt shock at hearing Owain say that he wished me dead."

Stephen shrugged, laboring over the other man's bonds as Fellis crawled across to join them.

She looked at Wynn, saw the sadness and rage in his eyes and wished things had been different for him. How terrible it would be to learn that you had been betrayed by one of the ones you most trusted.

Stephen had now moved to the other man's feet as Wynn massaged his stiff arms with an expression of grim fortitude.

Wynn looked up at Stephen as he sat back once the task was accomplished. "We must find a way to escape."

"Aye." Stephen arched dark brows. "But I know not how. We must figure out a way that will guarantee Fellis's safety, at least in part. They have taken our weapons and we are sadly outnumbered."

She blanched. "I am sorry for insisting you take me with you, Stephen. I did not think of anything except that I wished to be with you. Now I have made it more difficult for all of us."

Stephen shrugged, taking her hand. "Do not worry, love, you had no way of knowing what would happen. Had I wished to, I could have tied you to my bed to prevent your coming."

Fellis glanced at Wynn to see him watching them with open curiosity. She blushed, realizing how much they had just given away.

Stephen, seeing the other man's regard, said, "Wynn, as I was trying to tell you when we were set upon, I have a scheme in mind that will give us all what we desire. You would be free to wed Ardeth, and I to take Fellis as my own bride."

Wynn's lips tightened. "I know not what part Ardeth has played in this. How can I even think of marrying her, even if it were possible?"

Stephen met Wynn's troubled gaze with a level one of his own. "There is one thing I am certain of, Ardeth loves you. You too must know that, and also know that there is some explanation for why she did not tell you of her father's machinations." He looked to Fellis. "Part of loving is believing in someone. You must allow her to explain herself."

Wynn was thoughtful for a long time, then he turned a hopeful gaze to Stephen. "I can only pray that you are right." He nodded toward Fellis then. "Now tell me what plan you have that might make this tangle aright."

Taking a deep breath, Stephen began, "Last night Fellis and I..." He looked at her blushing face before continuing. "As you must have guessed, Wynn, we were together. Being with Fellis made me realize I could not allow things to go on as they were." He met the other man's gaze. "You see, I love her."

Fellis was so horrified at what Stephen was admitting that at first she didn't really hear what he was saying. Then as the words sank in she felt a wave of indescribable elation crash over her heart, the ripples settling into every part of herself and filling her with joy.

She launched herself into his arms, now heedless of the other man. "You love me!" Her blue eyes shone with the light of her own love for him.

He held her close, reveling in this moment of happiness with her. "But of course I do," he replied gruffly. "More than my own life."

Only when Wynn coughed discreetly did they start apart. Fellis made no effort to take herself away from Stephen.

"As you can see," he said to Wynn, "we care for each other. And knowing that, I began to think there must be some way for us to be together." He watched the Welshman closely. "Much of my plan will depend on you and your opinion of me."

Wynn shrugged. "Well, I must admit that I have had reason to change some of my views about the English since meeting you. You have proven yourself to be honest and straightforward in your contact with me." He grimaced, gesturing around them. "And judging by the way events have gone forward since last eve, I can only think that you have revealed yourself to be more friend to me than those I trusted."

Exhaling roughly, Stephen said, "Ah, well then, there is hope. You see, I began wondering if you would be willing to treat with me. Did Fellis's father agree to accept me as her husband, and King Edward accepted me as Lord Grayson's heir, I would be in a position to do just that. All we would need do then is gain King Edward's permission to go forward."

As Stephen spoke, Fellis heard him first with amazement, then growing optimism. Could Stephen actually make this work? Had he foreseen all the possible ramifications and problems that might arise in trying to do so?

Wynn replied, "So you presume your king would be disposed to agree to this arrangement if I was willing to accompany you to court?" His eyes narrowed. "How would I know that I would not be imprisoned or worse. All Welsh know of the might of English law and justice. We are not protected by the English laws that govern us as your people are, only persecuted by them."

Stephen did not waver as his gaze met Wynn's. "I swear by my own life and honor as a knight that your safety and freedom will be guaranteed."

The Welshman watched him for a long moment while Fellis held her breath. Then he held out his hand. "I will accompany you to court, Stephen Clayburn." His gaze swept the four stone walls around them. "That is, if we are ever freed from this prison."

Fellis watched as Stephen followed the path of the other man's gaze. He ran a hand through his thick dark hair. "As you say."

The hours of the day dragged on without anyone coming to their jail.

For the most part, Fellis stayed close by Stephen and he was not reticent about holding her to him and offering comfort. He tried his utmost to put a hopeful front on for her sake, but she knew that the situation was indeed dreadful.

Their prison consisted of one main chamber, approximately fifteen feet wide by fifteen feet long. At the north side there was a pile of fresh straw, which they made use of in arranging places to sit, though Stephen did precious little of that and paced the hard-packed floor impatiently.

In one corner was a separate stall with a sturdy wooden door. Fellis took her time in examining the tiny chamber and found nothing that might aid in their escaping.

They each thoroughly explored the whole structure and concluded that there appeared to be no way out. There were no windows and the thatched roof was in good repair. The door was bolted from the outside and refused to budge when they tried it.

As the hours passed, Fellis wondered what could be happening that their captors would have forgotten them. What could Owain be planning?

But as night fell with still no sign from him, Wynn suggested they try to get some sleep. None of them had had any rest the previous night and he added that, if they were to find a chance to escape, they would have need of all their strength.

Stephen stood holding out his hand to Fellis.

She placed hers into it and followed him to the stall at the other end of the structure. It was obviously meant as a confinement area for birthing and was laid with clean straw. Stephen closed the door behind them.

When Stephen held out his arms to her she went into them. The deepness of the night was like a thick cocoon that blocked out the rest of the world. Now that they were alone with nothing to separate them, there was only her love for him, and his for her.

No matter what tomorrow might bring she would have this night with Stephen, the man she loved.

When he dipped his head to claim her mouth she accepted him expectantly. Fellis reached up to twine her fingers in his thick hair, straining upward.

Stephen sensed her eagerness, but he held back, kissing her slowly and thoroughly, nibbling and sucking at her lower lip. This time he would not hurry their loving. He meant to savor every precious moment. For he did know that each could indeed be their last.

Stephen held her tenderly, kissing Fellis until she felt faint, her knees threatening to give way beneath her. She sighed with the pure pleasure of it as she sagged against him.

He leaned close, whispering into her ear, his hot breath causing a shiver of delight to run down her spine. "Let me undress you."

She reached out to rest her hand against the stone wall as he bent to raise first her cote and then her tunic, drawing each over her head in turn. In her haste to dress the previous night, she had not put on a chemise and was now bare to his questing hands.

Tenderly he ran his hands down her shoulders and over her sides to her hips, then upward over her ribs to cup the weight of her breasts. Stephen felt their fullness in his palms and closed his eyes on the wave of desire that washed over him when the nipples hardened against him.

He bent to nibble at the nape of her neck, her hair falling across his face in a silky caress. "Fellis, you are so beautiful, so beautiful."

She sighed, reaching out to clasp his shoulders as he bent further and his lips closed on the rigid peak of her breast. She nearly cried out, having to bite her lip to still the sound as a shaft of liquid heat pierced her lower belly.

Her hands moved to touch and she was thwarted by his clothing. "Let me," she said, reaching for his belt.

He stood perfectly still as she placed her trembling hands on the gold buckle. She fumbled a bit with it but he did not try to help her and that further heightened Fellis's passions. He was allowing her to participate in the loving as an equal. The realization was heady and drove her to try to please him as he did her.

When the belt fell to the floor, she put her hands to the hem of his garments. The only assistance he gave was to lift his arms and bend his knees to allow her to reach over his head as she drew them off.

With that done, Fellis raised her hands and placed them on his chest, her fingers exploring and learning the delicious contours of this glorious man. He was hers and hers alone.

Even if there were no more tomorrows for them, no one could take these moments from her. She would go from this life remembering the velvet touch of his hands on her flesh.

She leaned forward and kissed his wide chest, her mind seeing him the way she had the night before, all golden and powerful in the firelight. Without thinking, she ran her tongue over that smooth flesh, tasting him.

Stephen moaned so softly that she barely heard. Fellis knew that the sound had been wrung from deep inside him and it further emboldened her to explore him. As she kissed and licked at his chest, she reached around him, her hands closing over the solid mounds of his buttocks.

Stephen rocked toward her, one arm going around her as he lifted her face to his. She offered her mouth freely.

This time he kissed her fiercely, his lips demanding a response she was happy to give. Her blood raced with each thrust of his tongue and she gripped him all the more tightly.

Her breasts were crushed to his chest, feeling heavy and aching with need for him. "Love me, Stephen," she whispered against his mouth.

He lifted her in his strong arms and knelt with her on the hay, his lips never leaving hers. Then his mouth was slowly moving down her throat, lingeringly across the mound of her breast, then finally on the turgid tip.

She put her hands to his head, nearly swooning with the fire that raced down through her body and made her hips arch. She wanted him, needed him, but even more she wanted to give of herself to Stephen. With all the will she possessed, Fellis pushed him gently back from her. Her body ached with the desire he awoke inside her but she would not give in to her own yearnings.

Without words she guided him to lie back in the soft hay. When her lips found his, she kissed him deeply, as he had taught her. Her tongue circled his and she felt the pull of longing increase inside her as he answered back.

Stephen ran his hands over her delicate back and shoulders as Fellis moved down to kiss and stroke his small male nipples. They firmed to tiny nubs and she sighed against his skin, her breath warm and exciting. He felt rather than heard her say, "I love you."

When she dipped lower to caress his belly with her lips, his heart began to pound with a deafening beat. Then Fellis reached down, her fingers closing on the tumescent length of him and Stephen could not hold back a gasp as his heart ceased to beat for an indefinable moment, then started again with a lurch that left his head spinning with desire.

She was driving him mad with her delicate hands and soft mouth. Stephen could stand no more. Reaching down, he drew her up to lie along the length of him. His hands tangled in the glorious mass of her hair as he kissed her.

When Stephen rolled her beneath him, her legs opened without coaxing and he moved over her. With his first deep thrust, she rose up to meet him and his craving found its rapture.

Fellis's breathing became ragged as the throbbing cry of need inside her built to an indefinable pitch. Then the pleasure was breaking through her with a harmony that brought her every sense and feeling into perfect union with the universe.

A moment later, she heard Stephen moan and stiffen above her. She was suddenly filled with an incredible sense of power, tempered with incredible love and tenderness that she had brought him this same delight.

It was sometime later that Fellis opened her eyes to an inky blackness. For a moment she could not understand what had awakened her, then realized that Stephen was leaning over her. He put his finger to her lips.

He placed his lips close to her ear. "Shh, listen."

That was when she heard the sound that had obviously alerted him. A creaking of metal on metal, mayhap the sound of a rusty bolt being drawn. The noise was furtive, as if someone were trying not to be heard.

Stephen pressed her clothing to her.

Without being told, Fellis began to pull the garments on, little heeding whether they were right side out or upside down. What, she wondered, was happening? Had Owain waited till the middle of the night to murder them in their sleep? Her stomach tightened with fear and anger.

What kind of coward could not even face the ones he would put to death?

Fellis sensed Stephen opening the door of the stall. It made no sound at all as the hinges were not made of wood but leather. He stepped into the outer room.

Uncaring of whether or not she was properly covered, Fellis pulled her skirt down and followed him.

The chamber was as dark as the one she'd just left and Fellis strained to see something—anything. She could not. Then she heard a further creaking of rusty hinges as the outer door moved. Now she could make out a narrow line of weak light at the other end of the structure where the door lay.

Whoever was opening it seemed to be taking an inordinate amount of time to do so. As she watched, she saw Stephen move to stand against the wall beside it. Another shadow pressed itself to the wall on the other side of the portal—Wynn.

The door swung open. In the frail light of the new moon stood the silhouette of a woman.

Fellis knew instantly who it was. She made to call out softly to Stephen. He did not hear her, for he was already upon Ardeth.

Grabbing her from behind, he placed his hand over her mouth as Fellis raced forward. He whispered gruffly, "Do not make a sound."

Her brown eyes were large, the whites showing all around as she nodded. Fellis did not require more light to note her fear and nervousness. The Welshwoman's gaze swept the room for her beloved.

Wynn stepped out from behind the door and came toward them. His lips were thinned to a forbidding line. When Ardeth saw his expression, her eyes filled with unshed tears. Wildly she began to tear at Stephen's hand over her mouth.

He held her securely. "Hold now. I will uncover your mouth if you swear to remain quiet."

She nodded, her gaze never leaving Wynn.

As soon as Stephen had freed her, she ran to Wynn, throwing herself against him. Fellis saw him close his eyes as if it was all he could do to keep his hands at his sides.

Ardeth cried, "*Cariad,* I have come to help you escape."

Still Wynn did not reach out to hold her. He spoke stiffly. "Did you know that your father was trying to kill me?"

She began to sob. "Nay, I did not, my love. I only knew when you were brought here last night. I knew he was angry and that he wished to stop the marriage between you and the Englishwoman. But I did not know that he would harm you. You must believe me. You are my life. That is why I have defied him to come to you. He has forbidden anyone to come near you until he decides what to do with you. He says he must find a way to make your deaths appear to be an accident so that the English king will not send his army." Tears slipped down her cheeks as she peered up at her lover, her hands twisted together before her. "Even if my father never forgives me, I cannot see you die. Come, you must go." She drew back and ran to the door, then waited impatiently for them to follow.

Stephen was the first to react, with Wynn directly behind him.

Fellis hurried out after the two men. Ardeth bent down and struggled with some object on the ground, then came back dragging their weapons. "You see, I have come to help you."

Wynn reached toward Ardeth with a groan even as Stephen moved to rescue his sword from her.

But at the same moment, there was a shout of outrage. Fellis turned to see several soldiers, led by Owain as they leapt out from beside the main house. They had obviously been lying in wait for them.

Owain addressed his daughter directly. "Did you think I would not have you watched, girl?" The tone was furious but Fellis could also hear the hurt in the man, as well. "I did hope that you would see where your loyalty should rest." He looked to Wynn, who was now holding his own weapon. "This man is a traitor to our people and to you, Ardeth. He was willing to set you aside, no matter that you carry his child, in favor of the English bitch." He did not look at Fellis, who inched even closer to Stephen's side.

She put her hands over her ears to block out her father's words. "Nay, Father, I cannot listen to you. He did so only to help our people. Wynn loves me."

Owain made a cutting motion with his hand. "Enough." He turned his back on her, nodding to his men. "Take them."

Stephen hurriedly set Fellis behind him as he turned to defend them. Wynn backed toward them and directed Ardeth to take a position beside Fellis. The two women looked at each other, a strange current of understanding passing between them.

Fellis knew that they must both do what they could to help their men prevail. The other girl must feel, as she did, that they could not see them die without at least trying to assist them.

Then their opponents were upon them. Fellis watched as Stephen dispatched two of their number with a wide sweep of his sword. He circled, keeping Fellis and Ardeth behind him as he moved to ward off the next man. Wynn, too, made every effort to keep them at his back as he fought.

It soon became clear to Fellis that these were not well-trained soldiers who fought against them. But there was still danger as they were outnumbered by some four-to-one.

As Stephen held off two attackers, another came at him from the other side and Fellis knew she must help him. Searching about her for anything to use as a weapon, she spotted a large flat rock just behind her. Reaching down, she picked it up in her two hands, barely even feeling its weight in her panicky state. She dashed forward, raising the rock over her head as the man made a rush at Stephen's unprotected back. With all the force she could muster, she brought it down on his head. He crumpled to the ground, unconscious.

Seeing this, Ardeth picked up a small rock and the two women kept up a volley of stones to distract some of their foe while Wynn and Stephen fought on.

The fracas raged on and soon several of Owain's men lay injured or dead around them. Fellis was aware of their leader, where he stood back from the others, his hate-filled gaze taking in the action with obvious displeasure. By now few of his men were left, and to Fellis it seemed that some of them might have abandoned the fray. Mayhap they were not completely comfortable with the notion of killing Wynn.

It was only when Wynn was turned, with his back to the man he had once trusted, that Owain made his move. Like the coward he was, he raised his sword and ran at Wynn from behind.

Fellis called out to Stephen, who had just dispatched another. He swung around, intercepting Owain with a smile so cold it could freeze sunshine. "I am your man, Owain," the knight told him.

With a sneer of rage, Owain came at him, swinging his sword in a downward stroke that could have cleaved a man in twain. Stephen met the blow with his own sword and followed with an equally powerful thrust of his own.

They battled on, Owain proving surprisingly crafty in his swordplay. He even attempted to back Stephen toward the wall of the house, where he would not be able to maneuver freely, but Stephen saw what he was about and drove him in the other direction.

Finally, when Fellis thought she would surely faint with the agony of seeing Stephen block one swing after another, Owain made his fatal mistake.

In raising his sword above his head with both hands, he left his midriff unprotected and Stephen drove the point of his sword deep. With a gasp of shock and fury, Owain fell to the ground and lay still.

This seemed to make the few men remaining lose what little heart they had. As if by some unspoken consensus, they backed away and Fellis dropped the rock she was holding to the ground.

The whole episode had taken no more than a few minutes, but it was now getting fairly light. In that pale dawn, she saw Ardeth run to her fallen father.

Fellis looked to Stephen, who held out his arms to her. She ran into them and was enveloped in their protective strength. He kissed her, raising her face to his. But even as she felt his comfort, her heart ached for the other girl. Although he had been a traitor and a coward, Owain had been Ardeth's father.

Drawing back from Stephen, she went forward, reaching down and put her hand on the Welshwoman's back. ''Is he dead?''

Ardeth looked up, her brown eyes filled with misery. ''Yes.'' Her gaze went to Wynn, who moved to take her up in his arms. She said, ''I could not let him kill you in cold blood.''

Wynn held her head against his chest, his eyes showing his own sadness. ''Nay, *cariad,* you could not.''

Stephen came to Fellis's side. Seeing her kindness toward the other woman had reminded him anew of just how much he loved her. It was that mixture of strength and sweetness that had made him see her as much more than just a beautiful woman. She had fought alongside him this day, very probably saving his life more than once.

Looking down at her, he smiled tenderly. Despite her haphazardly arranged garments, she was the most lovely thing he had ever seen, with her silvery hair tangling about her and her blue eyes damp with concern for Ardeth.

As if sensing his attention, Fellis turned to him and held out her hand. ''My lord.''

He took it, his gaze telling her how very much he needed her. ''My love,'' he replied. Drawing her close to him once more, he kissed her boldly, reveling in his freedom to do so, to show the world that she was his woman and his alone.

When he pulled away, she gazed up at him, her eyes bright now with love, her breath coming quickly. Stephen wanted to kiss her again, to hold her in his arms forever. But this was not the time.

Stephen looked about them, his gaze going to Wynn and Ardeth where they stood nearby, lost in each other and their pain. He knew it would be some time before they were able to put this behind them.

Gently he said, "Wynn, I think we had best be on our way before someone decides to try and stop us. I for one have had enough of fighting this day."

Wynn nodded. "I, too, friend. And we still have much to accomplish before your troubles are sorted out."

Tightening his arm about Fellis, Stephen knew the other man spoke true.

Epilogue

Fellis gave a start as the horn at the castle gates sounded from outside her window.

Heavens above, she thought silently, raising her hands to her breast. Please, let it be Stephen! A whole month he had been gone with Wynn ap Dafydd, and not a word.

During that time, she had been torn between hope that the king would grant them permission to do what they wished and fear that he would refuse them.

She repeatedly told herself that the latter thought was a foolish one. King Edward would have no reason for denying their requests. Her father had given Stephen a letter that detailed his complete approval of the plan. Richard Grayson had in fact been so pleased with Stephen's solution to their troubles that he'd suggested the knight marry his daughter before going to court.

Stephen had declined, saying he could not try to force King Edward's hand by doing so. And though Fellis was disappointed and worried that the king might refuse them, she had told her love nothing of her feelings on the subject. His sense of honor was one of the things she most loved about Stephen.

Yet the days had weighed heavily upon her, especially when Ardeth had come to share her own fears with Fellis. Fellis had done her best to comfort the other girl and assure her that Wynn was safe as long as Stephen lived. Though they were not exactly close, Ardeth seemed to feel, as Fellis did, that their ordeal had brought them closer together. Their shared danger had made them understand each other and what they were going through as no one else could.

Stephen and Wynn had left for court only days after the kidnapping and fight with Owain and his men. Fellis felt that events had moved almost too quickly to fully absorb their importance.

The only thing that had given her any sense of purpose was her new duties at the keep. Fellis's mother had begun to expect her to help supervise the castle as a mistress might. As a woman she was finally learning to oversee the many tasks great and small that made life run smoothly for the occupants of Malvern.

Mother had taken advantage of Fellis's assistance to spend time with her husband. More than once the two had been seen riding off alone together on a warm afternoon. In spite of her own loneliness, it brought a glow to Fellis's heart to see them learning to love each other as they once had.

The horn sounded again and Fellis became certain the arrival must be an important one. She looked down at the skirt of her pale pink cote and grimaced as she saw the smear of honey that must have gotten there when she was helping bake tarts earlier in the day.

The horn blew again and Fellis leapt to her feet, her stomach fluttering. The state of her clothing was instantly forgotten as she was overcome with a certainty that it had to be Stephen.

She hurried from her room and down the hall.

She met Stephen on the stairs as he raced up them. They both came to halt at the same time, only three steps separating them. He was even more handsome than she'd remembered with his sultry dark eyes and strong features. He was taller, broader shouldered, more self-assured than any man had a right to be.

For a moment she felt suddenly shy. Although she loved him with her whole heart and soul and had touched him more intimately than anyone she had ever known, she was halted by a stab of anxiety that he would not still want her.

In the days before he'd left for court he'd not tried to be with her again. At the time she'd thought he was simply attempting to behave honorably. What if she had been wrong and he had realized that he did not really care for her as he thought?

But the moment his eyes met hers, she knew she had worried for naught. His love for her glowed from inside him like a bright flame. He smiled at her, his hungry gaze devouring her as he held up his hand. In it was a roll of parchment bound with a thick seal of red wax.

His voice was hoarse from running and, she thought, emotion. "The king has agreed."

She held her trembling fingers to her lips, unable to believe her deepest desire would really be granted. "To everything?"

"Aye," he replied, watching her closely.

Fellis swallowed, unable to take it all in. "What had my father to say?"

Stephen cocked his head to the side. "Did you think I would not come to you first?"

She had to ask again, make certain she understood. "King Edward agreed to all, the peace treaty, your becoming my father's heir, our marriage—all of it?"

He nodded, his thick hair falling across his forehead, making her want to reach out and brush it back. That was when the enormity of what he had just said hit her.

The king had agreed to their marriage!

Never again would she have need to hide her love for this wonderful man.

Joy soared up inside her on widely spread wings and Fellis fair flew into his arms. She wrapped her arms around his neck and held her face up for his kiss. "I love you."

As he leaned down, his lips claiming hers, she spread possessive fingers through that lock of hair.

Fellis forgot everything else in the sweet sensuality of his kiss, her lips clinging to his even as he drew back. "I just need to look at you for a moment," he said. "All these long weeks at court, I have thought of nothing but being with you again, holding you."

Her eyes opened wide as he reminded her of where he had been. "And Wynn?" she asked.

Stephen groaned, burying her face in his shoulder. "Has gone home to his own woman."

She smiled against him, breathing in the fresh, leathery, warm male scent of him. "Am I your woman?" There was nothing she desired more than to be his.

"As I am your man." He raised her face to his. He kissed her again until she was breathless and dizzy with wanting him. "When will you marry me?"

"As soon as my father will allow," she said.

He held her hips to the lower part of him and she felt his arousal. "Today would not be soon enough for me."

Her eyes shone as she blushed, but she did not try to move away from that most intimate part of him. "Then we'd best go tell my father," she replied.

He stepped back, holding out his hand to her. When she placed hers in it, he drew her next to him. Stephen unconsciously matched his strides to her slower ones as they went down the steps to the hall. She glanced up at him with devotion and pride. This tall, beautiful man was hers, ready and willing to match his pace to hers as they walked through life together.

Love filled her heart to overflowing. How different her life had been since he came into it. Only a few short months ago she had felt hopelessly trapped by the twisted ankle that had seemed to set the course of her future. It had appeared an insurmountable obstacle that cut her off from the things she dared not even admit she desired. A husband, a family, a life of her own choosing. She now knew that her deformity was simply a hardship she had need to overcome, as other hardships must be overcome.

Stephen had shown her that, not by telling her what she must do, but by treating her as if she had the right to decide how she was to live. They could walk through life together, just as they descended the stairs to her waiting father. Side by side.

* * * * *

Coming in July from

Harlequin®
Historical

DARLING JACK
by
MARY McBRIDE

He was the country's number-one Pinkerton
operative...she was his pretend wife.

"I can hardly wait for her next one! She's great!"
—*Affaire de Couer*

Available wherever Harlequin books are sold.

BIGB96-5

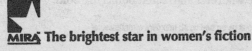

Bestselling authors

ELAINE COFFMAN
RUTH LANGAN
and
MARY McBRIDE

Together in one fabulous collection!

OUTLAW
Brides

Available in June wherever Harlequin
books are sold.

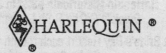

HARLEQUIN ®

BRIDE'S
BAY RESORT

UNLOCK THE DOOR TO GREAT ROMANCE
AT BRIDE'S BAY RESORT

Join Harlequin's new across-the-lines series, set in an exclusive hotel on an island off the coast of South Carolina.

Seven of your favorite authors will bring you exciting stories about fascinating heroes and heroines discovering love at Bride's Bay Resort.

Look for these fabulous stories coming to a store near you beginning in January 1996.

Harlequin American Romance #613 in January
Matchmaking Baby by Cathy Gillen Thacker

Harlequin Presents #1794 in February
Indiscretions by Robyn Donald

Harlequin Intrigue #362 in March
Love and Lies by Dawn Stewardson

Harlequin Romance #3404 in April
Make Believe Engagement by Day Leclaire

Harlequin Temptation #588 in May
Stranger in the Night by Roseanne Williams

Harlequin Superromance #695 in June
Married to a Stranger by Connie Bennett

Harlequin Historicals #324 in July
Dulcie's Gift by Ruth Langan

Visit Bride's Bay Resort each month wherever Harlequin books are sold.

HARLEQUIN ®

BBAYG

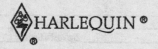

HARLEQUIN®

Don't miss these Harlequin favorites by some of our most
distinguished authors!
And now, you can receive a discount by ordering two or more titles!

HT #25645	THREE GROOMS AND A WIFE by JoAnn Ross	$3.25 U.S./$3.75 CAN. ☐
HT #25648	JESSIE'S LAWMAN by Kristine Rolofson	$3.25 U.S.//$3.75 CAN. ☐
HP #11725	THE WRONG KIND OF WIFE by Roberta Leigh	$3.25 U.S./$3.75 CAN. ☐
HP #11755	TIGER EYES by Robyn Donald	$3.25 U.S./$3.75 CAN. ☐
HR #03362	THE BABY BUSINESS by Rebecca Winters	$2.99 U.S./$3.50 CAN. ☐
HR #03375	THE BABY CAPER by Emma Goldrick	$2.99 U.S./$3.50 CAN. ☐
HS #70638	THE SECRET YEARS by Margot Dalton	$3.75 U.S./$4.25 CAN. ☐
HS #70655	PEACEKEEPER by Marisa Carroll	$3.75 U.S./$4.25 CAN. ☐
HI #22280	MIDNIGHT RIDER by Laura Pender	$2.99 U.S./$3.50 CAN. ☐
HI #22235	BEAUTY VS THE BEAST by M.J. Rogers	$3.50 U.S./$3.99 CAN. ☐
HAR #16531	TEDDY BEAR HEIR by Elda Minger	$3.50 U.S./$3.99 CAN. ☐
HAR #16596	COUNTERFEIT HUSBAND by Linda Randall Wisdom	$3.50 U.S./$3.99 CAN. ☐
HH #28795	PIECES OF SKY by Marianne Willman	$3.99 U.S./$4.50 CAN. ☐
HH #28855	SWEET SURRENDER by Julie Tetel	$4.50 U.S./$4.99 CAN. ☐

(limited quantities available on certain titles)

	AMOUNT	$
DEDUCT:	**10% DISCOUNT FOR 2+ BOOKS**	$
ADD:	**POSTAGE & HANDLING**	$
	($1.00 for one book, 50¢ for each additional)	
	APPLICABLE TAXES**	$_____
	TOTAL PAYABLE	$_____
	(check or money order—please do not send cash)	

To order, complete this form and send it, along with a check or money order for the
total above, payable to Harlequin Books, to: **In the U.S.:** 3010 Walden Avenue,
P.O. Box 9047, Buffalo, NY 14269-9047; **In Canada:** P.O. Box 613, Fort Erie, Ontario,
L2A 5X3.

Name:_____

Address:_____ City:_____

State/Prov.:_____ Zip/Postal Code:_____

**New York residents remit applicable sales taxes.
  Canadian residents remit applicable GST and provincial taxes.

HBACK-AJ3

Harlequin® Historical

If you're a serious fan of historical romance, then you're in luck!

Harlequin Historicals brings you stories by bestselling authors, rising new stars and talented first-timers.

Ruth Langan & Theresa Michaels
Mary McBride & Cheryl St. John
Margaret Moore & Merline Lovelace
Julie Tetel & Nina Beaumont
Susan Amarillas & Ana Seymour
Deborah Simmons & Linda Castle
Cassandra Austin & Emily French
Miranda Jarrett & Suzanne Barclay
DeLoras Scott & Laurie Grant...

You'll never run out of favorites.

Harlequin Historicals...they're too good to miss!